A Body at the Christmas Book Fair

Also by Helen Cox

Murder by the Minster
A Body in the Bookshop
Murder on the Moorland
Death Awaits in Durham
A Witch Hunt in Whitby
A Body by the Lighthouse
Murder in a Mill Town
A Body in the Borderlands

HELEN COX

A Body
at the
Christmas
Book Fair

QUERCUS

First published in Great Britain in 2025 by Quercus
Part of John Murray Group

2

A CIP catalogue record for this book is available
from the British Library

HB ISBN 978 1 52944 217 5
EBOOK ISBN 978 1 52944 218 2

Typeset in Swift by CC Book Production
Printed and bound in Great Britain by Clays Ltd, Elcograf S.p.A.

MIX
Paper | Supporting
responsible forestry
FSC
www.fsc.org FSC® C104740

Papers used by Quercus are from well-managed forests and other responsible sources.

Quercus
Carmelite House
50 Victoria Embankment
London EC4Y 0DZ

John Murray Group
Part of Hodder & Stoughton Limited
An Hachette UK company

The authorised representative in the EEA is Hachette Ireland,

8 Castlecourt Centre, Dublin 15, D15 XTP3, Ireland (email: info@hbgi.ie)

A Body at the Christmas Book Fair

CHAPTER ONE

The deep timbre of a brass band playing 'Once in Royal David's City' filled Kitt Hartley's ears and warmed her heart as she strode along High Petergate. Snow was settling on the spires and medieval gateways of York, like icing sugar might over warm mince pies. In the middle distance, beyond the crenelations of Bootham Bar, Kitt thought she could just make out a thick storm cloud forming in the black sky, the kind that might be full of hailstones and thunder claps rather than delicate snow. The weather was of little concern to Kitt just then, however. For one thing, the maroon trilby she was almost never seen without in the winter months and her thick, navy coat offered protection from the frosty conditions. For another, the bookshops along High Petergate were open late for Christmas shopping and could easily be dashed into if the heavens did open. And for another, well, how could anyone, let alone a librarian, mind what the clouds were doing, when this

1

portion of the city had been closed to traffic for a Christmas Book Fair?

Row upon row of book stalls had been crammed into the street, illuminated with the glow of a thousand fairy lights, and sheltered by heavy sheets of red and green tarpaulin to keep the merchandise safe from the elements. Thanks to the numerous food and drink vendors that had also set up shop at the fair, the air was a spicy cocktail of festive aromas emanating from cranberry-infused gin samples, roasted turkey baps and freshly baked cinnamon cookies. The mere smell of all these delicious delicacies was enough to make *that* feeling swell in your heart. That feeling that always seemed to be sprinkled in the air during the run-up to Christmas, just waiting for you to breathe it in: a warm sense of gratitude for whatever little chunk of happiness you might have managed to carve out for yourself in the year gone by.

The Christmas spirit seemed almost palpable in the streets of York that night, so it was little wonder that the many faces in the crowds, reddened by the late December chill, were also aglow with seasonal cheer.

Kitt's ice blue eyes widened at the sight of so much temptation. Her usually steady gaze darted around the many stacks of paperbacks and hardbacks waiting to be thoroughly inspected. Since starting her own private detective agency, Hartley and Edwards Investigations, Kitt had spent more time surveilling unfaithful spouses and less time curating the Women's Studies department in the Vale of York University Library. Which, in turn, had led to a dip in her usually voracious reading habit. With the students already having vacated the campus for Christmas, the library would be operating on skeleton staff, and she wouldn't be expected back there now until January. She planned to use her Christmas break from her part-time hours to catch up on all of her reading, and perhaps to add a few more volumes to her To Be Read pile. With this in mind, she couldn't think of a more fitting place to spend a Wednesday evening than at a bookish event such as this.

Though Kitt wanted nothing more than to start a meticulous perusal of each and every title on sale, she had promised to meet her friend Evie at the fair and, much as it pained Kitt to admit, it wasn't good form to prioritise book browsing over besties. Besides anything else, they had tickets to a special abridged reading of *A Christmas Carol* which Kitt really didn't want to miss, so she mustn't get too sidetracked. She and Evie had agreed to meet near the food stalls at six p.m. and if she knew Evie as well as she thought she did, right about now her friend would be ... ah, yes, there she was. Buying more gingerbread than anyone could hope to eat in a month from one of the stands.

Smiling, Kitt sidled up to her and said, 'Just a small snack on the way to the events tent, is it, Evie?'

At once recognising the voice of her dearest friend, Evie's head spun around, her blonde curls bouncing as she did so. Kitt chuckled when she realised that Evie's mouth was already full of gingerbread and she was frantically chewing in a bid to respond to Kitt's quip as quickly as possible.

Kitt gave her friend a minute to swallow her food, but even then Evie still had too much in her mouth to respond.

'Crikey, Evie. How much gingerbread did you cram in there? Slow down, will you?' Kitt said, holding a hand in the air. 'I do not need a trip to A&E over a gingerbread choking incident. If you don't mind, I'd like to get through my night off without any farcical episodes.'

Evie held a finger in the air bidding Kitt to wait just a few more seconds for a verbal response and then, at last, swallowed her intimidating mouthful. 'I take it that your desire to avoid farcical episodes is the reason you left Grace at the office tonight?'

'That,' Kitt said with a small shake of her head, thinking about just how giddy Grace, her assistant-cum-business partner at the agency, could be at times, 'and the fact that the pair of you are a nightmare when you get together. You encourage each other to spout even more nonsense than usual, not that anyone who had encountered you individually would think that possible. I never get any peace.'

'You make out like being ruthlessly teased every five minutes is a bad thing,' Evie said with a knowing grin. 'We provide you with a very important service. Can't have you taking yourself too seriously, can we, old chum?'

'Between you, Grace and Ruby, there's no danger of that,'

said Kitt. 'Oh, speaking of Ruby, she mentioned she might be around, but I'm rather hoping we can dodge her tonight. She's visited the office every single day in December trying to coax me into sampling her homemade mulled wine. Despite having studied many a dictionary closer than most in my time, even I don't have words to describe how vile it looks. You know I'm fond of her, but really, I'm running out of excuses.'

'Oh Kitt, this is what I mean about taking things so seriously. What are you like? It's only a drink. It's not going to kill you.'

'I don't know so much,' said Kitt, shuddering a little as she remembered the gungy consistency of the stuff.

Evie chuckled. 'Look, knowing Ruby, it probably isn't the most appetising concoction known to man, but it doesn't sound as though she's going to give up until you've tried some. Maybe you should just give her what she wants. Bottoms up and all that. Get it over with and that will be the end of the matter.'

'Have you met Ruby?' Kitt said with a wry raise of her eyebrows. 'That will in no way be the end of the matter. If I cave and drink one drop she'll bring another bottle into the agency every day between now and New Year. God only knows how the unbridled eccentricity of Ruby Barnett will manifest in liquid form, or what said liquid will do to my insides. I just have to ward her off for another ten days and then it will be January and hopefully she'll give up on her mission.'

Kitt had to wait a little longer than usual for Evie's response as she had shoved another large chunk of gingerbread in her mouth.

'Are you alright in yourself?' said Kitt, looking her friend up and down. 'I know you're fair-skinned but you're even paler than usual, if you ask me. You haven't been on another one of those sadistic diets, have you?'

Evie swallowed her gingerbread with a big gulp. 'Maybe.'

'Evie, for heaven's sake . . .' was all that Kitt said. She didn't want to make too big a deal out of the matter but she did worry about her friend and her obsession with her appearance. It had been just over ten years since Kitt's first sleuthing case. One that had changed the course of her professional life and left her closest friend with scars on her face that had faded but never fully healed. Even before all those chilling events had unfolded, poor Evie had been deeply concerned with how she looked, and Kitt couldn't help but wonder from time to time if those scars had only made her friend's somewhat unhealthy interest in her own appearance even worse.

'Oh, come on,' Evie snorted. 'Everyone tries at least one crash diet on the run-up to Christmas, don't they? I was reading about this parsnip diet. I wanted to fit nicely into my party dresses . . . Anyway, before you start on a rant about how clothes should fit me rather than me having to fit into them, on the subject of Ruby, I don't like your chances of avoiding her. No idea how she does it, but she always seems to appear just when you least—'

'Eeeeeee! There you are, Kitt love.' Ruby's voice rang out over the murmur of the crowds and the husky blare of the band who had now moved on to a rousing rendition of 'Good King Wenceslas'.

Kitt sighed before turning to face the woman, who was now well into her nineties and still going strong, hobbling her way towards Evie and Kitt in a dark hooded cloak. Instead of the walking sticks she often carried, she was leaning on an upturned broomstick for balance.

'Ruby . . .' Kitt said, doing her best to smile and at least look pleased to see her. It wasn't really Ruby's fault that she tried her patience so much. When it came down to it, the woman was just a bit lonely, and for that reason Kitt would have been mortified if so much of a hint of weariness ever showed on her face. 'I'm assuming you got that job you went for with York Witch Walks.'

'No, still waiting to 'ear back. Why would you think that?' Ruby said with a frown.

Kitt cast a glance at Evie and her friend did her best to smother a smirk. Kitt sometimes forgot just how much Ruby marched to the beat of her own drum. Over the years, she had seen this woman blithely pottering about in some unconventional get-ups to say the least. She should have known better than to assume that she was in the employ of one of the city's walking tours just because she was sporting a strange costume.

'The . . . broomstick?' Kitt clarified.

'Oh, it's the winter solstice today, love,' said Ruby. 'You know 'ow I've got to mark the sabbats and, I was just 'aving so much fun with all me celebrations I decided to keep the party going when I left the 'ouse. There's magic in the air today. I can feel it. And anyhow, it can't do any 'arm to do a bit extra and keep all the good spirits on me side and that. Don't want to displease the spirits. There's lots of 'em about between 'alloween and Christmas, you know? Get on their bad side and you never know what'll befall you. It's a road to wreck and ruin, it really is.'

'Indeed,' Kitt said, doing her best not to sound tart about Ruby's somewhat unique belief system.

'Now, I know you've been at work the last few times I've asked yer,' Ruby said, wasting no time in getting down to her most pressing business, 'so, I understand you wouldn't want to drink any of the 'ard stuff while you were on duty, so to speak, but I did bring me mulled wine with me on the off-chance of seeing yer. I think you said tonight was yer night off? Maybe you've got time for a tipple?' At this Ruby pulled a black glass bottle from her cloak and gave it a little shake. Kitt did her best not to remember what it had looked like when Ruby had poured herself a healthy measure of the stuff at the agency the other day. Presumably to prove to Kitt that a person could ingest the substance and still live to see another day.

'Well . . .' Kitt said, remembering Evie's words about getting the ordeal over with.

'I've brought some takeaway cups with me, just in case,' Ruby said, producing those from another inside pocket of her cloak.

'Come on,' Evie said, holding her hand out for a cup. 'I'll try a sip of it, too. Then we're all in on the game.'

'That's the spirit, love,' said Ruby, handing Evie and Kitt a white plastic cup in turn before uncorking the bottle.

'Does it have any magical properties?' Evie asked, while pointedly avoiding Kitt's glare. After the many strange dealings the pair of them had had with her over the years, Evie of all people should know better than to encourage Ruby on the topic of magic and spiritualism.

'Ohhh aye, love, that it 'as, that it 'as. Why do you think I'm so keen for Kitt to give it a go? It's a soothing tonic this one, an elixir you might even say. It opens the third eye. Once you drink this, you will see all that can be seen.'

'Oh . . .' said Evie, unable to disguise the disappointment in her voice.

'It wards off earaches and 'eadaches too,' Ruby quickly added, seemingly reading the room for once and realising that Evie was less than impressed with the idea of having her third eye opened.

'That's a small mercy because I can feel a headache coming on right now,' said Kitt.

'Its 'ealing properties know no bounds . . . good for the skin . . . not to mention weight loss,' Ruby said, ignoring Kitt's comment while filling their cups with a much more

9

generous serving of the beverage than Kitt would have preferred.

'Oooh, definitely count me in then,' said Evie, brightening for a moment before peering inside her cup and announcing: 'It's . . . it's . . . what colour is *that*? Not black . . . not brown . . . somewhere in between! And it's kind of . . . sludgy . . .'

Kitt tried not to take too much satisfaction in the expression of mild horror on her friend's face, but she did go so far as to shoot her an *I told you* look.

'Oh, all the best drinks are,' said Ruby. 'In my book an indiscriminate colour is a mark of a beverage of superior quality, and it's the black cherries that give it that wonderful rich thickness.'

Tentatively, Evie took a sniff and on inhaling the mixture her head jolted back an inch. Her eyes widened and she stared helplessly at Kitt as though perhaps she could think up an excuse to get her out of this.

'Don't worry Evie, it won't kill you,' said Kitt. It was a bit mean to throw her friend's words in her face, but perhaps on actually seeing the drink up close, Evie might at last understand why Kitt had been putting this moment off as long as possible.

Looking rather sorry for herself, Evie took a deep breath. 'Looks like the devil's oil spill,' she said just loud enough for Kitt to hear. If Ruby heard, she didn't acknowledge the comment. 'Oh well,' Evie added, 'down the hatch,' before tilting her head back and emptying her cup in a few gulps.

Scrunching her eyes shut, as though that would somehow make the experience more bearable, Kitt did the same. Doing all she could to ignore how the distinctly aniseed fluid stung at her throat, and the way in which the world around her so suddenly started to spin.

CHAPTER TWO

'Marley was dead: to begin with. There was no doubt whatever about that.'

These words were the next thing Kitt was truly conscious of.

The line, famously written by Charles Dickens, somehow jolted her back into her own skin after a period of unexplained absence. Evie was sitting next to her, staring intently at the low stage in the events tent. A piece of gingerbread passing from hand to mouth between small chuckles. Despite being, perhaps, slightly more giggly than usual Evie seemed her normal self, though for her part Kitt felt far, far from that.

She blinked hard a couple of times. Trying to ground herself in reality.

Quite how she and Evie had found their way, as previously planned, to the events tent for the abridged dramatic reading of *A Christmas Carol*, Kitt couldn't say. She clearly hadn't passed out or anything. If that had happened, she would be laid up somewhere and Evie would already have started teasing her about what a delicate flower she was to have fainted the second alcohol had brushed past her lips.

And yet, for the life of her, Kitt couldn't remember wending her way up the rest of High Petergate to the venue in which they now sat. Or showing her ticket. Or finding her seat. She didn't even remember saying goodbye to Ruby. Kitt had experienced a similar blank in her memory only once before and that had been after a whole night's worth of drinking from a bottle of very cheap vodka during her university days. What in God's name had been in that mulled wine that Ruby had served up?

The second that question formed in Kitt's mind, however, she decided she really didn't want to know the answer.

Though her vision was still a little hazy, Kitt tried to focus on the man on the stage. They had booked seats on the front row, which made it easier. The stage was not very high, Kitt would guess maybe three feet at the most, so they were sitting exceptionally close to the actor as he stood at the front of the stage. The actor in question was dressed in a black suit cut in the late Victorian style and wearing a fake bushy beard in a clear attempt to emulate the appearance of Charles Dickens himself.

As it was a dramatic reading of a book, rather than a play, there was no on-stage setting. Just a microphone stand and a tall wooden table on which the actor had placed a glass of water.

Some efforts had been made, however, to at least make the interior of the tent as festive as possible. A thick, green garland hung in waves around the top of the tent. And, much like the rest of the book fair, illumination was provided by strings of golden fairy lights.

Despite her bleariness, Kitt was at least able to emit a little chuckle at her favourite line from the book: 'There's more of gravy than of grave about you.'

She still had her sense of humour.

That had to be a good sign.

She may not be feeling her best but so long as she could just sit here in the cosy shelter of red canvas, be still for a while and listen to an energetic reading of her all-time favourite Christmas book, she was confident she could recover herself from whatever intoxicating spell the mulled wine had cast on her.

One thing was for sure, though, that was the last ingestible substance Kitt was ever accepting from Ruby.

'I wear the chain I forged in life,' the actor recited, 'I made it, link by link.'

This line in the book had always hit Kitt hard but had only hit harder since she had taken up her role as a private investigator. Being a card-carrying agnostic, she had no clear ideas about what may or may not follow a person into the next life. But she saw clear enough the chains that people forged for themselves in this one. For ten years now, just over, she'd been witness to cruelty and calculation she only could have imagined before, and alongside the victims and the families of their victims, the perpetrators inevitably created suffering for themselves. How did a person live with taking the life of another away? That was one thing about the business she was in that Kitt was sure she would never understand.

'My time is nearly gone,' said the actor on stage, in the booming voice he had adopted for playing the part of Marley's ghost. These words, however, seemed to give the actor pause, for he bent forward for a moment and placed a hand against his chest. With his other hand, which Kitt noticed was shaking, he reached over to his glass of water and took several gulps. Then he pulled a handkerchief from his coat pocket and mopped his brow. Despite the time of year, and the glacial temperatures outside, it was quite warm in the tent. All of those bodies sardined together on closely packed chairs were clearly generating a significant amount of heat. Was the temperature in the tent getting to this bloke? Difficult to be sure but even though she was in less than perfect shape herself, it was obvious to Kitt that, for whatever reason, the actor did not look well.

The pause only lengthened and the man frowned around the audience. His wide, intense eyes betrayed an odd mixture of disbelief and pain.

Kitt and Evie exchanged a look at this juncture; something was really wrong here.

Kitt reached out a hand to the man's arm. From her position on the front row she was just able to do this without standing. Of course, she might be interrupting some dramatic moment in his performance but that wasn't the feeling she was getting. Besides, it was well worth the risk of looking the fool on the off-chance that the man was as unwell as he looked.

'Are you alright?' Kitt whispered.

The man started at her words, as if he had not known that she was there, nor felt her hand touch the sleeve of his long, black jacket.

He shook his head back and forth frantically. His face contorted and seemed to sort of fold in on itself. To Kitt's eyes, his expression read like the very definition of agony. 'No . . . no . . . no! Cinnamon . . .' said the man.

'Cinnamon? What . . . what about it? You . . . need cinnamon?' Kitt said, trying to make sense of why, of all the words in the English language, the man would utter this one.

That said, there was a strong and unmistakable smell of cinnamon in the air. Kitt presumed it was coming from the nearby food and drink stalls but somehow, in the events tent, the smell seemed even more potent than it had outside. Perhaps the actor was feeling overwhelmed and sickly? Or did he have some kind of intolerance to cinnamon? If so, that must be a fairly rare allergy. Kitt had never heard of anyone being allergic to cinnamon before. Moreover, a

Christmas Book Fair was arguably the last place you should go if you were so afflicted.

'Cinnamon . . .' the man repeated, his voice croaky now. His eyes bulging and his mouth hanging open as he grappled with the pain he was so obviously suffering through. He clutched Kitt's arm with a desperate force. 'Sssssssss . . .' He seemed to be about to form the same word again but it was a word he was not destined to finish. To a symphony of gasps and cries from the audience, Kitt watched on as the man's eyes rolled back in his head.

CHAPTER THREE

Kitt found herself blinking hard for the second time in the last fifteen minutes as she looked at the man before her. He had fallen to his knees and was still conscious – just – but there was something most peculiar about him. She couldn't explain quite what she was seeing but if pushed to make a description she would have said it looked very much to her as though his body had become completely rigid.

'Somebody call an ambulance, now!' Kitt shouted out, knowing all too well the signs that a person was not long for this world when she saw them.

'I'll do it!' said Evie, pulling out her mobile phone.

With a hand still grasped tight around Kitt's arm, the actor convulsed and fell backwards, the violence of the movement dragging Kitt out of her seat and wrenching her arm with such force that she cried out at the sickening jolt of it.

Kitt heard Evie shout after her – mid-999 call – as she was pulled towards the stage.

'Help me,' the man croaked. 'Cinnamon!'

The man's body was still convulsing. The temptation was to hold him still but everything Kitt had read about what to do if a person had a seizure told her to ignore this instinct. When the person stopped convulsing, you were supposed to put them on their side. But what if they didn't stop?

Kitt watched on helplessly for what felt like a lifetime, vaguely aware of Evie's phone call to the emergency services to request an ambulance, and little else. In reality the time she stood there, watching, waiting, was probably less than a minute. After which, the man dressed as Charles Dickens lay completely still. His body stiff. His eyes wide.

At this juncture, a man with cornrows braided across his head appeared on the stage. The man was panting in such a way that it was obvious he'd had to push his way from the back somewhere to join them. He wore a yellow lanyard around his neck that identified him as a member of staff for the book fair. He was probably the guy in charge of sound for the performance, or something similar.

'I'm Jordan, I'm a first aider,' he said. Not wasting a moment before crouching next to the actor.

'Leonard,' he said to the man who was lying completely still on the hard wooden boards of the stage. But Leonard did not respond to his name. 'Leonard,' Jordan tried again, a little louder this time. He held his hand close to the man's mouth to see if he could feel any breath. A few seconds later he shook his head. 'God knows how long an ambulance will be.'

19

'I think they're supposed to respond to events of this magnitude within ten minutes,' said Kitt. 'But I don't think that's going to be soon enough.'

'Take it from me, there's a lot that can affect whether an ambulance gets here in that space of time, even in this kind of emergency,' said Jordan. 'We need to start CPR.'

Kitt looked again at the man she had now gleaned was called Leonard, fully prepared to use her own first aid skills to support any attempts at resuscitation. Something about his appearance, however, made her wonder how much good it would do. It wasn't just that the man's chest was completely still. A person might yet have CPR performed on them even if there were no signs of life. In fact, that was sort of the point of it. It was more to do with just how far gone the man already looked.

Jordan moved into a kneeling position and, interlocking his fingers, began chest compressions. 'I'm also trained in CPR. I'll take over when you tire,' said Kitt.

Jordan simply offered Kitt a rapid nod as he continued pressing down on Leonard's chest.

'Leonard,' Kitt said to the man. She had read that saying a person's name when they were unresponsive could help. 'Leonard, we're here for you. If you can hear me, take comfort in the fact that you're not alone.'

'His body ...' Jordan said, already breathless from his efforts. 'It's ... it's stiff ... really ... really stiff. I can barely do the compressions. It can't be . . . not so soon . . . but . . . it feels like rigor mortis.'

'You've . . . been around a lot of dead bodies?' Kitt said as gently as she could. She didn't want to judge the young man outright as being naive about such matters. But she knew from her research into the process the body goes through after a person had stopped breathing that it took at least two hours after death for rigor mortis to set in. Not being a medical doctor, she couldn't explain why Leonard's body appeared so rigid, but the likeliest explanation was not rigor mortis.

'I'm training to be a paramedic,' Jordan confirmed between ragged breaths. Kitt wouldn't have expected a young man like Jordan to tire from the repetitive action of compressions quite so soon, but then, there was no denying that the body was stiffer than expected. 'Been an ambulance care assistant for a year now. Seen quite a few bodies. I'm telling you, something isn't right with this one.'

'What do you mean, not right?' said Evie, now that she had finished her phone call.

Jordan did not get a chance to respond. Just as Evie said these words, a large crack sounded out. Something inside the body had definitely broken. Not uncommon when delivering CPR but the sound was loud enough for Jordan to cease his movements at once and frown. 'I know what a rib snapping from compressions sounds like . . . that didn't sound normal to me.'

'In what way?' said Kitt, looking Leonard up and down as though there might be some obvious visual clue.

'I can't explain it,' said Jordan. 'The body . . . it looks . . . something just isn't right.'

'What should we do?' said Kitt. 'Is there a protocol we can follow for this kind of bodily response?'

'Not that I know of,' said Jordan, before resuming his compressions.

Kitt and Evie exchanged a look of concern. It was clear from Evie's frown that, just like Kitt, she had noticed the oddness of Leonard's body. The strange, soured appearance it had taken on.

Jordan managed another three compressions before another ungodly crack came from the body and, though Kitt couldn't see precisely what was going on under Leonard's clothes, at the sound of the second snap she saw his chest sort of sink into itself in a way that didn't look at all natural.

Jordan's eyes widened. He waited a moment, stared at Leonard's face, and then, once again, shook his head. 'Something's wrong . . . I mean, look at him . . . it's . . . I've never seen somebody look like this minutes after an incident. I'm not convinced we should continue CPR.'

'You . . . you think there's no hope of resuscitation?' Kitt confirmed.

Jordan shook his head. 'If I thought there was a chance I'd continue, you know I would, but . . . well, just look at him.'

Swallowing hard, Kitt manoeuvred herself so she could

kneel on the stage, on the other side of Leonard's body. Gently, she released her arm from the man's grip and then pressed two of her own fingers against his neck.

She let out a little gasp as her hands pressed against his skin. 'He's cold,' she told Jordan and Evie in a half-whisper. 'So cold . . . like you say, it's as though he's been gone for hours.'

'That . . . can't be normal?' said Evie.

'I . . . I've never known anything like it. There's no body heat left at all.'

Jordan reached out and pressed the back of his hand to Leonard's face to confirm for himself what Kitt had said. 'I don't understand it, he only just went down. I mean, how many minutes could really have passed? Five? Not more than that. Body temperature can't fall that fast . . . I mean, not from what I've studied. I mean, can it?'

'I don't . . . think so. I . . . I don't know. I've never heard of it happening this fast. But there's no pulse and he's cold and . . . so stiff.' And there was something else but it was too strange a detail for Kitt to mention out loud.

The strong smell of cinnamon she had detected before, it wasn't coming from the nearby food stalls as she'd imagined but from Leonard himself. Now that she was up close with the body, there was no mistaking where the scent had originated. It was so pungent it almost made Kitt want to gag but, in fairness, she couldn't tell if that was just the after-effects of Ruby's mulled wine. Perhaps her senses were still playing tricks on her after that shock to the system. Or perhaps the mere sickliness of the scene in front of her was affecting her constitution. At any rate, she could think about how the body smelled later. Right now, there was one pressing matter to be settled. Was this man as far gone as he appeared? Or was there still a chance for him?

Kitt looked at her watch, and waited. Staring into the man's vacant grey eyes, feeling the cold of his skin against her fingertips, she knew in her heart he was gone and yet still she waited.

Hoping.

Willing a pulse to beat out.

A Christmas miracle.

Wasn't she long overdue one of those? But try as she might, she couldn't ignore the colour of the man's skin. Pale blue. A sign of what forensic workers called lividity.

But no . . .

It couldn't be.

Not so quickly.

There had to be something wrong with the lighting in this tent. Or perhaps she was just too unnerved by Leonard's appearance in general to make sound judgements. She had been unsettled by what Jordan had said about rigor mortis, and maybe her imagination was running away with her.

Yes, that had to be it.

Lividity wasn't usually visible for at least an hour after a person died. Leonard couldn't have stopped breathing more than five minutes ago. It could not be lividity.

That was what Kitt told herself even though some instinct in her, deep down, knew better.

Once a whole minute had passed, Kitt was certain her suspicions were correct but still she waited another minute. Everyone in the events tent waited with her. Silent. Still. While, somewhere, outside the tent in the near distance, the brass band could be heard playing 'God Rest Ye Merry Gentlemen'.

After the second minute had passed, Kitt knew she had no choice but to speak up.

She shook her head at Jordan.

'I'm sorry. There's nothing there. I think you're right. I'm afraid this man is dead.'

CHAPTER FOUR

'Right everyone, as the ambulance crew have already told you, I need you to stay back, some of you are still not complying with what you've been asked to do. We've asked you to do it for good reason,' Detective Inspector Malcolm Halloran shouted, after taking one look at the body of Leonard Bell when he arrived at the scene an hour later.

The time between Leonard's death and Halloran's arrival had been largely filled with letting the ambulance crew know that the man they had been called out to had died and trying to keep everyone who had witnessed the death in the events tent until the police could take command of the scene. Although the exact nature of this man's demise had yet to be ascertained, Kitt knew that the mere fact there had been an unexplained death made this situation a police matter. She had clarified this with the organisers of the book fair, who had confirmed with the police by phone and relayed this to the audience.

Since Leonard had already been established as dead by an ambulance care assistant, the ambulance crew arrived about half an hour later. Kitt noticed two things that happened as the two paramedics approached the body: firstly, both their expressions changed from neutrality to confusion and disgust. The second thing Kitt noticed was that neither of them touched or even went anywhere near the body.

The next thing Kitt knew, the paramedics had instructed everyone to stand as far away from the deceased as possible until the police arrived. Kitt had just assumed they didn't want anyone tampering with it or accidentally leaving forensic material that would muddy an investigation, but the severity of Halloran's reaction now that he was on scene made her think twice about that.

'Banks, we're going to need hazmat suits for this. Level A,' Halloran added.

'Sir,' said Detective Sergeant Charlotte Banks with a stiff nod. Banks, who had been married to Evie for several years, cast a worried glance in the direction of her wife before striding off to carry out Halloran's instructions. As a rule, Banks wasn't one for giving much away and her unmissable alarm about this situation was more than enough to set Kitt on edge.

'I'm . . . assuming an A grade isn't good in this instance?' said Kitt, completely taken aback by the order Halloran had just dished out to Banks.

'It's really not,' Halloran said to Kitt, before turning back to the already agitated and perturbed crowd. Everyone in the tent had spent their wait for the police talking in hushed tones about just how tragic an incident this had been. How sad it would be for this man's family to discover he wasn't coming home and how terrible a thing that was to endure a mere four nights before Christmas. Now that the police were here, however, Kitt could see a bit of agitation and self-interest creeping up on certain members of the crowd. Some were looking at their watches. Others were glaring at Halloran before muttering to the person next to them that they wished the police would get a move on.

Kitt knew from all the stories Halloran had told her during the years they'd been romantically involved that he was very used to managing a crowd like this one. Even if she hadn't known that outright about him, the tone he used when addressing the tent would have left her in no doubt about it.

'OK, listen up everybody. I know you'd probably rather be anywhere else but here, but since there has been a death this situation now warrants a police investigation. This means, there's going to be a bit of a wait. I need you all to remain in the tent until you've been given official clearance to leave and—'

'But I've got a babysitter to relieve, how long is this going to be?' a man called out somewhere in the crowd.

Kitt's eyes widened at the interruption and at the sight of Halloran's jaw clenching.

'You're not the only person in the room who has got other commitments, sir. And I'm sure this man, who is now dead, also had plans for later this evening.' Halloran pointed at the body lying on the stage. 'This is a serious incident otherwise I wouldn't have to hold you. We will process all of the information we need as quickly as possible. I assure you, I don't want you hanging around here any longer than necessary. But I do need you all to keep to the perimeter of the tent, away from the body. For anyone thinking this would be a good time to make a break for it, I assure you, you won't get far and you're only going to delay departure for everyone else. Cooperate and we'll be able to get this nightmare over with as soon as possible. It's no more fun for us than it is for you.'

There weren't any further outbursts, but a low grumble and murmur rose up from the crowd as the few stragglers moved to the perimeter of the tent.

'Before I go any further, I need to speak to you three individually,' Halloran said, looking between Kitt, Evie and Jordan.

'Why?' said Jordan.

Halloran looked long and hard at Jordan. Long enough that Jordan asked a follow-up question.

'Is . . . it's not to do with those hazmat suits you requested?'

'I'm afraid so,' said Halloran. Slowly, he turned to Kitt. 'Pet . . . you . . . you didn't touch the deceased, did you?'

At this, Kitt's whole body turned cold. 'Mal . . . I . . . yes,

I did. Several times. I reached out to him when he looked ill. He grabbed my arm when he had his seizure. I took his pulse to confirm his death. Why? What's . . . . what's going on here?'

The lines on Halloran's face seemed to harden and he ran a hand over his short-trimmed beard. After a decade in a relationship with this man, Kitt was more than familiar with that look. It always meant the worst had happened.

'What about you?' Halloran said, turning to Evie. 'Did you touch the body?'

'No, but I did sit next to it, with Kitt, while we waited for you to arrive. So, I definitely spent quite a bit of time in close proximity to it,' said Evie. 'And from the look on your face, I'm guessing that's bad . . . isn't it?'

'It's too early to be concerned,' said Halloran, though there was a dullness to his steel blue eyes that always overtook them when things were serious. Kitt recognised it at once as a sign that Halloran was a lot more concerned than he was letting on.

'I gave him compressions,' said Jordan. 'So, I definitely touched the body.'

'Look, the important thing here is not to panic. We don't know anything yet,' Halloran said. 'But we do have to take some precautions to keep everyone safe. Just in case.'

'In case of what exactly?' Kitt said.

'Just . . . in case, pet,' said Halloran, his voice almost breaking as he did so. And in that moment, Kitt felt her heart physically sink in her chest. Halloran couldn't even bring himself to say the words. But she could make some guesses about what was worrying him based on his questions about how close they had been to the body. That, and his request for hazmat suits.

At this juncture, Halloran turned to Jordan. 'So, you administered the chest compressions?'

Jordan offered Halloran a nod that was far too long and vigorous in response to a simple question. He seemed to be operating on autopilot. The guy was probably in shock. He was no doubt aware of some of the risks involved in coming into very close contact with numerous people during his ambulance training. Moreover, had he seen the body in the same state the paramedics found it in, he probably wouldn't have touched it in the first place either. Still, Halloran's unspoken insinuation that in trying to help save another human being he may have unwittingly put his own life in danger probably wasn't on his paramedic-in-training bingo card.

Looking at his wide brown eyes, Kitt couldn't help but feel sorry for the lad. He couldn't be much older than twenty-five from the look of him, and to face your own mortality at that age would be a difficult thing for anyone. Talk about a good deed never going unpunished.

'We're going to need to separate and quarantine you all, somewhere isolated. If such a place exists in York city centre in the run-up to Christmas,' Halloran said to Kitt, Evie and Jordan.

Kitt cast a glance in Evie's direction and her friend offered her a nod. She already knew what Kitt was thinking.

'Mal,' said Kitt. 'If it's all the same to you, I'll take my chances and be quarantined with Evie, rather than on my own.'

'You might be risking Evie with that course of action, pet,' said Halloran.

'I've already been sitting next to Kitt for an hour,' said Evie. 'I'd say if any damage was going to happen it was likely already done.'

'Alright,' said Halloran. 'That does mean we only have to find two spaces for quarantine, rather than three. But at least stand a couple of metres apart from one another until we've got confirmation that everything's OK.'

Taking stock of how close they were standing to each other just then, the pair inched a little further apart.

'Jordan, I would say these two are taking a risk in sticking together, so I'm going to strongly recommend that you quarantine separately,' said Halloran.

'I'll do whatever you say,' said Jordan. 'But ... you haven't really explained why you think we need to quarantine ourselves in the first place. And I'd really like to know that before I get isolated from everyone.'

Halloran paused. 'Well, please understand it's just a precaution at this stage. Everything is probably going to be fine but we can't take any risks.'

'You think Leonard was exposed to some kind of substance

or disease and that might have killed him, don't you?' Kitt said. She wasn't convinced that Halloran was ever going to get around to saying the words out loud unless she did it for him first. She couldn't much blame him for that. If the roles were reversed, if he had been exposed to something potentially deadly, she probably wouldn't want to think too hard about it either. As she spoke, Kitt tried to push the memory of Leonard's wide, searching eyes right before he died from her mind, and failed. Could that really be about to happen to her?

'Those things are possibilities,' said Halloran, 'and given the condition of the body, we can't discount that some kind of substance or disease might be responsible for Leonard's death. But even if that is the case, even if it is something contagious, there might be time to treat it before it becomes fatal. More to the point, if this man has been exposed to some kind of toxic substance, it doesn't mean you have been. It could have happened at any juncture. So, it really is too soon to worry. We just have to rule it out.'

Halloran paused here and Kitt took the opportunity to look from Halloran across to Evie. She'd known Evie long enough to recognise when she was forcing a smile. That was what her friend was doing right now, and it was probably in a bid to keep from crying. As if Evie hadn't been through enough over the years without being dragged into this. That said, that sentiment rather counted for Kitt too.

'I know this must be frightening, for all of you,' Halloran

said. 'I wish I had more time to reassure you. But I'm afraid we can't spend any more time than we have discussing the matter. I need you to take my word for the fact that any worrying you might be doing is premature. I need to get suited up and I need to get your blood tests run immediately. I've got a friend in A&E at the hospital and they can usually run bloodworks within a couple of hours. We should know more very soon. So, try not to panic. I just have to treat this incident as though it is a high alert. We can't risk somebody else suffering the same fate.'

'I understand,' said Kitt, unable to stop her eyes from wandering to the body that lay several feet away on the stage. Leonard had gone down so suddenly. And the look on his face, there had been no mistaking the terror in it. Or the agony. The band were still playing Christmas songs somewhere outside and just then they were performing 'Silent Night'. But from where Kitt was standing, all seemed far from calm and bright. And there was no heavenly peace to be found.

Kitt did what she could to focus on what Mal had said about quarantine being the most sensible procedure under the circumstances. He had to err on the side of caution when there might not be anything to worry about at all. They really had no idea what had caused this man to collapse as he did. Or caused his body to take on such a strange and disconcerting appearance. For all they knew, the police would check with his doctor and find that he had some very rare condition and had simply, by the course of nature, succumbed to it.

As much as Kitt tried to reassure herself, however, the nagging feeling in her gut did not subside as she peered down at Leonard's pale, contorted face. She had seen the torment in his eyes as he had died. There was almost an accusation in his stare, as though he were angry or full of a sense of betrayal. There was something about it that made it seem to Kitt that someone was to blame for what had happened, and that Leonard knew upon whom the blame should rest.

Kitt shook her head. She really was getting carried away. So much speculation when they didn't know anything yet. Likely all this was running through her mind because she was desperately trying to ignore the one question that would not leave her. For she couldn't help but wonder, given all the contact she had with Leonard in the moments right before and after his death, if his fate would become her fate too.

CHAPTER FIVE

Three hours later, Kitt learned that if anything could set a woman on edge, it was the sight of her romantic partner walking towards her in a blue hazmat suit.

Kitt's muscles tensed as Halloran entered the staff-only tent where she and Evie had been instructed to stay, while keeping a three-metre distance from each other at all times. There was one detail that gave Kitt cause to hope, and that was that Halloran had lowered the mask on his suit as he'd entered. That was surely a sign of good news about the blood tests she and Evie had taken? Unless he just couldn't bear to deliver the worst tidings to her with his face covered up?

'You're in the clear,' Halloran called over before he was even within six feet of them.

'Oh, Mal,' Kitt said. 'Both of us? You're sure?'

'Yes, pet,' said Halloran. 'Banks was very sorry she couldn't come along with me and tell you herself, Evie, but as you know resources are low and we're trying to work this crime scene as quickly as possible. She's busy giving Jordan the all-clear but she'll be along as soon as she can.'

'I know she will,' Evie said in a tone that indicated she'd been under no illusions about just how seriously Banks took her work when she married her.

'God,' said Kitt. 'I was so worried we'd been exposed to something.'

'Well, you're not the only one,' said Halloran. 'But there's nothing untoward in your bloodwork according to my contact. And neither of you have developed any symptoms of any kind? Shortness of breath or dizziness?'

'Oh no,' said Evie. 'I've been feeling very full of breath and not a hint of dizziness. The world is definitely standing still.'

'Hmmm,' said Kitt.

'What?' said Halloran, narrowing his eyes.

'Well, I did have a bit of a strange experience this evening but I thought it was down to drinking Ruby's mulled wine,' said Kitt.

'You . . . ingested *that*?' said Halloran. 'As in, voluntarily? Bloody hell, Kitt, I thought you knew better.'

'You know she's like a dog with a bone when she gets started on something,' said Kitt.

'Yes, I suppose I do,' Halloran said, his tone weary at the mere mention of Ruby who so often managed to rub him up the wrong way without even trying. 'What was the strange experience?'

'After I drank that godawful concoction, the world did seem to spin,' said Kitt. 'And I had a blank in my memory. I can't remember getting to the venue tonight. The next thing I remembered after drinking Ruby's wine was the performance starting. I couldn't remember anything in between. I didn't think anything of it at the time, especially since I'd ingested one of Ruby's homemade concoctions, but in light of all that's happened . . .'

'I thought you were a bit giddy on the way to the events tent,' said Evie. 'But I just assumed you were high on the fumes of all the old books on sale at the Christmas Book Fair.'

'What do you mean, giddy, exactly?' said Kitt, her nose crinkling somewhat at the suggestion. She was as happy as the next person to enjoy a good joke but giddy was not a word she ever would have imagined being applied to her.

'Well, you were singing,' said Evie.

'Singing?' Kitt and Halloran said in unison. Though while Halloran's voice was laced with amusement, Kitt's had the distinct note of alarm.

Evie nodded, her grin widening. 'You gave a very hearty rendition of the *Dogtanian* theme tune. And you followed that one up with the one from *Danger Mouse*.'

'Oh God, don't tell me any more,' said Kitt. 'I don't want to know. I suppose if I was singing, the odds are I was a bit . . .'

'Squiffy,' Evie finished. She had a love of all things vintage, including old-fashioned language, and could always be

38

counted upon to use a word that hadn't passed anyone's lips in fifty years just for the fun of it.

'Yes,' Kitt said, 'rather than suffering the after-effects of some unknown substance.'

'Ruby Barnett's homemade mulled wine *is* an unknown substance,' said Halloran. 'But yes, based on your description, and the timing of it – you experienced all this before you reached the events tent?'

Kitt confirmed that was correct.

'Then the odds are it's just a reaction to whatever the hell Ruby put in that drink. I think based on the blood test we can rest somewhat easy. But if either of you feel anything out of the ordinary, anything at all, you must report it straight away and quarantine yourselves.'

'I'm so glad Jordan is going to be alright too,' said Kitt. 'He probably had no idea when he delivered CPR that he might be putting his life at risk.'

'Probably not, but mercifully he didn't contract anything,' said Halloran. 'Banks is giving him the same advice that I've given you. Everyone in the audience has been checked over by one of the paramedics on scene. Nobody has informed us of any strange symptoms so far and have been advised to report it immediately if they experience any. Based on the fact that you two and Jordan aren't exhibiting any worrying signs, however, I'm confident the rest of the crowd should be OK. The three of you were the most likely candidates to have been exposed to something, if indeed there was anything to be exposed to in the first place. Which, of course, I still don't know for sure. These are just the measures we have to take under these circumstances.'

'I know there's a long way to go before figuring all this out but I must say I'm relieved that, at least for now, it seems as though any threat to life was localised and isn't going to affect anyone else,' said Kitt.

'You and me both,' said Halloran. 'And here was me thinking, when you rang, that you'd called just to check in and say you loved me. You know, most couples have traditions that are all about anniversaries and flowers and chocolates being exchanged. But for some reason you and I have a tradition by which you call me about dead bodies. Do you think that's something we should probably try to work on?'

'Oooh, will you give over?' said Kitt, smiling in spite of herself, and the morbid situation. 'Funnily enough, watching a man dressed as Charles Dickens keel over right in front of me isn't my idea of a relaxing night off. Neither is discovering I might have been exposed to a toxic substance and spending the evening in quarantine. Call me old-fashioned, but I'd take a few tipples at the pub over that any time.'

'And to be fair,' said Evie, 'Kitt has only called you about dead bodies on a handful of occasions.'

'Thank you, Evie,' said Kitt. 'That's probably about enough help from you.'

'I know everything has checked out OK physically,

at least for now, but are you both alright in yourselves after everything that's happened?' Halloran said, his tone becoming gentler as he looked between the two of them.

'In comparison with the poor man who died tonight under as yet unexplained circumstances, I'd say we're both fine,' Kitt said, looking at Evie for confirmation and getting a firm nod in reply. 'Mal, I've never seen someone die like that. I'm assuming that at some point you'll need us both to give you a full witness statement?'

'Yes, that'll ideally be done down at the station. Probably tomorrow now,' said Halloran. 'There's just too much else that's urgent here to tie up before we get on to witness statements.'

'Like trying to determine a cause of death?' said Kitt.

'Yes,' said Halloran. 'But it's not just that we haven't been able to determine the cause of death by examining the body. We couldn't even draw blood to run tests on it as we did with you because of the decomposition already present. So, we'll have to run other tests and, of course, an autopsy will have to be performed. The only thing we can say for sure is that something strange is going on with how quickly the body is demonstrating signs of decay. I don't mind telling you, the whole situation is creeping me out.'

'Be thankful you weren't there when the poor chap went down,' said Evie. 'It was like a horror film.'

Halloran nodded. 'The sequel is still playing out at the crime scene, I can tell you.'

'Thankfully I wouldn't know much about that,' said Kitt. 'Grace is the horror fan at Hartley and Edwards Investigations. But, you've already spoken to Jordan in detail, I take it? He's told you . . . what the body was like mere minutes after Leonard went down?'

'Yeah,' Halloran said. 'I had hoped with him being a paramedic in training that he might have some ideas about cause of death when the state of the body stumped the coroner. Not much chance of a trainee knowing something an experienced coroner doesn't but sometimes people new into the medical fold have the latest information and, frankly, in a situation like this I'm open to any learned opinion. But Jordan said he'd never seen anything like this and all he could vouch for was that it felt like rigor mortis had set in within a couple of minutes of the death occurring. Which is unusual, to put it mildly.'

'I think it is true though, Mal,' said Kitt. 'When Jordan first said that, I didn't really think it was possible. But then I looked at the body. It . . . it didn't look like a fresh corpse. The stuff you'd usually expect to happen hours after death was happening in minutes. I know some killers use sodium hydroxide to speed up decomposition—'

'Ugh,' said Evie. 'Do you have to? I see you've been indulging in your usual cosy bedtime reading. I need to get some new friends who read Enid Blyton at bedtime.'

'I'm not ill-disposed to Blyton if I'm in the mood,' said Kitt, offering her friend a wry smile at the same time. Admittedly, the reading pile on her bedside table had become increasingly gritty since she'd opened the agency.

'Yes, but I've seen bodies where that's happened to them,' said Halloran. 'I know what that looks like. That's not what's going on here. It's . . . it's something else. It's the strangest thing I've ever seen, and it's only got worse while we've been examining the crime scene. It's as though the stages of death have somehow been accelerated. That's why we need to get the body tested asap to see what's going on. Due to red tape, the very fastest I'm going to get a post-mortem is within twenty-four hours, the full report will take a lot longer but we should be able to get an initial cause of death confirmed once that has taken place.'

'And, call me a naive optimist, but I'm assuming we're still entertaining the idea that this might be a case of death by natural causes?' said Kitt.

'Until we've got a cause of death confirmed, we have to keep an open mind,' said Halloran. 'There may be some medical condition I'm not aware of that does . . . that to a body. But I've never heard or seen anything like it in all my years on the job. And failing that . . . well, I don't want to put any blinkers on the investigation, but we could be looking at foul play.'

'Since there was no violent act, so far as any of us could see anyway, if it is foul play, you must be thinking poison,' said Kitt.

'Aye. And, if that is the case, whatever the substance is

must be responsible for the rate of decay. It must be something that keeps . . . eating away at a person. The thing is, I don't know of any poison that does that to a body,' said Halloran.

'Me neither,' said Kitt. 'And it's something I've read a lot about over the years.'

'Name me a subject that isn't,' said Halloran.

'Crikey, dinner with you two must be a romantic dream,' said Evie. 'Nothing to make that roast beef go down a treat like a good chat about poison.'

'Don't be ridiculous, Evie,' said Kitt. 'Everyone knows it's bad form to discuss poison over dinner.'

'Yeah, you at least wait until the cheese plate has been digested,' said Halloran.

'If you've quite finished discussing your favourite brand of smoked cheddar, sir, I've got more news about the body.' These words, spoken in a strong Glaswegian accent, came from Banks who had slipped into the staff tent without anyone noticing.

'Oooh, Stealth Wife strikes again,' Evie said, holding a hand against her heart. 'Three years of marriage and I still don't know how you manage to skulk to such an impressive standard.'

'What can I say? I believe in finding ways of keeping a marriage exciting.' The officer paused then and there was a notable softening of her tone as she added: 'I'm glad to hear you didn't manage to get yourself contaminated by a toxic substance on a night out, which would be, of course, a very typical thing for you to do.' Banks offered Evie a small smirk. Which as far as Kitt was aware was a very rare sight when Banks was on duty.

Evie smiled back. 'You don't get rid of Evie Bowes that easily!'

'You said something was going on with the body, Banks?' Halloran said.

'Yes . . . I'm afraid it's already started bloating, sir . . . and foaming,' said Banks.

'What?' Halloran said, his mouth hanging open. 'But . . . but . . .'

'I know,' Banks said.

'What?' said Evie looking between Banks and Halloran. 'What does that mean?'

'When a body starts decaying—' Kitt began.

'Oh brother, I had to ask,' Evie said with a shake of her head.

'Do you want to know or not?'

Slowly, Evie nodded.

'It usually doesn't happen until a few days after death but dead bodies, they start to bloat and sort of foam at the mouth and nose. It's a well-recognised sign of decay among those who work with cadavers.'

'A few days?' Evie repeated. 'That poor chap really is decaying faster than expected.'

'You said that the body was cold to the touch only a few

minutes after Leonard stopped breathing?' said Halloran. 'And you're sure of that?'

'Stone cold,' said Kitt. 'I commented to Jordan about it right away. He felt it for himself. It wasn't anything to do with the cold weather getting to my hands or anything. There was no mistaking it and it was unsettling to say the least.'

'Yes, he told me that he put his hand against Leonard's skin to confirm what you'd said. I'm sorry, don't take this as me doubting your word, it's just . . . it's just difficult to really take it in. What should be happening to the body in hours is happening in minutes. What should be happening in days is happening in hours. Dear God,' Halloran said with a shake of his head. 'What the hell could cause a situation like that?'

CHAPTER SIX

'I wish I knew, Mal,' was the only way Kitt could think to answer Halloran's ominous question.

'Obviously there have been incidents in the UK of people being exposed to toxic substances, both by accident and on purpose, poisonings and the like,' said Banks. 'But I've not seen anything like this before, and I've seen some things over the years.'

'I'm a fully paid-up member of that club, too,' said Kitt. 'There is one thing I should mention. But I don't know if it was my mind playing tricks on me. When I was taking Leonard's pulse. I can't quite explain it, but there was a strong smell of . . . of . . .'

'Cinnamon,' Halloran and Banks finished the sentence for Kitt in unison.

'So, I wasn't imagining it . . .' said Kitt.

'No, you weren't,' said Halloran. 'There's no way of knowing if the smell is related to the cause of death right now but there's also no missing the fact that the corpse smells like an overbaked Christmas cookie.'

'Are you trying to put me off Christmas cookies?' said Evie. 'On second thoughts, I *am* trying to slim down. Say more stuff like that.'

Kitt shook her head at her friend before resuming her conversation with Halloran. 'It was the last word Leonard said,' Kitt explained.

'What was?' said Halloran.

'Cinnamon,' said Kitt. 'He repeated it several times. And the way he said it. As though he was afraid of it. Of . . . cinnamon for heaven's sake. It doesn't make any sense when I say it out loud but it must mean something for him to repeat it over and over like that. We just don't know what yet.'

At this juncture Banks's phone rang and she strode off into a corner of the tent to take the call. Despite the seriousness of the situation, Kitt couldn't help but smile after her. Given the company present, Mal would have just taken that call in front of everyone while perhaps being a bit careful in his own word choice so that those in attendance weren't exposed to any sensitive information.

But not Banks.

She was a stickler for protocol and not even marrying the love of her life would seemingly change those hard-boiled instincts.

'I'll make a note of what you've relayed, about cinnamon

being the last thing he said. Maybe it'll make sense later. Especially considering that the body reeks of the stuff,' said Halloran. 'I'm going to have to head back to the crime scene in a minute, but before I do, did you notice anything unusual happening before the performance?'

Kitt turned to Evie and raised her eyebrows in expectation.

'Don't look at me,' said Evie. 'I'm not the observant one of the two of us. Especially not when I've got a big bag of gingerbread in my hand.'

Kitt let out a little sigh. 'I don't know if anything unusual was happening before the performance because, as I said, I can't remember getting to the venue. I was two sheets to the wind on Ruby's mulled wine, remember?'

'So, when the performance started, you didn't notice anyone hanging around? Nobody suspicious?' said Halloran.

'I'm sorry, love,' said Kitt. 'But if I was giving acapella versions of the *Dogtanian* theme tune I really don't think I was in a fit state to be noticing things like that. The only reason I'm as alert as I am now is that the crisis situation jolted me out of my daze and the adrenaline must have kicked in. I suspect I'm going to have a long sleep and a sore head in the morning. Not much good to you on the observation front, I'm afraid.'

'Sir,' Banks said, returning from the phone call she'd taken.

'Any news, Banks?'

'We've located next of kin, sir. A wife. And, we've ascertained the victim's place of work.' Banks paused here, clearly not wishing to give away any more detail than necessary in front of Kitt and Evie.

'With the body decaying at this rate, we don't have time to pussyfoot around, Banks,' said Halloran.

'Sir, he worked at the Defence Medical Agency on the outskirts of Clifton.'

'I know the place,' Halloran said. 'It's a military agency.'

'Wait . . . I thought the man who died was an actor . . .' Evie said.

'Most of the people at the book fair are just locals volunteering. Like Jordan, helping out backstage but he's training to be a paramedic. I'm sure Leonard was another one who put his name in the hat,' said Kitt. 'The Defence Medical Agency . . . I think I remember the protests when that place opened. People were up in arms about something like that being built on the edge of the city.'

'I'm amazed you weren't part of the protests,' said Halloran.

'If we lived in a completely peaceful world where nobody was ever a threat to anyone else then maybe I would feel like I could afford to be,' said Kitt. 'Absolute pacifism is, very sadly, a luxury no country can afford. Plus, it's a bit rich to get all riled up about something like that when RAF Fylingdales has been sitting in the heart of the Yorkshire Moors since the early sixties. It's not like the county of Yorkshire has some kind of exemption certificate from the realities of the world.'

'If only,' said Evie. 'Wouldn't that be nice.'

Kitt smiled at her friend's comment and then turned back to Halloran. 'But Mal . . . if he works at a medical agency. Well, they might deal with all kinds of substances . . . maybe even diseases too. Do you think Leonard might have been exposed to something on the job? Perhaps even by accident or without his knowledge? It surely can't be a coincidence that he works at some kind of medical facility and has had something like this happen to him? An unexplained death with an advanced rate of decay? There simply must be some connection, mustn't there?'

'You know the job almost as well as I do by now. We can't go in with any assumptions. There's still a chance of foul play. That somebody who knew where he worked might just have wanted it to look as though he'd had some kind of accident on the job. If this guy's death has anything to do with his place of work, however, I can be sure of two things. One, it will be a media frenzy.'

'There are already reporters outside,' said Banks. 'I've given them no comment for now but the hazmat suits didn't escape their notice. We'll probably have to say something to them to keep them from drawing their own conclusions and starting a panic.'

Halloran sighed and nodded to himself. 'I'll give them a

statement that the suits are just a precaution for now until we ascertain a cause of death and hope that pacifies them.'

'What's the second thing you can be sure of?' asked Evie.

Halloran's jaw tightened before he answered. 'That it'll be an absolute catfight getting any information. Most of the work the Defence Medical Agency do is classified and even with a dead body they can insist on filing certain information for their eyes only.'

'I could see if we've got an Information Sharing Agreement with them?' said Banks. 'I don't know if we do with that agency but it's worth a look.'

'I don't remember them being on the list,' said Halloran. 'But let's double check.'

'If they won't share any information with you that ... that would definitely complicate things, to put it lightly,' said Kitt, thinking back to her last major case which had played out on the border of Scotland. She, her assistant Grace and a man Kitt had offered work experience to – Joe Golding – had stumbled on a classified case the government were working on. It had been one of the most difficult mysteries Kitt had ever unravelled. It clearly hadn't put Joe off the job as he had gone on to start his own private investigation agency over in Manchester, but after that experience, Kitt didn't like their odds of getting information about an unexplained death out of a military institution.

'Let's keep an open mind and hope, for now, for some other explanation,' said Halloran. 'Perhaps when we inform his next of kin, his wife will be able to offer some useful insights.'

'Will you go straight there?' said Kitt.

'Pretty much,' said Halloran. 'I need to make sure all the tests are requested first. At the rate this body is decomposing there won't be anything but a skeleton left to analyse if the tests aren't performed quickly enough.'

Kitt sighed. What a terrible fate to befall anyone. She could only imagine the struggle Mal would have explaining the situation to Leonard's wife. What a terrible heartbreak to endure. 'I'll be at home when you're done,' she said to him.

'Me too,' Evie said to Banks.

Both the officers nodded and made their way out of the tent.

'I hate when they have to inform next of kin,' said Evie.

'Worst part of the job, no doubt about it,' said Kitt.

'And right near Christmas time too,' said Evie. 'I'm sure there's never a good time of year to receive that kind of news but Christmas must be up there with the worst.'

'Unthinkable, really,' said Kitt. 'We never got to this part in the reading but when Scrooge has his epiphany in *A Christmas Carol* he promises to honour Christmas in his heart and try to keep it all the year.'

'Yeah,' said Evie. 'I think I remember that bit from the Muppet version.'

Kitt rolled her eyes at Evie and shook her head. 'Yes, well,

I don't know how anyone could hope to keep a promise like that after hearing news that a loved one had died so brutally, so unexpectedly.'

'Kitt . . .' said Evie. 'What do you think is going on with the body? I mean, why do you think it's decaying so fast?'

'I don't know,' Kitt said. 'My money is on that facility Leonard worked at. It might not be a purposeful poisoning. It could be down to negligence of some sort. Or, it might be the result of a workplace accident that either Leonard didn't report or they simply didn't understand the consequences of when it happened. But, whether Leonard's employer is involved in what's happened to him or not, there's no doubt that this is no ordinary death. I don't know what it is exactly, but something very unusual is going on.'

CHAPTER SEVEN

Kitt awoke with a start to a familiar meow.

'Iago?' she said, her voice still husky in her sleepy state. Lifting her head just enough to see what her black cat was up to, she caught the illuminated digital display on her alarm clock.

One a.m.

She had barely been in bed for an hour, yet, somehow, it felt so much longer.

Groaning, she looked around for the cat, who was strangely persistent in his meowing. The door to the bedroom was open, an unusual detail in itself, and Iago sat in the frame. His yellow-eyed stare glaring back at her through the dimness. Beyond his silhouette, Kitt could see a shaft of warm light coming from downstairs.

Kitt's brow furrowed. Sighing, she threw off the bedsheets. She could have sworn she'd turned off all the lamps on her way up to bed. But then again, after the surreality of the evening behind her she hadn't exactly been her usual self. And who could blame her? Though it was most out of character, she might have missed one of them, she supposed.

The second it was clear Kitt was getting up, Iago slunk down the stairs in front of her. Following after him, Kitt came to realise that the glow from the living room was not an electric light after all, but a fire blazing in the hearth.

Had Halloran returned from his shift and had too much on his mind to come to bed? If so, perhaps he had decided to sit by the fireplace for a while. It wouldn't have been the first time, but, then again, they had an understanding that he would wake her if ever he decided on that course of action. She hated to think of him sitting alone with the responsibility of a difficult case weighing on him. Far better that they sat up together into the early hours. Even if he couldn't talk about the case for confidentiality reasons, at least he wouldn't feel quite so on his own with it all with her there to squeeze his hand.

On reaching the foot of the stairs and peering into the living room, Kitt could see, at once, that there was indeed a man seated in one of the two armchairs angled next to the fire. But the man in question was not Halloran.

Kitt knew she should be more alarmed by this discovery, and yet she was quite calm in herself. She was more curious than disturbed. Who *was* this late-night visitor? And what was he doing here?

Taking a few steps closer to get a better look at the figure sitting in her living room, who was drinking from a small glass of what looked like some kind of crimson punch, Kitt squinted harder in her bleary state. Very soon after, her mouth dropped open. 'You're, you're . . .'

'Charles Dickens.' The man finished the sentence for her in a most matter-of-fact tone. As though a visitation from a Victorian-era author was a very natural thing to expect four nights before Christmas, or was it technically three nights before Christmas now that midnight had already come and gone?

Kitt blinked hard and shook her head but the figure remained. It was him alright, and no mistake. She had seen his photograph on countless book jackets. But what on earth was he doing in her living room? Sitting in front of her fire. Surrounded by the festive ornaments she dragged down from the attic every December, featuring snow-covered cottages and deer standing pensively in icy forests.

'Oh, for heaven's sake,' Kitt said with a sigh, 'I'm dreaming, aren't I?'

'Given that I've been dead for over a hundred and fifty years, I'd say, yes, the odds are that you *are* dreaming,' said Dickens, placing his glass down on a small coffee table, next to a large snow globe that contained a miniature model of York Minster.

'You're wearing your glasses,' Kitt said, gesturing to a pair of small, round spectacles resting on the nose of her unexpected guest. The arms of them so wire-thin, they were almost invisible to the naked eye. 'I thought I'd read that you didn't like people knowing that you wore glasses.'

'I don't, but since we're in your head and not mine, I have no control over my attire. You could have me dancing around your hearth in a pink tutu if you wished.' At this Dickens held up a hand and hastened to add, 'But I beg you to spare me that indignity.'

'I shall do my best but the human dreamscape can be an unpredictable thing,' said Kitt with a shrug.

A flash of concern rippled over Dickens's face at this comment. He seemed to be chiding himself for putting the idea of him pirouetting about in a pink tutu in Kitt's head in the first place.

'I suppose you'll want to know why I've come here,' he said at last, perhaps thinking it best to move the conversation on.

'I suspect you're here because my mind is trying to process what happened earlier, that's all,' said Kitt.

'Is that so?' said Dickens.

'It's the most logical explanation. The man dressed up just like you at the book fair, he died and I'm still trying to make some sense of it.' Slowly, and with a frown firmly fixed on her face, Kitt charted a path over to the vacant chair and took a seat. Iago jumped up on the armrest and narrowed his eyes at their unwelcome visitor. Uncaring that he was considered a literary great. Only interested in the fact that this intruder was trespassing on his well-defined territory.

'I shall leave it to you to be logical even in your dreams,' Dickens said. 'But, however you want to believe I came to be here, you should know I do come bearing an important message for you.'

'An important message?' said Kitt, trying to stifle a wry chuckle and failing. 'You're just a figment of my subconscious. And possibly a precursor to the world's worst hangover.'

'Well, consider this, then. If I am, as you say, a figment of your subconscious,' said Dickens, 'then surely it is even more vital that you listen to what I have to say. You know better than most the importance of trusting one's instincts. If I am part of you and I'm here telling you there's a message you need to hear, well, it is worth taking the time to heed such a message, don't you think?'

'I'm not sure I followed all that,' said Kitt. Was it possible to feel weary in a dream? A person was already asleep after all and yet that all-too recognisable feeling was undoubtedly creeping over her. 'But, OK, I'll hear you out.'

'Yes, well ... how magnanimous of you,' Dickens said, his tone as arid as Kitt's could be at times. 'You can believe what you will about me and how I came to be sitting by your fireside, but I'm here to tell you that there is a reason you witnessed that man dying tonight.'

'I know,' said Kitt.

'You do?' said Dickens, raising his eyebrows in what looked to Kitt a lot like quiet admiration.

'Yes, the reason is, we booked front-row tickets to a reading of *A Christmas Carol*.'

Dickens's eyes became sharp slits. 'Don't be a Scrooge. It didn't end well for him, you know?'

'Yes, it did,' said Kitt. 'He arguably got the greatest gift anyone can get in this world: a second chance when he least deserved it.'

Dickens opened his mouth to argue, then closed it again. He took a moment to clear his throat before speaking. 'You know full well what I mean. The point is, right now, I need you to be a Bob Cratchit and believe in something.'

'I believe in what I can see, hear, taste, touch and smell. Isn't that enough?' said Kitt.

'Maybe not, not for this case.' Dickens pressed his fingers into a steeple as he spoke and looked long and hard at Kitt.

'Case?'

'The case of that poor man's death. The one who died right in front of you,' Dickens confirmed.

'I'm not on that case,' said Kitt. Confused by Dickens's assumption that she had any involvement beyond being an eyewitness to an unsettling incident. 'This is Halloran's case. A police matter.'

'And when has that ever stopped you before?' said Dickens.

'Well, never . . .' Kitt admitted. 'But I have no stake in this business. I just happened to be in the wrong place at the wrong time. That's all there is to it.'

'I think, before very long, you will change your mind about that,' said Dickens. 'Something is about to happen. Something that will compel you to find out the truth behind the death of Leonard Bell. You see, believe it or not, like it or not, you were there for a reason, Kitt, and you need to heed what I'm telling you. That man's terrible end was no accident. There are people to bring to justice. Time will play an important part in making that happen.'

'Time always plays an important part in bringing people to justice. That's hardly some personalised revelation,' Kitt said, while masking her surprise at how real all this felt. She could almost sense the heat from the fire against her skin. See the light glinting off the silver tinsel on the Christmas tree. Feel the softness of Iago's fur as he brushed against her. She could smell the logs burning. And yet, she knew it was nothing more than a hallucination. Likely brought on by one of the many hidden ingredients in Ruby's homemade mulled wine.

'I thought you might be reluctant,' Dickens said, his eyes lowering to the carpet before meeting hers again. 'I had hoped my urging you to get to the truth of this matter would be enough for you. But since it has not been, you should know, you will not be left alone until this man's killer is unmasked. The memory of that man cannot rest, and so, until the truth is uncovered, neither will you.'

'That ... sounds ominous,' said Kitt. 'I've already got an assistant who spends every waking minute planning her next prank on me and the local witch stopping by my office every day for an unsolicited visit. Aren't I already being bothered enough without further interference from you?'

Dickens's brows furrowed and his eyes and lips seemed to sharpen.

'Betwixt tonight and Christmas Eve, you will be visited by three spirits. Each with an important insight about the end that man met tonight. Those insights will guide you to the truth. Without them, you may never find it.'

'Spirits?' said Kitt. 'Now I really do know that this is Ruby's wine having its way with me.'

'You will see,' said Dickens. 'The peace of that man's soul will rest on you this Christmas. Do not turn away from your calling, Kitt. If you don't speak for Leonard, who will?'

'But, if you already know the truth about what happened to this man, why even send more spirits to visit me? Why can't you just tell me now?' Kitt thought this was a pretty clever question that might stop Dickens in his enigmatic tracks and force him to tell her what she needed to hear.

Dickens, however, merely smiled.

He didn't say any more.

Slowly, the image of him began to fade until Kitt was left to sit by the fire with Iago, while wondering just how seriously she should take Mr Dickens's warning.

CHAPTER EIGHT

'I think that's about the most comprehensive witness statement I've ever taken, but I'll let you know if there's anything
else we need from you,' Halloran said as he pressed a button
by the security door at York Police Station.

'Nothing wrong with being thorough,' Kitt said. Smiling,
she glanced over her shoulder to make sure nobody was
looking and quickly pressed her lips against Halloran's
before striding into the reception area. With its overpow-
ering smell of stale vending machine sandwiches and its
hard, yellow lighting, the draughty corridor of the local
police station wasn't exactly the most romantic setting for
locking lips with the man who had become such a rock to
Kitt over the past decade. But Halloran hadn't made it home
last night. By his own admission, he had only managed a
few hours' sleep in the break room, which gave Kitt some
idea about just how serious a case this was. Given that it
was now early afternoon, this meant Halloran had only had

three hours of shut-eye in the last thirty, and who knew what the next few days would bring in light of this as yet unexplained death? If nights at the office were going to be the norm for the foreseeable future, Kitt decided there and then that she had to steal her kisses from him when she could.

'Do you think you'll make it home tonight?' Kitt asked, once the security door was shut firmly behind them. By its very nature, the station wasn't supposed to be an inviting place to spend your time but some vague attempts at Christmas cheer had been made. Somehow though, these festive additions only made the place look even bleaker than usual. Several lengths of balding red tinsel had been stapled around the window frames and Deirdre, who had worked part-time on the reception desk for longer than anyone could remember, had brought in a small artificial Christmas tree that danced – so far as any inanimate object could dance – and played an off-key electronic rendition of 'Rudolph the Red-Nosed Reindeer' whenever anyone got within a foot of where it stood on the counter.

'I don't know for sure, pet. We've checked and we don't have an Information Sharing Agreement with the Defence Medical Agency, so that's a real spanner in the works. It sort of depends on whether we have a cause of death confirmed and what that cause might be. If this man has been poisoned in some way, I'll have to make a follow-up statement to the press to assure everyone of public safety.

Most of the calls we've had in this morning have been from newspapers asking for further comment. But . . . I'll do everything in my power to get home as quickly as possible,' said Halloran, before running his hand through Kitt's long red hair and adding in a quieter voice: 'I don't relish nights away from you.'

'I know that, love,' she said, patting his trimmed beard.

Giving her witness statement about the events that had unfolded at the Christmas Book Fair had been more difficult than Kitt had envisioned. She kept flashing back to the way Leonard's face, Leonard Bell to give him his full name, had looked right after he had collapsed. The sounds his body had made when Jordan tried to administer compressions. Talking about the incident had only heightened the intensity of these invasive memories and Kitt was beginning to wonder if she was ever going to be able to think of anything else for the foreseeable future. She had seen vacant dead faces before. But she had never seen such terror and torture writ across a person's face as it had been across Bell's.

All of this had left Kitt wondering, yet again, just how much of a toll being involved in cases like this was taking on her. She wasn't even investigating this one directly, and yet somehow had managed to see some sights she would never forget.

She hadn't mentioned her strange dream about Charles Dickens to Halloran. Usually the pair of them would have laughed over such an odd subconscious glitch, but in the cold light of day it didn't seem appropriate to discuss mad visions of dead authors bearing stories of her being the chosen one to crack this particular case. The reality of it all was simply too gruesome for light to be made of anything. Besides that, the dream had been a bit of a concerning sign of the lasting effect Ruby's mulled wine had on her. Halloran had enough on his plate without worrying about Kitt's wellbeing, and without her adding yet more absurdity to the mix.

Kitt was about to say a reluctant goodbye to Halloran but before she could speak someone off to the left of her cleared their throat. On looking over in the direction of the sound, Kitt saw it was Banks.

'Sir, we've just had word from pathology. They want to see us about their preliminary findings on the autopsy.'

Halloran nodded. 'Proof that marking something as urgent still does hold some weight around here, I suppose. God knows what we're about to learn about that body. By the time that poor guy was taken to the mortuary he looked like something not of this world.'

Kitt took in a deep breath and slowly let it out. Doing all she could not to dwell too hard on what Halloran had just said. She hadn't developed any worrying symptoms in the last twelve hours and having checked in on Evie via text, she knew the same was true for her, but she still couldn't help but feel a little bit on edge. As yet, they had no idea what had caused Leonard Bell to go out that way. Until that was determined and Kitt had had it confirmed by a medical professional that she couldn't have been exposed to anything that might mean she suffered the same fate, she would be on high alert for any irregularities in her vitals.

'You can head straight to pathology, Banks. I'll follow on in just a minute,' Halloran added.

As it happened, however, Halloran's turn of phrase was a little too optimistic. For at that moment, the door to York Police Station flew open and a man came darting up to the reception desk.

'Help me. Oh, please help me, this is urgent!' said the man.

Deirdre, who had been in the middle of eating her lunch – what from this distance looked to Kitt like a cheese and pickle sandwich brought from home – stood from her stool behind the desk and opened her mouth to speak. Before she got a word out, however, the Christmas tree sensor activated. The tree began to wriggle and jiggle, and a flat electronic rendition of 'Rudolph the Red-Nosed Reindeer' filled the air.

The man who had entered curled his lip at the gyrating tree and glared at Deirdre.

'Sorry!' she said, grabbing the tree and shoving it in a cubby under the desk, which muffled the irritating tune but didn't completely silence it. 'What appears to be the problem, sir?'

'I-I-I need to report ... well, a murder,' said the man, looking momentarily over his shoulder while running a hand through his short grey hair which had receded almost to the apex of his head.

The man's words naturally caught Halloran's attention. He shot a look at Banks before striding over to the desk to learn more. Banks followed after him and Kitt followed a few paces behind her. Could the murder this man wanted to report have something to do with the dead body in the mortuary? The one that was decaying at an alarming rate? Or was it possible that two completely separate deaths had occurred in the small city of York, less than twenty-four hours apart?

On approaching the desk, Kitt took a moment to study the man who had made such a disturbing and unexpected announcement. He was a short but slender man with gold-framed spectacles. He wore a long, grey trench coat and had a black satchel tucked under his arm. The most noticeable thing about him in that particular moment was his inability to stand still on the spot. He was hopping around from one foot to another, but then if he had just witnessed, or maybe even committed, a murder, then it was no surprise that the man was quite beside himself.

'I'm Detective Inspector Malcolm Halloran, sir. This is Detective Sergeant Charlotte Banks. Whose murder are you reporting?'

To Kitt's ears, Halloran's voice was overly light considering the seriousness of the matter. He was no doubt trying to set the man at ease; to make him feel as though he could disclose whatever he knew about the murder he had mentioned. But behind that easy tone was a reserve Kitt recognised all too well in her partner. He knew, as well as she did, that you could never trust anyone in a murder case. Sometimes, not even the person reporting it. Not until you had gone to all possible lengths to discount them as a suspect, and, sometimes, not even then.

After Halloran's words, there was a pause and the man looked at the officer with wide bulbous eyes. The green pupils at the centre of them looked sick with worry. 'The murder I'm reporting,' he said. 'Well . . . it's my own.'

'Your . . . own murder?' Halloran repeated. It was subtle, but Kitt could hear the shift in his tone; there was now a slight weariness to it. If she had to guess, she would say that, given this man was very much alive, Halloran had already mentally dubbed him as a time-waster on a day when that was the last thing he needed. She couldn't much blame Halloran for his assumptions. He was dealing with the most startling of cases and didn't have time to waste. For her part though, Kitt was intrigued by this man's statement. What would make him say that he was there to report his own murder?

'I know how that sounds, really I do,' said the man. 'But don't let the fact that I'm standing here alive and well right now fool you. I can guarantee you that if I don't get your help then in five days', God, for all I know even fewer than that, I will die. Just like Leonard Bell.'

CHAPTER NINE

'What's your name, sir?' said Halloran. At the mention of Leonard Bell, there had been yet another distinct change in his demeanour. He had relayed to Kitt, in passing, that Leonard Bell's wife had been too distressed to answer any questions when he and Banks had broken the news of her husband's death. Halloran had sent officers to follow up with her that morning, but, unfortunately, she had not been able to think of anyone who might have wanted to harm her husband. She had expressed concern over his work at the agency. Described it as all-consuming and insinuated that it had, at times, caused Bell great stress. But she had stopped short of being able to provide a motive for someone wanting to see him dead. Thus, anyone else who was going to step into the fray and potentially offer some suspects to get the investigation started was of great interest to Halloran just then.

'Sorry, what am I thinking?' said the man. 'I should've

introduced myself. I probably sound insane. But then, you see, there's no time for pleasantries. No time at all . . . but, I understand you do need to know who you're talking to. I'm Kevin, Kevin Ripley.'

'Perhaps we should step into a quiet room to talk about what you have to say,' said Halloran.

'With all due respect, inspector. There's simply no time for that. For all I know five days is a generous estimate for the amount of time I have left. For all I know, I could die in the next hour, or the next minute.'

Halloran swallowed hard at Ripley's words and stared at him. Like Kitt, it was obvious he wasn't sure exactly how much of what Ripley was saying could be relied upon just then, but it was obvious, no matter what was going on in real terms, that Ripley feared for his life. His whole body was a portrait of agitation. And his eyes, they darted this way and that, widening now and then as the realisation that his number could be up at any moment seemed to hit him over and over again.

'Alright, let's ascertain the basics,' Halloran said at last. 'What exactly do you know about what happened to Leonard Bell?' he asked.

Ripley looked around the reception area. Down along the skirting boards and up to the ceiling. His eyes narrowed at something. Kitt followed his gaze to see he was glaring at a security camera. Ripley had insisted there wasn't time to find somewhere private to talk and yet, it seemed, he was still intent on keeping what he had to say as quiet as possible. He manoeuvred himself so that his back was to the camera and lowered his voice. 'Everything *they* don't want you to know.'

'They?' said Halloran.

'The Defence Medical Agency,' said Ripley. 'I work for them. Just like Leo did. We were lab partners on a special project. I shouldn't, of course, be telling you any of this but that's on them. They've created this mess by dabbling with things they can't control. And now what's happened to Leo is very likely going to happen to me unless I get some help.'

So, Ripley was suggesting the Defence Medical Agency were somehow responsible for the death of Leonard Bell? Kitt had suspected that the moment she had learned of his employment there. But how exactly had they created this mess, as Ripley had phrased it. And had it been deliberate?

Halloran no doubt had all the same questions Kitt did but, in order to make sure nothing was missed, he would have to ensure his questions came in a considered, logical order.

'What exactly did happen to Mr Bell?' said Halloran.

'You mean ... you don't know?' said Ripley, frowning between Halloran, Banks and Kitt. 'There were images on the lunchtime news of police officers in hazmat suits. Someone at the local news station caught the scene on camera. The report said this all happened last night so, forgive me, I thought you would have ascertained his cause of death by now.'

'Tests don't run as quickly at police level as they do at military and government level,' said Halloran. He wasn't quite gritting his teeth but Kitt could feel the annoyance behind his words. If she'd heard him rant about the delays in test results once, she'd heard it a thousand times. 'We were just about to get an initial report from the pathologist but if you've got insider information, now's the time to share it. Especially if your life is in jeopardy. I certainly wouldn't want to see another person suffer a fate like Leonard Bell did. There's not much left of the poor bloke now.'

Ripley winced at Halloran's words. Kitt knew this interview tactic well and had used it herself on more than one occasion. It wasn't the kind of approach you'd use on next of kin, it was too harsh for that. But if someone was an acquaintance of a wronged party, you could sometimes shock them into revealing information quicker if you used emotive language or alluded to a graphic crime scene, as Halloran had. Kitt understood Ripley's reservations about revealing all if he worked with the Defence Medical Agency. An entity like that would not look kindly on him spilling state secrets to save his own neck, and that was putting it politely. But something very sinister was going on here, and Halloran could offer Ripley protection if necessary. The priority right now was to get Ripley to share all he knew. After all, if his life was also in danger, perhaps others were too.

Ripley looked over his shoulder again to see if there was anyone else in the station, but there was just him, Halloran,

Kitt, Banks and Deirdre. He looked long and hard at Kitt before speaking but seemingly assumed her to be a plain clothes officer by the fact that she was standing with Halloran and Banks. Right now, she certainly wasn't going to correct him. Her somewhat insatiable curiosity had well and truly been stoked and, more than anything, she wanted to know from the horse's mouth whether she was in any danger after making contact with Leonard Bell just before he died.

'Forgive me, I didn't mean anything about the tests not being back yet,' Ripley said, taking in a deep breath. 'To be fair to you and your team, even if you had already got the test results back, there would have been no clear way of identifying the substance found in Leo's blood. You'd have known there was something awry but there's no way the substance could be identified.'

'Substance?' Halloran said, exactly as Kitt would have done were she not already well-versed in letting Halloran take the lead in his own workplace.

Ripley nodded. 'Bell ingested a toxin we were working on at the agency, presumably without any knowledge of what he was ingesting. I can't think that anyone would willingly drink a lethal substance . . . unless perhaps he was under some kind of duress.'

'When you say you were working on this toxin . . . you mean made. Don't you? You . . . you made a lethal toxin?' said Halloran, his voice laced with a mixture of disbelief and obvious disdain.

Ripley sighed. 'It wasn't on purpose. And we were tasked to formulate it. We were just following orders. That's what one does in a military career. But to be clear, the agent was never supposed to be lethal. The original design was supposed to incapacitate enemy soldiers. Nothing painful, you understand. It was simply supposed to attack a person's nervous system in a manner that kept them immobile. Sort of like an anaesthetic but with a longer-lasting effect that could be relied upon to stay effective for a more accurate period of time. Something that could be controlled with precision in the field. We originally designed the agent to stay in the subject's system for twenty-four hours – long enough to capture and transport them to prison. After that time, the toxin was designed to eradicate itself from the host's body, leaving no trace at all that it was ever there.'

'But instead of creating something that left no traces in the body,' said Halloran, 'you manufactured something that kills people.'

'I can see you're angry, Inspector Halloran,' said Ripley. 'But that really was never the intent. It was supposed to be humane. Anyone captured would regain mobility and be able to be questioned and cooperate with the authorities.'

'And this agent,' Halloran said. 'You said Bell ingested it? So, is it in liquid form?'

Ripley nodded. 'We worked first on a liquid agent and then were set to do trials in vapour form to see if merely inhaling the agent, rather than either ingesting it or being injected with it, had the same effect. That way, troops could gas an entire room of enemy soldiers, knowing that no pain or long-term harm would befall the people they were neutralising. And, say there was a civilian unexpectedly mixed up in there, or a child, they wouldn't be hurt. In short, they could safely take out large contingents of the enemy without having to use lethal force. But we never got on to those secondary tests because it became clear in the first human trial that something had gone very wrong with the formula.'

'Went wrong how?' said Halloran, when Ripley paused.

'I wish I knew,' said Ripley with a shake of his head. 'Nothing like this was supposed to happen. All of our data models, somehow, I don't know how, they didn't accurately reflect the toxin's impact on the nervous system. Somewhere, a calculation must have been out and in the live trial . . . the reality was very different.'

'Different in what way, exactly?' Banks pushed after exchanging a look with Halloran.

Ripley's eyes darted to the lino flooring and he pressed his lips together. It looked to Kitt as though he almost couldn't bring himself to meet their gaze. As though he were ashamed of something. Something that had resulted from him 'just following orders' as he had put it. 'As I've said, this agent was supposed to be toxic, but the intention was always to keep the host alive . . .'

At these words, Kitt felt tears fill her eyes and she fought to hold them back. They had created something deadly in that lab, and now, for reasons Kitt had yet to understand, people were paying the price. It wasn't just the memory of Leonard Bell's wide searching eyes that had caused this well of emotion. But the hard stab through the heart she felt at what humanity was coming to. After all the lessons that history and literature had taught them, was finding new ways to kill each other, even by accident, the best the species could do?

No wonder Kevin Ripley couldn't meet their eye. Just as his now deceased lab partner had recited upon the stage before he died, these men had already forged their own chain in this life, link by link. And Ripley knew it.

'The toxin turned out to be deadly,' said Halloran. 'I understand that. How did you come to understand that?'

Ripley took a deep breath before speaking, as though it was taking all of his strength just to stay on this subject. 'In its current form, the toxin seems innocuous for a five-day incubation period. So, initially we thought we'd failed. That the toxin simply didn't have any effect. During the first human trial it quickly became apparent that after that five-day incubation period, the agent becomes lethal and the host drops dead ... It is a painful death and, as you've no doubt seen with Leo, it has extraordinary effects on the body post-mortem.'

Halloran sighed. Closed his eyes for a moment and then opened them again to glare at Ripley. Nobody would necessarily have guessed it about him, but Kitt understood her partner to be something of a pacifist. He would use force if it was in self-defence or to protect an innocent. But that was as far as his violent tendencies went. He hadn't even taken arms training even though the opportunity had been offered to him many times. Kitt could only imagine some of the thoughts that would be running through his head right now.

'So a person could be walking around with this toxin in their bloodstream for five days without knowing a thing about it, and then just drop dead?' said Halloran.

Ripley offered a meek nod. 'I'm afraid so.'

'And how did Leonard ingest the toxin?' said Halloran, his voice much more level than anyone might expect under the circumstances. No matter what information you were given, regardless of how alarming it may be, this was the job. Compartmentalise your emotions. Stay rational. Ask logical and pertinent questions.

'I don't know,' said Ripley. 'I only know he must have ingested it somehow to die the way he did, and for the mere sight of his body to prompt you to wear hazmat suits. But he can't have drunk it intentionally and the only other way of administering the toxin in its current form is by injection. If Leo had been injected with something he would have known about it. My guess is, somebody slipped it into his drink at some point without his notice. Either someone who he trusted or someone skilled at misdirection.'

'And, how do you know you have ingested the substance? Are there tell-tale signs if you suspect and know what to look for? Or has someone threatened to do the same thing to you?' Halloran said.

Ripley shook his head. 'No, if only they had threatened me first. They could have had whatever it was they wanted. There's nothing I value more than my life, I can tell you. And there are no tell-tale signs. At least not without a blood test. The host has no idea the substance is in their system until it starts to kill them. The only warning sign is a very strong smell a few minutes before.'

Kitt could guess with ease what that smell was, but she knew Halloran needed Ripley to confirm it without any prompting.

'What kind of smell?' Halloran duly asked.

'The closest thing it can be compared to is cinnamon.'

If Kitt had doubted Ripley's somewhat wild story up until now, this detail cemented him as, if not a credible source, then certainly someone in the know about what had really happened to Leonard Bell. So far as Kitt knew, that particular detail, the part about the body smelling of cinnamon, had not been leaked to the press, so it was a fair assumption that Ripley's story had some truth to it. Privately, however, Kitt admitted that a big part of her also wanted to believe Ripley's tale. Firstly, because, by Ripley's account, it did not seem as though it were possible to suffer the same fate as Bell simply by having had contact with him. And secondly, because it was extremely unlikely that anyone had slipped the substance into her drink. Of all the wild ingredients in Ruby's homemade mulled wine, a lethal synthetic agent concocted by the Defence Medical Agency probably wasn't one of them.

Moreover, if Bell was working on the drug at the Defence Medical Agency then the odds were that this was a targeted attack. Exactly what the motivations were behind this attack had yet to be revealed. Possibly, it had been perpetrated by somebody working for a third-party agency. Perhaps even a foreign agency. But on this logic, it seemed unlikely that she, Evie or Jordan were in any immediate danger and a rich, warm sense of relief flooded through Kitt at this realisation.

'So, since nobody's threatened you and there are no early tell-tale signs, can I assume you've done a blood test to confirm the toxin is in your body? We'll need to see those, you know. We'll need to verify what you're saying,' said Banks. The angles on Banks's face always somehow looked sharper to Kitt when she was at work. She routinely wore her hair in a tight bun that pulled all the skin back half an inch. It was a look that made Kitt think twice about being easy or friendly with the woman, even though she was married to her best friend. Kitt had to admit, however, that this aesthetic probably served her well when trying to convey to would-be time-wasters that she wasn't to be messed with.

'I have copies of the blood test I took,' Ripley said. 'Of

course, I understand the need to verify my story. I'll hand those over and you'll see, there's something unusual in my bloodwork. Compare it with Leonard's results and, I guarantee, it will be a match.'

'When did you take this blood test?' asked Banks.

'When I went into work at the agency this morning, I was informed of Leo's death,' Ripley said. 'Being a defence agency, they, of course, have eyes and ears all over the city so they knew what had happened to Leo almost before he did. When I heard about what had happened, I wondered, just for a split second, if he had used himself as a guinea pig for some new formulation of the agent he hadn't told me about. He was a decent man and it was the kind of thing he might do, risk his life for the good of his country. But something told me deep down that probably wasn't the case. It's not like the agent we were working on was desperately needed by a particular deadline or was some kind of life-saving substance.'

'Quite the opposite,' said Halloran.

Ripley nodded. 'I suppose I deserve that. The most likely scenario is that the agent had been slipped into a drink and that Leonard unknowingly ingested it. Of course, if that was the case, the big questions are, who and why? Why would someone do that to Leo? There were a few reasons I could think of given the line of work we do. And if they did it to him, did they also do it to me?'

'So, to answer Banks's question more concisely for you,

you ran a blood test this morning to see if the agent showed up?' said Halloran.

Ripley nodded. 'I'm sorry. My mind is all over the place. There's so much to tell. And for all I know I'm going to drop down dead right in the middle of telling you. There is so much I shouldn't say but must, simply must, if I want to stay alive. The agent is in my bloodstream, there's no mistake about that. You know my life wouldn't be worth living if the agency knew I was here right now talking to you, but the threat of all that didn't even enter my head when I saw those blood test results. I want to live. And I certainly don't want to die the way poor Leo did. If I live out the rest of my life in a witness protection programme, that's good enough for me.'

Kitt marvelled at the idea of having to be protected from people who worked at a military agency sanctioned by their own government. She wasn't a woman who entertained conspiracies, but from her limited experience of dealing with the world of classified information she knew that such situations probably cropped up more often than most would imagine.

'If you're talking about the rest of your life, I'm assuming there is a way to flush the agent out of your system before it kills you?' said Halloran.

'Ordinarily, yes,' said Ripley. 'It's never prudent to develop any kind of toxin without also developing an antidote. But there's a problem.

'Of course there is,' said Halloran. 'Heaven forbid our lives were ever made easy. Go on then, what is it?'

'It's the other reason I know Leonard can't have injected himself willingly with the agent. All samples of the toxin and all of the synthesised antidote were stolen from our facility in Clifton,' said Ripley, growing visibly paler as he relayed this information. 'Whoever stole it is probably the same person who killed Leo. And now, whoever they are, they're trying to kill me.'

CHAPTER TEN

Halloran was silent for a few moments as he digested what Ripley had told him about the theft. When he did speak again, it was Banks he turned to.

'We're going to need to pull up all CCTV footage of the roads leading to and from that facility,' said Halloran, before turning back to Ripley. 'When did the theft take place, exactly?'

'It was ten days ago now. From what I understand about the incident, the security systems went down at the facility around three a.m. and didn't go back up until five a.m., so it was somewhere in that window. But with the security cameras down, there was no record of who broke into the agency and there's very little else I can tell you because any intelligence about that break-in has been classified SPO.'

'Security Personnel Only,' Halloran said with a sigh.

'So, the information about the break-in has been classified, even from you?' said Banks. 'Even though you developed the toxin and the antidote that were stolen?'

'I think you may have an inflated idea of how much power and sway I have,' said Ripley. 'A biochemical scientist in the military is one tiny cog in an incredibly complex machine. Just because I was instrumental in developing the toxin, doesn't mean I have any ownership over it. The substance belongs to the military. They would have no qualms about classifying information about it, or its whereabouts, even from me.'

'You said the security systems were down for two hours. That seems a long time for security to be down at a military facility without anyone noticing,' said Halloran.

'Oh, people noticed,' said Ripley. 'As I say, I don't know how the building was infiltrated or exactly what happened during the time that the facility was being robbed because the information is being withheld. But from the debriefing we were given the next day, we were at least told that the security team put the facility into lockdown when the system didn't return to normal after a few minutes.'

'In a few minutes, couldn't whoever was responsible have done what they needed to do and escaped?' said Banks.

'Given the size of the compound I'd say that was unlikely,' said Ripley. 'But I admit, it's not impossible. Especially if this person was a professional and knew what they were doing. Still, our security team would have had to be sure there wasn't some minor glitch with the tech before initiating lockdown protocol. It's a serious move, you understand? Nobody can go in or out under such circumstances and superiors are immediately notified of a security breach. All of their employees have to present themselves at pre-designated stations to ensure safety, and to make sure that there isn't a rogue employee at large.'

'I'm assuming lockdown protocols override the usual security systems, then?' said Halloran.

'Not on a technological level,' said Ripley. 'If someone hacks in and disables all of the cameras and the door locks, as they seem to have done when this theft took place, well there's nothing security can do about the cameras unless they can undo what the hacker has done. But the door locks can be manually locked one by one by the security team. This way, at least you can stop people going in or out of the building. So that's what they did ... Despite this precaution, despite working non-stop to try and reinstate the cameras, whoever it was who stole that antidote was not caught. Everyone in the building underwent a thorough search before leaving.'

'In a complex full of classified artefacts and documents, they realised that quickly the toxin and the antidote had been stolen?' said Halloran.

'Goodness, no,' said Ripley. 'The military are efficient but they're not *that* efficient. At that point, the security team didn't know if anything was actually missing. It's just protocol to conduct body searches of the staff before they leave the premises under such circumstances. There may be details that I'm not privy to, given information about the breach has been compartmentalised. But considering what followed during the days after the theft, it was clear that nobody on staff that day left with the toxin and the antidote. So, that points to an intruder from the outside and, whoever the intruder was, they weren't captured.'

'What exactly did follow in the days after the theft?' asked Halloran.

'A lot of interrogation of staff. Sweeps of the building for forensic evidence. It was obvious they had not caught the culprit. Or recovered what had been taken,' Ripley explained.

'Compromised security systems and no culprit found. Either this is an inside job, or it's the work of a professional who does this kind of thing every day. Anyone who worked there would know that they'd be searched on the way out. So they wouldn't take the toxin and the antidote themselves. But they may have helped whoever did get in and out as quickly as possible,' Halloran said before running a hand over his beard. 'If that person was on the security team it would be even easier for them to orchestrate the escape of a third party.'

'Or even steal the substance and the antidote for themselves,' said Banks. 'If you're the one doing the body searches, couldn't you get away with something like that?'

'That couldn't happen unless two of the security personnel

were in on it together,' said Ripley. 'Even the security team are subject to body searches before leaving the premises. Protocol accounts for corruption at every level. It has to. Our national security depends on it.'

'We can't rule out that two members of the security team were in on it,' said Banks. 'And even if they weren't, that still doesn't mean that someone on the inside wasn't helping someone on the outside.'

'I would have to agree with you,' said Ripley. 'As you can imagine, all of the staff on shift that night were rigorously interrogated about their whereabouts during those two hours. They had to repeat their stories several times over to our superiors. Their interviews were recorded and pored over. No discrepancies were found in anything they said and all of them had alibis for the vast proportion of the time the systems were down.'

'Vast proportion is not all of the time,' said Halloran. 'And if the person behind it does work at the facility that would explain why they didn't find an intruder when they searched. Still, we have to keep all avenues of investigation open. Ten days out from the incident we'll be reliant on council footage of the surrounding area. The National Highways only keep their footage for seven. Let's hope the council have got a few cameras pointed in that direction. In the meantime, is it possible to create a new batch of the antidote?'

'Oh, it's possible,' said Ripley. 'But it won't benefit me, I'm afraid. It takes three weeks before the antidote synthesises to a point where it can be used and, as I've outlined, the agent slowly overtakes the nervous system over a period of five days.'

'Do you have any idea when you might have ingested the toxin?' Halloran said, his voice a touch gentler than it had been thus far.

'I have no idea,' Ripley said with a shake of his head. 'The toxin itself doesn't have a strong odour or taste. So, it would be difficult to detect in any strong-flavoured drink, such as coffee. Which means, it could have happened any time I've had a drink in recent times. I could have four days left to live, I could have only one, or less. I suppose that's another reason why I'm not too worried about the agency catching up with me about all I've told you. Whatever the consequences of my actions are, they might not matter for too long.'

CHAPTER ELEVEN

Halloran exchanged a concerned look with Kitt at Ripley's words and paused before speaking to the man again. 'Obviously, though the creation of a substance like the one you describe is reprehensible in itself, I understand that you never intended it to be used in this manner. I am going to do everything in my power to recover that antidote and bring whoever is behind Leonard Bell's killing to justice.'

'I appreciate you taking the time to listen to what must seem like the paranoid ramblings of a desperate man,' said Ripley. 'I don't mind admitting to you that I'm desperate. I know, in a way, some might see this as poetic justice. Death by a toxin I had a hand in creating, perhaps that even has something to do with why Leo and I were targeted. But I am grateful, so grateful, for your help.'

Halloran didn't acknowledge Ripley's desperation verbally. Kitt guessed that he was likely too angry over all that he had heard to offer Ripley much sympathy at this juncture. But he did give a firm nod to confirm he under-stood Ripley's sentiments and situation. 'I realise time is of the essence, I really do,' said Halloran. 'But I need to make sure I've got all the key information before I start investi-gating this, otherwise it could lead to mistakes.'

'Anxious as I am for you to get underway with finding the culprit, and hopefully the antidote with them, I under-stand,' said Ripley. 'What else do you need to know?'

'I need to know why,' said Halloran. 'I'm sure you would have mentioned it before now if you knew exactly. But I'll even take hunches or inklings at this stage. Do you have any idea why you and Bell were targeted?'

'There are any number of reasons why we might have been, which is why I didn't venture a straight guess while I was appraising you of the situation,' said Ripley. 'In our line of work, much as you try to ignore it as a possibility, you know there are people out there who want to know what you are working on and will go to extreme lengths to get it. The thing is, in this instance, whoever wanted what we were working on had already stolen it.'

'And it's not as though they can interrogate you further about the substance once it has taken its effect on you,' said Banks.

'Precisely,' Ripley replied. 'So I'm wondering if it was some kind of warning to the agency. If Leo and I might have been the test subjects in a malicious demonstration of power. There are certainly people out there who would like the Defence Medical Agency to know they can match their power. There are also people who the agency has wronged, who might seek revenge.'

'Whoever stole the substance wants you to know that they were willing to use it,' said Halloran. 'And they know that the agency knows they have the antidote. Are they likely to understand how long it takes to synthesise more of the antidote?'

'I don't think so,' said Ripley. 'It's not like we attach a list of instructions to these things. But, I wouldn't like to bet my life or anyone else's on it. They may have an idea how long it takes to synthesise more of the antidote. If so, they might use the toxin again soon.

'Somewhere bigger for a more public demonstration of the toxin's power?' said Banks.

'Oh my, I can only hope not,' Ripley said. 'Even if I survive this episode in my life, I'm not sure I'd be able to live with myself if I was responsible for . . . something like that.'

'Whether we think it's a credible theory or not, I'm going to have to inform MI5. Something of that magnitude . . . it's a threat to national security,' said Halloran.

'If that is what's happening here,' said Ripley, 'it might explain why Leo and I were targeted. We were the chief researchers on the project. We know how to synthesise more antidote. Other people would be able to figure it out from our lab notes in our absence but it would take them much longer.'

'So, by taking you two out, whoever has the toxin and the antidote holds all the cards for longer,' said Halloran.

'Yes . . .' said Ripley. 'But, I don't know what the odds are of us catching people who work like that. And I have wondered if rather than pointing the finger at some mysterious third party with some kind of terrorist agenda, our energies might be better served looking closer to home.'

'How close to home are we talking?' asked Banks.

Ripley sighed before he spoke. Whatever he was about to say next, he was clearly in two minds about saying it. 'There is something about the timing of the theft that concerns me. And that lends weight to your immediate, and very reasonable, speculation that this might be an inside job, or that someone on the inside might have at the very least aided the person who stole those substances.'

'I'm listening,' said Halloran, and so was everyone else. Banks, Kitt, and even Deirdre who was trying to pretend she was stapling a large pile of documents. She'd only managed to staple two bundles in the time Ripley had been talking.

'Leonard and I were duty-bound to report our findings about the agent, about its capacity to kill, but once we fully understood what we had inadvertently created, we were of course horrified. We'd worked in the defence sector too long. Seen too much. Knew that just because we recommended the agent wasn't used, didn't mean that our recommendation would be followed by those who would immediately see its potential in the field. We even debated destroying the substance and all files containing the formula so that it could never be used, either by our employers or by some other third party who might get their hands on it.'

'But you were too concerned about the consequences of such action?' said Halloran, when Ripley paused.

Ripley nodded. 'You have to make some difficult ethical decisions when you work in this profession. But the way this agent worked . . . there was no argument about the fact that it brought about one of the most inhumane deaths a person could think of. Though Leo and I were appalled by what we had created, we both knew that there were people higher up in the ranks of the agency who would welcome this invention. Who would back it. Pour their energies and the agency's budget into developing it further for the supposed tactical advantage of Great Britain.'

'My experience with military agencies is limited,' said Banks. 'But I'm guessing you'd face some pretty heavy discipline for destroying something that would be deemed so valuable by the higher-ups?'

'Your guess, Detective Banks, would be more correct than you know. I hope you believe me when I say the creation of this formula was a complete accident. I never would have agreed to work on something so heinous. And neither would Leo. Once the agent had worked its way through a host, there would be little of the body left for families to bury, cremate or mourn. We knew that. But, as you so rightly point out, we dreaded the consequences if we out-right destroyed all of our work. So, we took the coward's way and I suppose you could say we both paid the price for that decision.'

'How does this relate to the timing of the theft being suspicious?' said Halloran.

'Leo and I put together a dossier about the unexpected effects of the agent. Outlining in detail why the agent must be destroyed, along with the files that described how to synthesise it. There are other ways of killing enemy soldiers. There simply isn't a need for an agent like this in warfare.'

'But your superiors disagreed,' Halloran said.

'I don't know that they did, exactly. It was never openly discussed. But the very night we submitted our report, believing ourselves to have done the right thing, the agent and the antidote were stolen from the lab,' said Ripley. 'When that happened, discussing our dossier became a moot point. Our superiors were only interested in recovering the agent and the antidote. And, in fact, they interrogated me and Leonard about the theft. They claimed that they thought we might have orchestrated the theft because we had recommended the destruction of the agent and didn't trust the Defence Medical Agency to destroy it.'

Ripley paused here and his lip trembled. Tears filled his eyes and it took him a moment to compose himself before he spoke again. 'Of course, the irony of those interrogations are not lost on me. If either Leo or myself had known that we would ingest the agent ourselves, we would have been even more ardent about getting our hands on the stolen antidote than they were.'

'In fairness, given what you wrote in that report, I can see why they might have been suspicious of you,' said Halloran. 'But the timing also casts suspicion on them, doesn't it? And that's what you're getting at.'

'I believe it does,' said Ripley. 'Though even I'm not sure if the agency would go this far. It seems so extreme. That they would orchestrate their own fake theft of the agent and the antidote, and then poison the two people who had recommended it be destroyed. If they wanted to develop the agent further against our ethical wishes, why not just dismiss us? Compel us to sign NDAs?'

'I agree that it's far-fetched,' said Halloran. 'But I'm also aware that some pretty far-fetched stuff goes on in the world of both military and government intelligence when they think nobody is looking. I'm not saying I'm buying it as a theory in full. But how strongly did you argue for the destruction of this agent in your dossier?'

'Both Leo and I were adamant in the document that destruction of the agent was the only ethical path to take ... We may also have hinted, off the record to our direct superior, that we would go to the press if the agency continued research. But that was strictly off the record,' said Ripley.

Halloran sighed. 'Do you not think that was a bit of a risk?

Even off the record? You know better than I do that military agencies do not take threats lightly. They can't afford to. Based on what you've told me, it seems to me that they might have believed you would take the information to the press even if you did sign NDAs,' he said. 'That you might rely on the infamy of the headlines to protect yourselves from any consequences. If anything befell you, or they tried to sue you, they would be pretty much confirming the stories as true when all they'd really want to do was keep plausible deniability.'

'It's only in retrospect that I realise what a risk we took in hinting that we would go public with this information if our recommendations weren't followed,' said Ripley. 'We were just both so incensed, furious not just at the agency, but at ourselves. Despite every precaution, we still managed to manufacture something we would never wish to be in military hands, even that of our own country. We weren't thinking straight when we made that insinuation,' he added. 'But even after all I've seen, I never thought that the agency would resort to something like this.'

'We don't know that they did, yet,' said Halloran. 'But, if they did think you might not adhere to any NDA you signed, they might have decided to take more extreme action if they wanted to pursue this agent and they knew it was likely to be controversial if the project was ever leaked to the public. Which would mean the interrogations you were subjected to were just a tactic to make it seem as though they were looking for the stolen toxin and antidote when in fact they knew exactly where they were all along.'

'You've summarised my concerns about the agency's conduct exactly,' said Ripley. 'I don't know who to trust in all this. Part of me was hoping that you'd dismiss the idea that the agency would go this far outright. That you might be able to think of a simpler explanation. Outlandish as it seems, even to me, when you work in a place where classified information is part of your daily bread, you rather come to redefine the word far-fetched. I think my employer does a lot of good in this world, otherwise I wouldn't work for them. But I stop short of trusting them completely. Especially with what essentially amounts to a bioweapon as powerful as this one.'

Again, Ripley paused and the reality of his situation seemed to hit him all over again. 'The reason I've come to you is just so that somebody knows. What's happened to me. I mean, I would hate to be found, you know, for my body to be found and for nobody to ever know the truth. Or at least some of it.'

'I understand that,' Halloran said, his voice softening.

'If I'm honest, I don't really know how far you're going to get with this investigation,' said Ripley. 'My employers are not obliged to cooperate with you or MI5, even if you do have a dead body on your hands that they might have something to do with. Even if I die and you have *two* dead bodies. They have a special kind of protection. So maybe all this is pointless, but I . . . I just had to do something. I couldn't just wait to die. I beg of you, I will do anything to help but I really don't want to die. Not like this.'

'I'm going to need you to tell me all of this again on record,' said Halloran. 'But I will set the wheels in motion while we square away the particulars. I think at this point, it might be more sensible to focus on working out where and when Leonard was poisoned.'

'Agreed,' said Banks. 'We know it must have been five days prior to his death. Whereas we don't know for sure when Mr Ripley was poisoned. If we work out the where and when of Leonard's poisoning that is likely to lead us to the who.'

'Which is the most crucial piece of information to saving your life,' Halloran said to Ripley. 'Whoever poisoned Leonard, whether the agency acted as a collaborative entity, whether it is a rogue employee at the agency or whether it is an unknown third party who stole the toxin from your superiors, they are almost certainly the same party who poisoned you and, by extension, the same party who stole the toxin and the antidote in the first place.'

'That makes sense to me,' said Ripley. 'However, I have taken the liberty of copying my diary, which details all of my movements for the past five days. I've also copied my lab notes that detail our discovery that the toxin was lethal. These are kept in private notebooks, away from the official reports I submit to the Defence Medical Agency. So many times in our line of work, you take your work home with you, puzzling through problems and reflecting on results. So you will have those to work from. It's probably best I hand these over now, as I have no idea how much time I have left. And here are the blood tests I underwent this morning, I repeated the test three times to be sure. Even though, of course, I knew right away what had happened. Will there be . . . many people working on the case?'

Halloran lowered his eyes at this question. It was obvious what Ripley wanted to hear but Halloran had never been one for stretching the truth. 'It will be our top priority to solve Leonard Bell's murder in the hope of preventing yours. But I can't lie to you, resources are tight.'

'Perhaps, I might be able to help with that problem,' Kitt said, speaking at last after wanting to so many times before.

'Under the circumstances, I'm open to any help whatsoever,' said Ripley.

'I think you may have mistaken me for a police officer,' said Kitt. 'Your problem seemed urgent, and indeed it is, so I didn't want to interrupt you to make a formal introduction before.'

Although privately Kitt admitted that her curiosity over what Ripley was going to tell Halloran had more to do with her keeping quiet than her concern for the urgency of the matter, she felt it was a plausible enough excuse for having kept her true identity a secret this long.

'You're . . . not a police officer?' said Ripley, his brow furrowing. Kitt couldn't quite tell if it was in anger, confusion or concern.

'No, I'm a private investigator,' she said quickly, hoping that the fact she could be of help with the case might distract from any anger Ripley was feeling over her not identifying herself sooner. 'I consult with the police on cases from time to time. In this instance, however, I was providing a witness statement when you arrived. You see, I was with Leonard when he died.'

'My God,' said Ripley. 'I'm so sorry. It's . . . Seeing what that agent can do to the human body, it's not for the faint-hearted.'

'That much we can agree on,' said Kitt.

'Though if private investigation is your trade, I'd imagine your heart to be anything but faint.'

'I think we can agree on that too,' Kitt said with a small smile. 'I'm not sure what help, if any, I can offer in recovering this missing antidote, but I'd be happy to look into any avenues that can't be covered by police resources.'

'I will appreciate every scrap of help I can get. It's very difficult to not imagine, moment-to-moment, that it's already happening. That you're already dying,' said Ripley, scraping his fingers through his grey hair.

'I think that's to be expected given the circumstances,' said Kitt. 'But we've got to hope that we've enough time to recover this antidote for you before it's too late. Otherwise, blind panic is going to keep us from saving you.'

'I can't thank you enough,' said Ripley, his eyes still watery over all he had relayed to them thus far. 'I will pay you of course.'

'Oh no, I couldn't take money off you when your life is in jeopardy,' said Kitt.

'Oh, but I insist,' said Ripley. Had the circumstances not been so dire Kitt would have smiled. Leave it to a British person to insist on paying a fee even as their life hung in the balance.

'Let's agree that if I recover the antidote before the police, you will donate my fee to a deserving charity. That's the right thing to do, especially at this time of year,' said Kitt, confident this would settle the argument.

Ripley offered a nod that assured her it had.

'I don't want to delay you any longer. There's no time to waste. But here's my card,' Kitt said, pulling a business card out of her pocket and offering it to Ripley. 'It has the agency address on Walmgate on there. When you're all done here, please come and visit us. I'll be in all afternoon trying to get to the bottom of the paperwork.'

'I appreciate it,' Ripley said, accepting Kitt's card. 'I appreciate any help from all of you.' At this Ripley looked from Kitt, to Halloran and then to Banks. 'I'm sorry, even with what I do for a living . . . I'm still in shock that this has happened. I don't know who is behind this or exactly why, but the cruelty of it astounds me. I'd take a knife or a gun or even strangulation over this. Whoever poisoned me and Leo with this agent, they mean business. They mean to kill me, just like they killed him.'

CHAPTER TWELVE

Thanks to Kitt's rather eccentric assistant and business partner, Grace, there was no mistaking that it was Christmas time at Hartley and Edwards Investigations. Grace had spent the first two days of December hanging thick, gold tinsel around every available bookcase and filing cabinet. A large Christmas tree stood in the corner in which they usually made the tea. For the festive season, Grace had switched out Kitt's usual favourite, Lady Grey, for a range of Christmas-flavoured teas so that the whole office consistently smelled of peppermint, ginger and orange.

The tree itself was ablaze with a million yellow fairy lights and an oversized white angel stood at its apex. The expression on the angel's face was one of mild disdain and, given the ornament's lofty position, Grace had got it into her head that the angel was actually a tyrant of the angel nation that looked down on fellow, lesser angels and humankind. Kitt had made the mistake of showing mild amusement the first time Grace had mentioned this idea. And thus, had subsequently been 'treated' to a whole anthology of *Tales of Tatiana the Tyrannical Archangel*. These stories detailed the various judgements Tatiana passed on the humans who entered Hartley and Edwards Investigations and were the kind of stories that could only be dreamed up in the startling imagination of Grace Edwards.

Grace listened carefully to all that Kitt told her about what had unfolded with Leonard Bell and Kevin Ripley, as well as the possible role of the Defence Medical Agency in his predicament. When Kitt had finished, Grace shook her head, seemingly trying to digest what was, even to her, a strange and surreal tale.

'What do we know about this Defence Medical Agency?' Grace asked.

'Not a great deal,' said Kitt. 'Just that they are a military operation and that one of the things on their agenda is developing new weapons – including bioweapons – for use in the field. Halloran seems to think it will be a nightmare getting any information out of them because most of their work is classified.'

'Classified . . .' Grace repeated, taking a moment to sip from a hot chocolate she had made for herself. 'I don't remember that case you, me and Joe worked up in the Borderlands being that much fun, and that turned out to be all about classified information.'

'My thoughts exactly,' said Kitt. 'But at least, in this

instance, we know who we're up against from the start. We didn't have a clue on that case. And the Defence Medical Agency is military rather than government so maybe that will make a difference.' Despite her best efforts, Kitt was unable to say any of this in a particularly convincing tone.

Grace was about to say something else, but she was interrupted by the door opening and Ripley himself walking in. As he did so, he brushed a small covering of snow off the shoulders of his winter coat and then strode towards the one face in the room he recognised.

'I hope I'm not interrupting anything too important,' he said, as he approached Kitt's desk.

'I think, considering the situation, there is nothing more important than talking to you right now and getting a jump on recovering that antidote,' said Kitt. Between getting to the office and Ripley arriving she had received a text from Halloran confirming that they had checked Ripley's blood tests against Leonard Bell's. The same unknown substance was present in both of their results, and so it was now official. This poor man was going to be dead in five days or fewer unless Halloran or Kitt could uncover the antidote.

'I'm so lucky you're able to make my case a priority,' said Ripley.

'Please, sit down,' Kitt said with a small smile. 'Could we offer you a drink of any kind? Any time is considered a good time to put the kettle on around here, but that counts double for mid-afternoon when you're starting to flag a bit.'

'No, no thank you,' said Ripley. 'I'm not sure if it's paranoia or just that my stomach has been turned over by this whole business but I'm struggling to eat or drink anything at the moment. Silly really. As though somebody is going to bother poisoning you with a lethal agent twice.'

Kitt could see that Ripley was trying to make a small joke about his predicament, but she couldn't bring herself to partake in it. Even Grace's face was solemn as Ripley took a seat.

'I don't want to waste too much time with pleasantries, I imagine you're already quite frustrated by how much time police protocol has taken,' said Kitt. 'But just so you know, this is my associate, Grace Edwards. She works with me here at the agency and, just like me, keeps all information confidential. We may bring in other associates as necessary to try and find the antidote quicker, and they are all bound by the same rules of confidentiality.'

'I greatly appreciate the reassurances,' said Ripley. 'But I don't mind telling you I'm past caring about who knows and who doesn't. My main concern was that I got to the police before I was stopped by the agency. Now that I've managed that, I'm not too concerned about what happens next in that department. I'll no doubt be out of a job for bringing the police into this matter, and a private investigator to boot. But I've been prudent about savings over the years. If I survive this . . . I mean, if I don't end up . . .' Ripley trailed off for a moment not wanting to say the words out loud that everyone in the room understood implicitly. 'If I'm careful . . . I'll have enough to keep me well enough until my state pension kicks in. No job is worth my life.'

'I agree,' said Kitt, and she took the briefest moment to glance around her surroundings and reflect on those words. Her eyes rested momentarily on the large bookcase filled with volumes about criminology and law. When the idea first struck her several years ago, she hadn't given much thought to starting a private investigation agency. It had just felt like the right thing to do at the time. But how many occasions had she found her own life in jeopardy since then? More than she'd like to think on. And each time a little part of her had wondered, despite the justice delivered, regardless of the hefty fees rendered, was it worth it? The personal cost of finding the truth for wronged parties had been much higher than she'd ever imagined.

'Before we get into the particulars,' said Kitt, 'there's something very specific I wanted to ask you. Something that I absolutely must get straight from the outset.'

'I'll do my best to answer any questions you have, of course,' said Ripley.

'This one should be pretty straightforward,' said Kitt. 'We just need to know, in as much detail as you can give us, what we're looking for. What does the toxin and the antidote look like? How is it stored? Was it in a particular kind of container?'

Ripley nodded. 'Inspector Halloran asked the same questions. Naturally, you need to know exactly what you're looking for. Had the toxin behaved as expected and been considered a success, we would have manufactured much bigger-batch doses of both the toxin and the antidote. As it stands, we were still in test stage so only a small amount had been synthesised. Ten vials of the toxin and twenty vials of the antidote. We made more of the antidote in case it was discovered that one vial wasn't enough to counteract a negative reaction.'

'So all told there are thirty vials missing,' said Grace.

'That's right,' said Ripley. 'But the vials are small. Ten millilitres each, small bottles made of clear glass. The labels on the toxin read YX8 – which was the name given to the substance. The antidote labels read ANTI YX8. So, if you find a vial or several vials, you'll be able to tell if you're holding the toxin or the antidote by the labels.'

'Is there anything obvious about storing these substances that might give some sense of where they're being held? Do they have to be stored at a certain temperature, for example?' asked Kitt.

'Temperature is not important as long as it doesn't exceed thirty degrees Celsius. So on a very hot day, you might have to refrigerate the substances, but I can't think it would make much difference in British wintertime. What does make a difference, however, is direct sunlight. Both the toxin and the antidote lose all potency if they are kept out in prolonged sunlight. A batch can be ruined in as little as ten minutes of sunlight exposure, we've found.'

'So it would have to be somewhere dark, a cupboard, a drawer, a refrigerator ... Hmmm, now that I'm starting to list things, that doesn't really narrow it down, does it?' said Kitt.

'Not really,' said Ripley, his eyes lowering to Kitt's desk. 'Whoever has stolen these substances wouldn't have them out on display anyway. The odds are they are hiding them somewhere. But you asked if they were in a particular container. Last I saw them they were in a wooden box about twelve inches long. But whoever stole them may have transferred them to a different container.'

Kitt nodded. 'Well, at least we know what we're looking for. And we'll do everything we can to make sure that the antidote is in our hands as quickly as possible.'

'I – well – suffice to say, I very much hope that is the case,' said Ripley, failing to disguise the sense of reservation in his tone as he handed over a thick brown envelope. 'In the meantime, I took the liberty of making you a copy of my diary for the last five days and my laboratory notes, just as I did the police.'

'I'm sure they'll be useful,' said Kitt. 'Thank you for taking the trouble when the last thing you likely want to be doing is standing at a photocopier.'

'I see it as a necessary evil. One that I hope will save my life,' Ripley said. 'I expect you'll want to know what I told

Inspector Halloran in order to decide which leads you want to follow up when it comes to the missing antidote?'

'That would be helpful,' Kitt said, reaching for a notebook and pen, as was her custom whenever a client was giving her information. The mere gesture, she was certain, made people think carefully about what they said. This simple device could, in Kitt's experience, save a lot of time on the job.

'I believe Inspector Halloran is focusing his attentions on my employer,' said Ripley. 'He said he'd get straight in touch with my direct superior, a man called Nathan Greene, to whom Leo and I submitted our dossier about the agent. And to whom we made the ill-advised insinuation that we might take what we knew about the agent to the press if they insisted on continuing development of the toxin. Looking back now, I don't know what we could have been thinking to say something like that. Even if it was supposed to be in confidence.'

'I don't think anyone could reasonably expect consequences like those you and Leonard have suffered,' said Kitt.

'Perhaps you are right,' said Ripley. 'But I'm keenly aware that that moment of folly may cost me my life. So, with all due respect for what you do here, I think the inspector has a better chance of getting something out of my employer than yourselves. To call the Defence Medical Agency tight-lipped about the things they do is an incredible understatement but the inspector at least has the gravity of the force behind him. I could be wrong, of course, but my instincts tell me those matters are best left with the inspector.'

'I am sure you know best when it comes to who your employer is most likely to speak to,' said Kitt, while privately thinking that Ripley might be surprised about just how effective some of the tactics they had used over the years at the agency to loosen the jaws of those reluctant to talk to them had been. At the end of the day, all agencies and companies, even those run by the military, were only made up of people. And people could usually be influenced to share information, by one means or another. Halloran had a strict rule book to play by but, as long as Kitt didn't break any laws, she was free to try a range of schemes to move an investigation forward.

'The inspector did say, however, that dealing with the Defence Medical Agency was going to eat up pretty much all of his resources for at least the first day of the investigation. So, he suggested, at least in the first instance, that you look at anyone else,' Ripley explained.

'Is there anyone else we could speak to or perhaps surveil who might shed light on the whereabouts of the antidote? Even if we just did surveillance, if we're looking at the right people, they might lead us straight to it.'

'Well, just like Inspector Halloran said, I think the key to recovering both the toxin and the antidote probably lies in what happened to Leo,' said Ripley. 'So the best thing I can do is tell you what I know about people he didn't get on well with in the workplace. Although I was friends with Leo, that's where I saw him for the bulk of the time, so that's the part of his life I know most about. The list of people he had issues with is short. And it's difficult because, just because two people have an issue, it doesn't immediately mean they're going to orchestrate the theft of a lethal toxin and kill you with it, and your lab partner.'

'Was there anyone who had an issue with both of you?' said Grace.

'That's really how I've had to narrow it down,' said Ripley. 'Which makes the list even shorter. It's not like me and Leo set out to make enemies, which might sound a perverse thing for a military employee to say, and yet it's true.'

'But there were some people in the workplace who took issue with you and Leonard? Or what you were doing with the toxin?' said Kitt.

'I don't know about the toxin, most people who work for the Defence Medical Agency are realists about the kind of world we live in, even if ethical dilemmas do surface from time to time,' said Ripley. 'But, there is someone who springs to mind now that I've had time to really think about it. A man named Tyler Simmons.'

'Who is he?' asked Kitt.

'He used to work for the Defence Medical Agency, he was dismissed a few months back for not following security protocol close enough. He was taking things home, classified documents, that he shouldn't have been. He had also not followed safety protocol on a trial he was working on and there were dire consequences for the subjects involved. Me and Leonard became privy to what he was doing and reported him for it.'

'This trial he was working on, was it a bit like the toxin you developed?' Grace said.

Looking at her assistant, Kitt guessed she might be wondering the same thing she was: exactly how many noxious substances were being cooked up in this place on an annual basis?

'Similar,' said Ripley. 'But in our case, we followed all of the safety protocols. All of our models predicted that this substance would not be lethal. The tests we'd conducted on living tissue didn't show any abnormalities. But then, of course, at that point we didn't know about the five-day incubation period. So after forty-eight hours had passed and there were no abnormalities shown, we deduced that it was safe for human testing. Simmons skipped several of these steps and several human test subjects paid the price.'

'So, after you and Leonard reported him, the Defence Medical Agency dismissed him,' said Kitt.

'Yes, and Simmons was not happy about it. He claimed he'd been unfairly dismissed and that sacrifice was necessary for progress to take place.'

'Easy to say when the sacrifice wasn't his,' said Kitt.

'My thoughts exactly, and Leo's for that matter,' said Ripley. 'I might not have thought any more about Tyler

Simmons after he was dismissed, but his dark shadow has loomed in the workplace long after he left.'

'How so?' asked Kitt.

'I think he's romantically involved with somebody who still works at the agency, a woman named Margaret Cryer.'

'She's a colleague?' said Grace.

'Yes,' Ripley said, 'she joined the agency a couple of years back now. At first, me and Leo thought we were getting on well with her. But then, over time, and particularly recently, things took a darker turn.'

'In what way?' asked Kitt, when Ripley sustained a lengthy pause.

'It's difficult to put my finger on. Over time, she seemed to get very short-tempered with us. Her manner was always quite abrupt but she changed from abrupt to indisputably snappy no matter which way we tried to keep the peace with her. First she was passive-aggressive and then outright aggressive. Most recently, she started verbally threatening us to stay off particular projects. She basically told us that we should be delegating certain projects to her because of her impressive track record.'

'Was the toxin project one of those projects?' said Kitt.

Ripley thought for a moment. 'Yes, it was. She was particularly threatening about that project, now that I think about it.'

'What kind of threats did she make?'

'Mostly about reporting us to superiors for any

corner-cutting or protocol not followed. I suppose looking to do the same thing to us that we had done to Simmons. Please understand though, unlike Simmons, neither myself nor Leo did anything heinous. But military agencies are tight-run ships and frown upon even the slightest breach of protocol. Even if some form or action you're supposed to perform makes no logical sense and slows a job down considerably. She seemed to be making a kind of catalogue of complaints against the pair of us. And she would threaten to take this list of crimes to our superiors and essentially cost us our jobs. Being fired from a place like that, as we saw when Simmons was dismissed, you're not going to get another job anywhere else credible. So, it was quite the threat to make.'

'When did the threats begin?' said Kitt.

'Around the time that Simmons got dismissed for breaching protocol,' said Ripley. 'A few months back now. Funnily enough she's kept her cool with Nathan Greene who is the person who did the actual firing, but then again, though Leonard and I had more senior positions in the lab Nathan Greene is her superior and ours, and there's no doubt she is ambitious.'

'And you say Simmons is romantically involved with this woman?' said Kitt.

'That's what I've heard, though I admit I've never seen them together,' said Ripley. 'I understand a person being mad about getting dismissed, and that maybe Simmons holds me and Leo responsible, but I don't really know why Margaret and Tyler would go that far. It seems to me that the cost to them would be great if they got caught. But . . . something in my gut just tells me it's worth mentioning. Especially since, again according to office rumour, Simmons has largely been living off-grid since he was fired.'

'Off-grid how?' said Grace.

'No mobile phone, no online presence. Using cash. Generally making himself difficult to find,' said Ripley. 'I don't know why a person really does that unless they are up to something they shouldn't be.'

Kitt nodded. 'It's too early to say what involvement either of them may have but from the sound of it both Tyler Simmons and Margaret Cryer are a solid place to start. Halloran is working on the agency as a whole. We can look into individuals, and the fact that Simmons is no longer at the agency might make it easier to approach him. Though if he's off-grid, maybe we'd be better off trying to find him through her.'

'I've got Simmons's last known address but I don't know how much time he spends there, so maybe surveiling Margaret would be the best bet in the first instance. Just . . . be careful, if you do approach him,' said Ripley in a tone that sent a shiver right through Kitt. 'I've also heard that since he's been fired he's become quite unpredictable in terms of how he reacts to other people.'

'What do you mean?' said Kitt. 'He's violent?'

'Not that I've heard of ... yet,' said Ripley. 'But he's become very shouty and verbally aggressive according to the couple of people who have managed to cross paths with him. And, to be honest, he's always been one of those people I wouldn't put much past. I was never quite sure, you know, what he was capable of.'

'OK,' said Kitt. 'We'll take the necessary precautions.'

'What I don't understand is how Margaret or Tyler would have managed to poison Leo without his notice,' said Ripley. 'He wouldn't socialise with either of them. I can't really see Margaret getting close enough to pull something like that off in the workplace – especially when there are numerous security cameras – and he would have mentioned it to me if he'd seen either of them outside the workplace. We know that the agent takes the victim over the course of five days, almost to the hour. So if Leo died at around seven p.m. last night—'

'Leonard must have ingested the agent at around seven p.m. five nights prior,' said Grace. 'So that would mean it happened around seven p.m. on Friday night.'

'It's not an exact science,' said Ripley, 'but I would say you were looking at a window of anywhere between six and ten p.m. that evening. So, definitely after Leo left the office. I did see Leo and his wife that evening but we didn't meet until nine. He was at a rehearsal for the book fair before that. I've let Inspector Halloran know and alongside looking into the agency, he's going to systematically question the volunteers at the book fair and also look into video footage that was taken of the rehearsal that evening for promotional purposes.'

'I'll get in touch with Mal and find out if there's anyone who volunteered at the book fair and is perhaps further down the pecking order that he wants us to handle,' said Kitt. 'Assuming the book fair rehearsal started at six, three hours of the window in which the poisoning might have taken place span that rehearsal.'

'If I remember correctly the rehearsal did begin at six,' said Ripley. 'From what he and Eleanor, Leo's wife, said when I met them for a drink, Leo left his house at around five thirty and was at his rehearsal until nine. But I must admit I might be getting that wrong. I think I would have noticed if anything untoward had happened while we were drinking together though, and I certainly would have noticed if either Margaret or Tyler were in the bar – as would Leo, but we were making merry that night and weren't on high alert so, I suppose, it could have happened in the first hour of our drinks together. All the details of where we were and what time we left are in my diary.'

'We'll definitely look into the people at the book fair that Halloran isn't already questioning,' said Kitt.

'Anyone extra that you can follow up on will be a help, I'm sure,' said Ripley. 'Though I hesitate to suggest it given how recent her loss is, I have been in touch with Eleanor and I think she would be a good person to talk to. Leo will have told her a lot more about his dealings with the people at the book fair than anybody else. I've explained what's happened to me and she's agreed, considering my life is in danger, to talk to you in addition to any interviews she does with the police.'

'Are you as close to her as you were to Leonard?' asked Kitt.

'Probably not quite. I mean, I worked with Leo every day, so we had more opportunity to have in-depth talks. But she's a good friend, is Eleanor,' said Ripley. 'I mean, they both are ... were in Leo's case. We were all quite close, before Leo died. Regular drinking buddies. I don't quite know how much she'll want to see me now, given that I had a hand in creating the substance that killed her husband, but she said she doesn't want to see the same thing happen to me that happened to Leo and will tell you everything she can remember about his movements last Friday night.'

'Sometimes people clam up around the police just because the whole process seems so official. We'll take her details and start there,' said Kitt. 'Halloran will be probably best placed to glean any information about the night of the break-in to your facility. He has access to all kinds of data I don't. But I certainly can ask some different questions to those the police might ask Eleanor, see if something sparks in her mind.'

'I appreciate it,' said Ripley. 'Had we all known that something like this would happen, we'd all have been a lot more vigilant.'

'Hindsight is always twenty–twenty,' said Kitt. 'While Halloran is focusing on your employers I can look into Tyler and Margaret, and at other places you might have been in the last few days where the poisoning might have happened. We'll cover all bases, no matter how absurd a lead might seem. We'll make sure we rule absolutely everything out. No stone unturned.'

'I'm grateful,' said Ripley, pausing for a moment as he gathered the strength he needed to say the next sentence. 'And if the worst happens, if we don't find the antidote in time, I can only think detailed breakdowns of all my movements will be very helpful in bringing the killer to justice. Even if I'm not here to see it.'

'I know it's difficult,' said Kitt. 'But try not to think that way. For all we know, you only ingested the agent yesterday and we've got days to figure this out.'

'I hope you're right, Ms Hartley,' said Ripley.

'Kitt . . . please,' said Kitt.

'Kitt,' Ripley corrected himself. 'The thought of dying as a result of my own scientific research is bad enough. But to die not knowing who did this to me, or why, is a fate that cuts even deeper. If there's anything else I can do to help don't waste a second in getting in touch with me. I'll do everything I can to try and get to the bottom of this myself, naturally. Keep my ears to the ground for any intelligence that might come my way. But Kitt, Grace, I fear that my life is very much in your hands.'

CHAPTER THIRTEEN

'Grace, bring up all you can online about Nathan Greene, will you?' Kitt said, the moment Kevin Ripley had left their offices.

'Ripley's superior at work?' Grace clarified. 'I thought we were starting out by looking into Tyler Simmons and Margaret Cryer.'

'We are,' Kitt confirmed. 'But it's just struck me that Nathan Greene is the only person that both of the victims, or shall we say intended victims in the case of Ripley, and all of the suspects mentioned so far have in common.'

'Oh yes,' said Grace. 'You're right. They've all worked at the agency with Greene at some point.'

'Not just with Greene, but under him. He is a direct superior to all of them. Halloran mentioned a theory when we were listening to Ripley's original testimony. That this scheme may not have been cooked up by the agency itself but by a rogue employee or third party.'

'And you think it might be this Nathan Greene guy?' said Grace.

'I don't know . . . but perhaps he's connected somehow. He was the person to fire Simmons. Cryer, from what Ripley tells us, seems to be keeping the peace with him even though he fired her romantic partner. Which makes me wonder if she is as ambitious as Ripley thinks or if she is, for some reason we don't know about yet, afraid of him.'

'I'm trying to put myself in that position,' said Grace. 'If someone fired my romantic partner I think I would at least feel a bit awkward about working with that person. And I think it would be a pretty difficult feeling to hide. But Ripley didn't mention any awkwardness.'

'No he didn't. Which could mean a number of things, including the possibility that for some reason Greene and Cryer are colluding with each other,' said Kitt.

'Why would they do that?' said Grace.

Kitt shook her head. 'I have no idea, at present. But it's something we've got to keep in our minds. Nathan Greene somehow seems to be at the centre of all this. He was the person who Bell and Ripley told, off the record, that they'd go to the press if their recommendations weren't followed. And he was the one they submitted their report to. It's not enough to say categorically that he's involved but just because Halloran is looking into him and Ripley has given us other suspects to consider, that doesn't mean we shouldn't keep the name Nathan Greene at the forefront of our minds,' said Kitt.

'I hear what you're saying. There are quite a few possibilities here. Maybe Ripley and Bell had something on Greene that he didn't want his superiors to find out,' said Grace. 'Or Greene wanted a promotion for successfully synthesising the substance and saw Ripley and Bell as an obstacle to that. Or, maybe he was working for another third party and was going to sell the formula to them and Ripley and Bell would have suspected. Or—'

'Yes, can I just stop you there, Grace,' said Kitt. 'I think it's best that we put the process of looking for evidence before the process of generating wild theories.'

'Spoilsport,' Grace said with a small smirk. And with that she slumped behind her computer, at the same time creasing the deep purple maxi dress she was wearing with gold trim around the hem. Kitt could always tell how well Grace was getting on with her family at any given time by how much her clothes reflected her Indian heritage. The dress certainly had accents to it that wouldn't be out of place on a beautifully designed sari. Kitt smiled as she tore open the thick envelope of diary notes and lab documents Ripley had handed over to her. She had never met Grace's family, who lived over in West Yorkshire, but Grace had had what must have been well over her hundredth serious argument with her dad a couple of months back. Kitt was glad they'd seemingly buried the hatchet before Christmas.

It was a particularly empty time of year to be sour at anyone and, as Bell's death and Ripley's predicament underlined, nobody ever knew how much time they had left in this world to make amends.

'So, how hard can it be to find a man who works for a covert military agency online,' Grace said, frantically tapping away at the keyboard and frowning at the screen.

'I have faith that if anyone can track down this bloke's online presence, it's you,' said Kitt. 'Anything you can find will be of some help in understanding who this guy really is, I'm sure. Once we've got what we can on him, we'll move on to looking into Simmons and Cryer. I think it's more likely we're dealing with a rogue individual. I can't see the agency itself authorising the poisoning of two employees, even if they were worried about them leaking information about the toxin. But then again, maybe that's me being naive.'

'Or maybe just hopeful,' said Grace. 'That we can actually trust the institutions that were built in the first place to protect us.'

'A girl can dream,' said Kitt as she flicked through the pages Ripley had provided. She was looking for one thing in particular: his lab notes from the night of the theft. The night he and Bell handed all their research over to Nathan Greene. Could it really be a coincidence that they recommended all work on the toxin be discontinued and then it disappeared in the early hours of the morning?

The moment Kitt landed on the pages Ripley wrote on that fateful day, she began to read.

12th December

The results of our first, and hopefully last, human trial have been tabulated and submitted to NG today. The singular small mercy is that only one life was lost to the trial. The five-day incubation period left us believing that the toxin had no effect whatsoever and could have led to yet more deaths. Had we decided to reformulate immediately and retest, rather than wait for thirty days to understand any long-term effects of the substance, the losses could have been even worse. Accidentally claiming one life, even in the name of science and greater safety in our country, is one life too many for me. I shall never forget the look on that man's face when we found him. I know, in my heart, that it will haunt me forever.

LB and I agonised over our accompanying report. Ensuring every word was selected for the very purpose of deterring the MDA from any further study on this toxin. I have the terrible feeling that in being party to its creation, I have done something that can never be undone. Though that is true of many research projects in the past, in this case it is coupled with the wish that there was, in fact, a way of undoing it.

NG says he will submit our research and our report to his superiors tomorrow. However, he took pains to tell us that he disagreed with our assessment that research should be ceased because of what he called a hiccup. A hiccup?! What happened to that man was no hiccup. He argued that although we had not managed to synthesise the toxin to the expected specifications, we may have inadvertently created something far more useful to the world of defence.

LB and I at once refuted his insinuation and made a personal appeal to NG not to go down that path. One that is ethically bankrupt and could backfire terribly. What if an enemy power manages to procure vials of the toxin, or manages to synthesise a more powerful version of it for themselves? LB and I have worked too long in the world of defence to believe that the upper tactical hand our superiors imagine could last long at all.

NG didn't outright dismiss our concerns but talked instead of the security measures that would be taken to ensure the strict compartmentalisation of the substance. Measures that would make it impossible for nefarious third parties to get their hands on it. Speaking to LB after the fact, it's clear that he is as unconvinced as I am that they will succeed in keeping such a powerful substance secure. Once foreign powers know that substance exists, there will be plots afoot to either reverse-engineer what we have created or steal any stockpile of the agent we may create.

Our guess, based on hints dropped by NG, is that the agency plans to develop this toxin to the point that there is no longer a five-day incubation period. To the point that the lethal effects are instantaneous. Having seen what this substance did to our first human test subject, I am filled with horror at the idea of people all over the world, even if they are would-be enemies, suffering a death like that due to something I had a hand in creating.

NG seems strangely insistent on the research continuing, however. I have been taken aback by his perseverance on this matter despite our protests. I could understand people higher up the ladder only seeing the possibilities of this formula in the field. In fact, there are *quite a few I can think of who would be overjoyed by what we have inadvertently synthesised. But I thought NG was built more like LB and me. After the conversation I've had with him this evening, I fear I may have been very, very wrong.*

Kitt took in a deep breath and slowly let it out. So, Nathan Greene had been 'strangely insistent' about the research continuing and Ripley could think of people higher up the ranks who would be very happy to continue research into this toxin in order to make it more lethal. Both of those strands in Ripley's notes made Kitt's tummy turn over.

Her greatest concern, however, was that from Ripley's point of view, who presumably knew him quite well, there was something out of sorts about Greene's behaviour the very night that the toxin and the antidote disappeared. He stopped short of saying that Greene was acting suspiciously. He hadn't quite used that word. But from the tone of his notes it was clear that Ripley knew something was going on with Greene, something he couldn't put his finger on.

'I'll keep digging,' said Grace. 'But so far, all I have found on Nathan Greene is a photo on the website of a private members' golf club.'

Getting up from her desk, Kitt walked over to where Grace was working. Staring at the screen, Kitt's eyes flitted around the rows of members' photos until they landed on one captioned *Nathan Greene.*

Given the amount of balding that was taking place, Kitt

guessed Greene to be somewhere in his early sixties. He had lost all of the hair at the crown and had two sections remaining either side that were salt and pepper in shade. His considerable forehead was interrupted by two bulging brown eyes that somehow looked too big for his head. In his blue checkered polo shirt, he didn't look particularly intimidating. But taking into account everything Ripley had shared both in-person and in his report, Kitt wagered that it was a different story when he put on a suit to go to work.

'He doesn't have any social media accounts. No X or Facebook. Not even an Instagram,' said Grace.

'Yes, well, that doesn't really surprise me,' said Kitt. 'I suspect he is quite vague about what he does for a living to those who know him. And I doubt he's the kind of person who volunteers lots of information about himself online. There are probably guidelines for the Defence Medical Agency about such things.'

'I will keep looking to see if anything else comes up on him,' said Grace. 'I'm not sure we're going to get very far in covertly investigating him if all we've got is a photo of him at his golf club.'

'These private members' places are always rife with gossip,' said Kitt. 'And you know how useful gossip can be sometimes. If we get really desperate, we could pay a visit and see if we can get any information out of anyone. But, we're not that desperate yet. At least we know what he looks like. Let's keep that photo of him handy so we can show it to people we're questioning if necessary.'

'I'll send a screenshot to both of our phones,' said Grace.

'I appreciate it, from what I read in Ripley's report I—'

Kitt was interrupted by her phone ringing.

'Speak of the devil,' she said, before answering Ripley's call.

'Kitt? It's Kevin,' said Ripley.

'Yes Kevin, I'm here,' said Kitt.

'I just wanted to confirm that I've arranged a time for you to speak with Eleanor tonight, Leo's wife. Will seven p.m. work for you? If so, I will text you the address.'

'Seven p.m. works just fine. We'll be there,' said Kitt before thanking Ripley for arranging the meeting and ringing off the line.

'Bell's wife?' said Grace.

Kitt nodded. 'We'll see if there's anything the police didn't get out of her. Or perhaps if there's anything she didn't want to tell them.'

'Do you think she knows anything about Nathan Greene?' said Grace.

'I imagine there are strict protocols for what agency employees can and cannot tell their spouses,' said Kitt. 'But there's nothing to say that Bell didn't break protocol. And if he did, Eleanor might not want the police to know that. Also, sometimes things just slip out. Maybe Bell told her some things confidentially after a few too many drinks, or maybe he even talked in his sleep. One thing's for sure, if she does know anything about Nathan Greene, especially about his behaviour over the last ten days or so, I intend to find out what that is.'

CHAPTER FOURTEEN

Kitt and Grace walked side by side through the dark December streets, just off Nunnery Lane, on their way to Leonard Bell's house. Or more accurately, the house in which Leonard Bell used to live. There, the wife of the deceased, Eleanor Meadows, was expecting to see them.

Kitt had received yet more text messages from Halloran prior to setting off. They had begun systematically interviewing the people Leonard Bell had come into contact with during his rehearsal for the Christmas Book Fair on the night he was likely poisoned. They had also requested CCTV footage from the bar in which Leonard, Ripley and Eleanor had been drinking later that night. Halloran had promised to let them know of any developments so far as he was authorised. Until then, it was down to Kitt and Grace to take a second run at Eleanor Meadows and see if there was anything she could remember about her husband's final days that might shed light on what had befallen him.

'Do I greet Bell's wife as Mrs Meadows?' Grace asked. 'I've never been sure of that. What's the deal when a person doesn't change their name after marriage?'

'Yes, greet her as Mrs,' said Kitt. 'That's the official title for a married woman whether they've changed their surname or not. At any rate, I don't think greeting her as Ms is a good idea so soon after her husband's death. It might seem like a pointed comment about her change of status. Better she correct us to Ms if that's what she prefers.'

'Righto, I'll follow your lead,' said Grace. 'Definitely don't want to put my foot in my mouth with somebody so recently bereaved.'

'You didn't have to come along to something this late, you know,' said Kitt. 'Your dedication is admirable but just because I don't have a life doesn't mean you have to suffer the same fate. I would have understood if you had a hot, pre-Christmas date.'

Grace snorted. 'And who am I going to meet in this line of work? Eligible adulterers? Credit card fraudsters with a heart of gold? And after my last blind date, I've pretty much given up on finding romance.'

'Was that the guy who called you Gail all night?'

'No, that was the guy before the last one. The last one was the guy who wouldn't use a spoon because, and I quote, he doesn't trust spoons. He insisted on drinking his starter soup through a straw.'

'Well, if you decide it's something you want—'

'Oh, it's something I want. Just not with someone who's more eccentric than I am. I'm sort of the last station stop before eccentricity bleeds into madness.'

'On that much we can agree,' said Kitt. 'I have confidence that there's someone for everyone who wants to find love. And not everyone does, you know? Some people are happy with the quiet life.'

Grace chuckled at Kitt's cynical comment.

'This is their street coming up on the left, White Rose Lane. I've always loved this road,' said Grace.

'Me too,' said Kitt, turning onto the street and looking along the long rows of grand houses built of brown brick. With the lush garlands hung on almost every door, the Victorian lampposts that lined the pavements and the black, wrought-iron railings surrounding each property, there was no denying that it was an almost Dickensian scene. Which, of course, got Kitt thinking about the strange dream she'd had, and how her hallucinated version of Charles Dickens, who had sat in front of the fire during her REM cycle, had said that time would be important to the solving of Leonard Bell's murder.

With Kevin Ripley's life depending on either her or Halloran uncovering the missing antidote in the next couple of days, perhaps even sooner, Kitt privately admitted that whatever part of her subconscious had dreamed him up had been right about that particular element of the case. She could only hope the part about future visitations didn't come to pass. The last thing she needed was to be haunted by spirits sent by deceased literary figures when she was trying to focus on saving a man's life.

'I used to walk down this road on my way to the library,' Grace said, referring to the days when she used to assist Kitt in the Women's Studies department at the Vale of York University. 'I used to imagine the grand lives of the people who could afford to live here,' Grace continued. 'I thought their lives would be nothing short of perfect, of course. I imagined they had afternoon tea at three p.m. without fail, like the Queen used to. And they never had a bad hair day. Or a flat tyre. But then . . . something like this happens to someone who lives here, in one of these perfect houses with their high ceilings and ensuite bathrooms, and you realise it doesn't matter how much money you've got, nobody has forever.'

'Are you feeling quite alright, Grace? That was almost philosophical,' said Kitt, teasing in the hope of lifting the mood a little.

'Hmmm, you're right,' said Grace. 'Must be the time of year or something. Christmas somehow gets you thinking, doesn't it? About endings and beginnings?'

'I suppose it does,' said Kitt. Thinking again about how she had begun the agency without realising the true ramifications. The jeopardy, the stress and the sights she couldn't unsee. One way or another, there would be an end to it at some point. And she certainly didn't want to push her luck so far that her career as a private investigator was stopped in its tracks by the erection of her own tombstone. When the end to all this came, she wanted it to be on her terms. 'Cases like this one don't do much for helping with seasonal existential crises,' Kitt said with a shake of her head. Trying to shake herself out of the pensive mood Grace had quite easily lured her into. 'Here we are though, number seventy-nine. We'll have to save any further existential discourse for later.'

Kitt stepped through the gate and Grace followed on, closing the gate behind them. Though the curtains in the big bay window were drawn, light shone from the nooks and corners the drapes didn't quite cover, making it clear that somebody was sitting in the front room, likely Eleanor Meadows, waiting to receive them.

Kitt rang the bell and, after a minute or so, a woman Kitt presumed to be Leonard Bell's wife answered the door. Kitt was struck by how well-presented the woman was. She wore a yellow chequered dress that came down to the knee over a pair of leggings. It was fitted and looked very stylish when paired with the turquoise chiffon neck scarf draped around her neck. Kitt wasn't sure how she had managed to arrange the extravagant layers of fabric in such a striking formation but the entire arrangement seemed to be held in place with a single pin.

And the care Eleanor had taken over her appearance didn't end with her attire.

139

Her hair fell in immaculate auburn waves which had been brushed out to perfection in the manner of a 1940s film star. Though Kitt hoped she hadn't gone to any special trouble just because she and Grace were visiting, she had to admire Mrs Meadows for maintaining her personal standards at such a difficult time. Kitt was pretty sure that brushing her hair would be the last thing on her priority list if anything terrible ever happened to Halloran.

'Mrs Meadows?' Kitt clarified, and when she was given a nod to confirm, she added, 'Kitt Hartley. I believe Kevin Ripley arranged for you to speak to us.'

Mrs Meadows offered another weak nod in response to Kitt's words, before saying: 'You'd better come in.'

Kitt and Grace exchanged a look. Kitt guessed her colleague was thinking the same as her: that the efforts made in Eleanor's appearance were simply an elegant way of masking the terrible hurt she was going through. The woman's demeanour was so meek, so fragile, it was clear to Kitt they would need to tread carefully with their questions. No matter how much of a brave face Eleanor might be putting on, her manner as she spoke and moved told Kitt that the brave face in front of her wasn't to be believed.

On following the woman into the property, Kitt's nose was at once filled with the scent of citrus and ginger. It was the kind of smell that seemed too good to be true, a manufactured fragrance rather than a natural one, probably from a scented candle burning somewhere. The hallway was a light, warm space, brightened by several lamps and had been made even cosier with numerous indoor plants. As the trio turned into the living room, Kitt had to keep herself from gasping at the picture-perfect scene before her that looked as though it had been torn out of a copy of the Christmas edition of *Good Housekeeping*.

Silver garlands hung around the fireplace, accented by red wicker stars that had been tastefully positioned on the walls. The Christmas tree almost touched the ceiling, which, considering how high the ceilings were in these properties, made it quite the intimidating feature. The cushions on the sofa had also been selected to complement the silver and red theme adopted around the room. In fact, Kitt was struggling to see anything that didn't look like it had been expertly placed by an interior designer.

'Can I get you anything?' Mrs Meadows said. Though she was quite full-figured, her face looked somehow gaunt. The effects of such sudden grief no doubt, and given her comportment, Kitt at once declined the offer – even though she had noticed Grace was about to open her mouth to ask for something. This interview was likely to be difficult enough for the woman without Grace making culinary requests. Kitt was determined not to put this new widow to any more trouble than absolutely necessary.

'We won't take up much of your time, Mrs Meadows,' said Kitt. 'We appreciate you even taking the time to talk to us given the tragic news you've had.'

'Please, call me Eleanor,' said their host. 'I'm probably not at my best, and you'll have to account for that. But if I can help Kevin. I mean, if I can stop him dying the same way Leo did . . .' The woman's face crumpled at those words as she no doubt imagined the horror on her husband's face that Kitt had seen for herself, back at the Christmas Book Fair. It took a moment, but Eleanor managed to compose herself. 'Well, I'll do anything I can to stop that from happening.'

'We know from what Kevin told us that the agent takes five days to . . . to overtake the nervous system,' said Kitt, trying to keep her language as clinical as possible. She did not want to add to this woman's terrible imaginings about her husband's demise one bit. 'So, we know, for a fact, that Leonard must have ingested that substance sometime in the last five days. Kevin keeps a meticulous diary of his movements. I don't suppose your husband did the same? Although perhaps, if he did, you've already handed it over to the police? It's just that . . . that kind of document would give us so many leads to work from. To narrow down where he was five days ago. Who he came into contact with. Who had the opportunity to poison him.'

'I wish I could tell you he was that organised,' said Eleanor, shaking her head. 'He and Kevin were chalk and cheese in that respect to the point that I always wondered how they got on so well at work. Kevin crossed every t, dotted every i, whereas my Leo was more akin to a mad professor.'

Kitt offered Eleanor a small smile to acknowledge the

endearing tone in her voice as she talked about her late husband's tendency to live a life of disarray. Inwardly, however, Kitt suppressed a sigh that they weren't going to have Leonard Bell's movements for the last five days he was alive handed to them on the proverbial plate. It wasn't the tedious work that would be involved in unpicking his whereabouts that irked her. After all, it was probably the same jigsaw Halloran was trying to put together right now using financial and phone records, and all cases required that kind of initial grunt work to some degree. It was the fact that Kitt was keenly aware of how precious every hour was on this case. She had told Kevin to be optimistic about how long he had left. But she couldn't afford that luxury. She had to work as though every hour and minute might be Kevin Ripley's last. Because the truth was, it just might be.

'Not to worry,' said Kitt, trying to reassure herself as much as Eleanor. 'It just means I need you to remember all you can about the day we believe Leonard was poisoned, five days before he passed away. Do you remember, where you were and any interactions you had with Leonard?'

'The police did ask me this,' said Eleanor. 'So, once we'd established that the day in question was a Friday, I was able to tell them all about it. I'm self-employed and Fridays are my self-imposed day off because I work most weekends.'

'And what is it that you do?' Kitt asked. She was relatively sure she could trust Eleanor, but she had made a habit of checking into anyone who gave them information. Did they live where they said, do what they claimed to do for a living? Were they, in essence, the person they were purporting to be? So, to get the ball rolling on the fact-checking as far as Eleanor was concerned, it seemed prudent to ask about what kind of work she did so they could verify this detail later. In visiting her, they had already verified her home address, so that was a good start.

The little dent in Eleanor's forehead told Kitt that she was confused about why Kitt would waste time in asking questions about her business practices when every minute counted to save Kevin Ripley's life, but she answered the question anyway.

'I am a personal stylist,' Eleanor explained. 'It's only part-time but it pays quite well and it's something I've always had a knack for. That's why this place looks like a department store showroom. I sometimes do consultations with clients here and if you're styling people's wardrobes, it's important to make a good first impression by showing them you can style your own home.'

'Makes sense, and your home does look wonderful,' said Kitt. 'So, what do your Fridays off look like?'

'I tend to spend it catching up on the housework and maybe indulging in a little bit of junk television. But that Friday, the Friday we believe my Leo was poisoned, that was a little different.'

'In what way?' asked Grace.

'Leo was tense. He didn't tell me why. But apparently

Kevin told the police that he and Leo were being interrogated over the agent that ultimately killed my husband and the antidote being stolen from the lab. I didn't know any of this at the time, of course. I didn't know about the toxin and the antidote going missing and the fall-out that was happening over that.'

'From what I understand about the secrecy of it all, Leonard was probably under orders not to tell you anything about the toxin,' said Kitt.

'Oh, I expect he was,' said Eleanor. 'But, the thing is, Leo's mood had nothing to do with work that Friday. Or, at least, that's not what he told me. When I asked him what was wrong, he actually said he'd been having repeated run-ins with someone at the book fair he was volunteering at.'

'What kind of run-ins?' said Kitt.

'Oh, I don't know, exactly,' said Eleanor. 'I think someone at the book fair saw his application papers when he first signed up and noticed he had listed the Defence Medical Agency as his employer. It's a bit of a controversial place to work for obvious reasons. Not everyone agrees with the defence agenda, you know? And, well, we've never held that against people when it comes up. We know it's a sensitive issue. But this person at the book fair was apparently quite aggressive and I think they had several heated political arguments about that. Leonard did seem very upset about it. I think because he just wanted to get away from everything that was happening at work and, of course, it even managed to follow him to his rehearsals for the Christmas Book Fair.'

'Did he say when these altercations began?' asked Kitt.

'He'd been putting up with them for about three weeks when he told me about it all,' said Eleanor. 'And apparently they had a particularly nasty encounter on that day, the day he was poisoned.'

Three weeks.

That morning, Ripley had told them that the toxin and the antidote had been stolen ten days ago. Was another ten days before that enough to find a way of infiltrating a military facility? And if so, how would said person make that happen if they were a mere civilian and didn't have any connections to anyone at the facility? Unless they knew someone on the inside . . .

'Do you remember the name of this person that had such a problem with him?' said Kitt.

'Um . . .' Eleanor paused, thinking for a moment. 'I think his name was Jayden . . . No, wait, that's not it. It was Jordan. Yes, definitely Jordan. Don't know a last name though, sorry.'

'Jordan?' said Kitt. 'You're sure?'

'As . . . sure as I can be,' said Eleanor, turning her head sidelong when she saw Kitt's expression change. 'Why?'

Kitt's blood ran cold as she thought back to the moments after Leonard Bell collapsed. Jordan had appeared within seconds. Had he known something was going to happen to Leonard Bell in advance? Had he been lying in wait for it all to unfold? And had it been his decision or hers to stop CPR?

His, she decided.

Definitely his.

She had taken his word about him being an ambulance trainee. But what if that had been a cover story? What if whoever poisoned Leonard Bell had hired Jordan as well to make sure that once the poison overtook him, he definitely didn't come back? Not that there seemed much chance of that based on Ripley's statement.

'I don't know if Kevin mentioned it, Eleanor, but I was present at the book fair when your husband died,' said Kitt.

'He did tell me that, yes,' said Eleanor.

'I did interact with this Jordan person you're describing, he was there too,' Kitt explained. There was a long pause then as Eleanor and Kitt looked at each other.

'He was there, when Leo died?' Eleanor said.

'Yes,' said Kitt. 'But that in itself isn't a smoking gun. It's more of a concern that your husband told you of a particularly nasty run-in he'd had with him on the day he'd been poisoned, and that he'd had repeated issues with him prior to that.'

'You don't think that he ... that he was the one who stole the toxin from the lab and poisoned Leo and Kevin?' said Eleanor.

'I don't think we have grounds to accuse him of anything yet,' said Kitt.

'No, but having repeated conflicts with a man who is sadly no longer with us isn't exactly a good look,' said Grace.

Kitt sighed. The way Jordan had stepped up to save Leonard's life and the fact he was training to be a paramedic had left Kitt with the general impression that Jordan belonged in the good guy category. But what if that had all been a cover for some sinister plot she hadn't realised at the time? 'Did you tell the police about the falling-out Leo had with Jordan?'

'I – er no, I didn't,' said Eleanor. 'I-I didn't get a chance. I told them he'd been tense on the Friday before he left for his rehearsal. Before I got any further with what I was saying, they told me about what Kevin had said about the interrogations at work about the missing toxin. In comparison, a falling-out with someone at a volunteer job seemed pretty insignificant and I wasn't exactly thinking straight when I talked to the police anyway. So, I just sort of assumed that I'd misunderstood and thought Leo was tense about the falling-out when really he was under suspicion at work for something far more serious.'

Kitt frowned. If Halloran or Banks had conducted the interview with Eleanor she wouldn't have been interrupted mid-flow like that. But from what Halloran had told her down at the station before she gave her witness statement, both he and Banks had both been completely consumed by their attempts to get communications going between themselves and the Defence Medical Agency. So, Halloran had sent someone else to talk with Eleanor, someone who had interrupted a witness giving their testimony. That interruption had possibly cost the police a crucial piece of information about Leonard Bell's death.

The person who claimed he wanted to resuscitate Leonard Bell had had several heated arguments with him about his choice of employment. The worst of them on the very day he was poisoned. Could that be a coincidence? Kitt again searched her memory of those terrible moments after Leonard Bell collapsed. Had Jordan given up a little too easily when it came to saving Bell's life? Had he even had any intention of trying to save Bell's life in the first place?'

'It's not that easy, you know?' said Eleanor.

'What isn't?' said Kitt.

'Breaking into the kind of place where Leonard used to work. I know protestors are well-organised these days. Glueing themselves to roads during rush hour, throwing oil over works of art in museums. Albeit over the protective glass rather than the piece of art itself. But do you really think that a volunteer at a book fair could have an argument with somebody one week and orchestrate what happened to my Leo the next? I think that kind of thing takes a lot more planning. I was never privy to much about Leo's job but even I understand that military-level security is no joke.'

That depended on whether Jordan knew anybody on the inside at the Defence Medical Agency, Kitt thought.

'I hear what you're saying,' said Kitt. 'Perhaps this Jordan person isn't a prime suspect but, he had a pretty serious and ongoing conflict with somebody. Very soon after the most serious incident, that person died. So, regardless of how likely I think it is that Jordan could have pulled off the poisoning, right now it's a piece of evidence we can't afford to ignore.'

CHAPTER FIFTEEN

On hearing what Eleanor had to say about Jordan, Kitt had decided to bring extra resources onto this case. Halloran might be handling Nathan Greene and the Defence Medical Agency but, besides that line of enquiry, there were Margaret Cryer and Tyler Simmons to look into, and now with Jordan from the Christmas Book Fair in the mix, the suspects were starting to rack up. Had time not been so much of the essence, Kitt would have made do with just her and Grace. But, in this instance, any delay due to lack of resources could cost Kevin Ripley his life. As such, Kitt had stepped into the hallway to put in a call to Joe Golding. A man who had completed some work experience with the agency a couple of years back before setting up his own agency in Manchester. She had given him the abridged version of events and appraised him of the likely risks. His caseload was slow on the brink of Christmas and he understood the consequences for Kevin Ripley if they failed, but the promise of coming to Kitt's cottage for Christmas dinner, along with Grace, Evie, Banks and Halloran, once the case was done and dusted seemed to be the deciding factor in his decision to drive through to York that evening, find a cheap hotel and do what he could to help.

When Kitt re-entered the living room, Grace and Eleanor turned to face her.

'Is Joe available?' said Grace.

'He is,' said Kitt, before looking over at Eleanor. 'He's worked on several high-profile investigations on the other side of the Pennines and, I can assure you, he is an asset to any team. I trained him myself. Having him on the case with us increases the chances of not only saving Kevin's life but getting to the bottom of who really killed your husband.'

Eleanor flinched at Kitt's words and inwardly she admonished herself for being so forthright about the fact that Leonard had been murdered. It wasn't like it was a secret that had been kept from Eleanor, Halloran would have explicitly explained the circumstances of Leonard's death when he broke the news, but Kitt was certain that this new widow did not need constant reminders of the situation.

'I'm so very sorry,' said Kitt. 'I didn't mean to be so businesslike.'

'It's OK,' said Eleanor, but her lips quivered as she forced them into a smile in a bid to compose herself. 'In a way, it's good. I do need people who will treat his death like business that needs to be resolved.'

'It might seem clinical, cold even to do so,' said Kitt. 'But I assure you the tragedy of what's befallen you and your husband is not lost on us. Being somewhat businesslike in this kind of situation is just the best chance we have of keeping our emotions in check well enough to conduct the investigation.'

'I do understand that,' said Eleanor. 'And I don't want this to drag on and on. Answers won't bring him back but at least there'll be justice for whoever did this to him. The worst thing in the world would be if whoever did this got away with it. It's bad enough having lost him. But for there to be no justice for what happened ...' Eleanor reached towards a box sitting on a nearby coffee table and pulled out a tissue. Gently, she pressed it against her face and closed her eyes, seemingly trying to compose herself.

'I've brought more than one killer to justice in my time,' said Kitt. 'I can assure you that neither myself, nor the police officers assigned to your husband's case, will stop until the person responsible is found. Whoever did this to your husband will not get away with it.'

Eleanor opened her eyes at this and her eyebrows rose into an arch as she tried to process the pain of the situation. 'I appreciate all you are doing for me, and my Leo.'

'Given what both you and Kevin are going through right now, it's only right that we do everything we can.'

'On the subject of making sure who did this won't get away with it, Kitt,' said Grace, 'we were just talking about the rest of Leonard's actions on the day we think he was poisoned and something's come to light. As Kevin told us back at the agency, he met Eleanor and Leonard for a drink after the rehearsals for the book fair finished at nine.'

'Yes, I remember,' said Kitt. 'Kevin said that he did think that the drink you had might be in the window of when Leonard was poisoned, but he didn't see anything untoward so wasn't convinced that it happened while you were out for that drink. Also, with the bulk of the window being at the book fair rehearsal, it's probably more important to focus our attentions there.'

This was the reason Kitt hadn't read through those particular notes, as yet. Kitt could understand how a person going about their daily business on their own might be easily poisoned without their knowledge. But for two people working at a military institution not to notice something untoward when they were out for a drink together, well, that seemed far less likely. Surely, in that situation, the odds were better of at least one of the two of them noticing something suspicious. For that reason, the killer, whoever they were, would probably not have thought it prudent to poison Leonard Bell under those circumstances. Divide and conquer, wasn't that the favoured military strategy?

'Well, I don't mean to make Kevin out to be a liar,' said Eleanor, 'I'm sure he's just giving his own take on what happened. And maybe he's more convinced it happened earlier and is trying to steer you in that direction. But if you ask me, I not only think it's possible that Leonard was poisoned when we were out for that drink. I think it's quite likely.'

'Why do you say that?' said Kitt. Doing her best to hide her surprise. 'Did you see someone suspicious hanging around your table?'

Eleanor shook her head. 'That's just the thing. I told the police all about this, but they were more focused on the Defence Medical Agency and what I knew about them, which I admit isn't much. Still, I tried to tell the police that we went out for a drink to the Book and Candle Bar in St Helen's Square.'

'Oh, I hadn't realised it was there, I love that bar,' said Kitt, momentarily forgetting the severity of the situation. 'The completely candle-lit bar is so atmospheric and the way they've lined the walls with second-hand editions of all the classics makes it quite a charming venue for an after-work drink . . .'

Kitt trailed off then, noticing the expression on Eleanor's face. Her head tilted to one side and her brows had furrowed. Kitt guessed she was likely confused about how Kitt could get excited about the decorating in her local watering hole at a time like this. People who met her in the guise of private investigator would likely never guess she was also a librarian. And anyway, it wasn't exactly an appropriate situation to be waxing lyrical about interior design. But, in Kitt's defence, the decor did involve books. And books were always exciting.

'I'm sorry,' said Kitt, now thinking it was a bit rich that she had judged the officers who had questioned Eleanor initially for interrupting her testimony when she had just done exactly the same thing. 'You were about to tell us why you think it's so likely that the poisoning took place that evening at the bar.'

'Like I told the police,' Eleanor said, 'we weren't vigilant about our drinks. It didn't cross our minds that anyone would touch them. There was some Christmas music on and we got up to have a bit of a dance, me, Leo and Kevin. I always loved it when something like that happened because Leo couldn't dance to save his life, and of course that's what made it entertaining. He was good at most things, being so intelligent. Being a terrible dancer somehow made him all that more loveable.'

Eleanor began to laugh but then, perhaps on realising that she would never witness her husband's questionable dancing again, the chuckle turned into a stifled sob.

'So, your drinks were left unattended while you were at the Book and Candle?' Kitt said. She could see that Eleanor was doing her best to hold herself together and thus it didn't seem prudent or fair to make a fuss of her emotional wobbling. Focusing on the business at hand, no matter how gruesome it may be, was how she was going to be of most use to everyone right now.

Eleanor nodded. 'We were up and down, on and off, for a few songs at a time. Our drinks were still sitting exactly where they had been when we came back to the table, and anyway, we didn't have any reason to suspect they'd been tampered with.'

'But, despite Kevin's reservations, I think someone might have taken that as an opportunity,' said Grace. 'And what's more, if that was when it happened, the poisoning must have been done by somebody who was watching your table for some time.'

'Wh-what makes you say that?' asked Eleanor, her eyes widening.

Kitt understood all too well the feeling that was coursing through Eleanor right now. She had herself been watched and followed by adversaries on several of her other cases. The idea of somebody tracking your every movement was unnerving to say the least. It was somehow far more sinister than a person who might attack you at random, unprepared. Someone who waited in the shadows, formulating a plan about how best to attack you, likely had a much higher chance of doing you damage. Plus, the idea of someone lurking on the periphery while you went about your life tragically oblivious was enough to give anyone the chills.

'Whoever did this must have been watching the table to know when you left the area,' said Kitt. 'But also to know which drink to poison. Which begs the question, why was only Leonard's drink targeted?'

'What do you mean?' said Eleanor, her eyes widening. 'You mean, why didn't they kill all of us?'

'Not quite,' said Kitt. 'But Kevin subsequently found out that he had been poisoned. So, he was on the target list of whoever is behind this. And yet, he can't have been poisoned the same time as Leo because otherwise he also would no longer be with us.'

'So, if you're going to poison two people anyway, why do so one at a time when you have the opportunity to poison both at once?' said Grace.

'Exactly!' said Kitt.

'You're right,' said Eleanor, the frown, which had only momentarily left her face in the time Kitt and Grace had been talking to her, deepening. 'That doesn't add up at all. I mean, if both Leo and Kevin were targets, why wouldn't you kill two birds with one stone . . . so to speak?'

'Perhaps they needed to keep Kevin alive a little longer for some reason?' said Grace. 'Perhaps they needed him for something. Something Kevin wasn't even aware of.'

'Could be,' said Kitt. 'Or, perhaps they were interrupted or accidentally drew attention to themselves while committing the crime and only had time to poison one glass. I'm sure there are several possible reasons. But without knowing the motive behind these actions, it's going to be impossible to narrow it down to the right one. Which leads to the most important question, and likely one the police also asked: Can you think of anyone who would want to harm your husband, and perhaps Kevin to boot?'

'I was just discussing that with Grace while you were on the phone,' said Eleanor. 'It's to do with Leonard's work.'

'You think there's an individual there who might have targeted Leo and Kevin specifically?' said Kitt. She tried to keep her tone level at this point. She wasn't sure if Ripley had already told Eleanor about the people he suspected in the workplace. But, it was so easy for confirmation bias to creep into a case, she wasn't going to add to it. If she mentioned somebody on Ripley's list then that amounted to two people independently naming potential suspects, without any help from Kitt.

Moreover, the people who worked alongside Ripley and thus had access to the toxin before it was stolen, or perhaps had a hand in stealing it for themselves, were the most likely suspects in this case. They would pursue the lead on Jordan, there was no question about that. If you picked a fight with someone who died a few days later, you should expect to be questioned. Especially when you didn't volunteer the information that you had a problematic relationship with the deceased. But if Eleanor could name someone at the Defence Medical Agency facility who might have benefited from Leonard's death, Kitt wanted to hear it. If the name of that person was Margaret Cryer, Tyler Simmons or Nathan Greene, all the better.

'I'm not sure about them targeting Leo and Kevin,' said Eleanor. 'I'm not sure if they would go that far. I didn't think to mention her to the police because, as far as I know, nothing happened with her on the day Leonard was poisoned or in the few days leading up to it. At least he didn't mention anything.'

'Her?' Kitt said.

'A colleague of Leonard's,' Grace clarified. Grace, who had trained alongside Kitt to become a private investigator, was doing a good job of keeping her face neutral, also aware of the dangers of confirmation bias.

'Her name's Margaret. Margaret Cryer,' said Eleanor.

Again, Kitt was careful to keep her expression level. 'And, you think she might have some involvement in what happened to your husband?'

'I must stress that I can't prove anything,' said Eleanor. 'I'm not trying to get people into trouble here. I'm just telling you about Leo's office relationships as I understand them, so it's definitely speculation. Another reason why I probably didn't think of her when the police were here.'

'We understand,' said Kitt. 'It's our job to find the evidence. You just tell us what you know about this individual.'

'Well, that's just the thing,' said Eleanor. 'I can't really tell you anything about her because Leo was very private about his work. He was under orders not to tell me certain things so I never pushed. I didn't want to put him in that position, you know, of getting into trouble at work over me. But he did once let it slip that this Margaret Cryer person was causing him trouble.'

'What kind of trouble?' said Kitt.

Eleanor shook her head. 'I'm afraid I don't know. He'd had a couple of drinks when he mentioned it but even then he was quite tight-lipped. From what he said, it seemed like she was sort of jealous of Leo and Kevin and wanted their jobs. But, it's difficult to believe that somebody would kill another person over a promotion.'

'I'm afraid I'm not able to discount it on that basis,' said Kitt. 'And I can tell you now that you've shared what you know, this is not the first time Margaret Cryer's name has been mentioned in our enquiries. So I shall be asking her a few questions, if I can find a way of crossing paths with her. I'm sorry to say that I've seen people commit murder for much less than a promotion. And, at any rate, I don't want to rule anything out at this stage. We need to keep an open mind if we're to find this antidote before . . . well. Before it's too late.'

Eleanor pursed her lips and nodded. 'I understand that. I suppose, the one thing I can say is if Margaret does have something to do with this it might explain why Leo was targeted first.'

'Why do you say that?' asked Grace.

'I don't know the ins and out of it, but I did hear Leo, once or twice, tease Kevin that Margaret at work had a romantic crush on him. I'm assuming it's the same Margaret.'

'Do you think there was any truth to Leo's teasing?' said Kitt; in her experience, unrequited workplace romances could sometimes head down a very dark track.

'I'm afraid I just don't know enough to comment on that,' said Eleanor. 'I never saw how she was around him, if you know what I mean.'

'If she did have secret feelings for Kevin, maybe she only ever intended to poison Leo,' said Grace. 'Maybe in some twisted way, she thought that by poisoning Leo, she would get to either take his place or see Kevin get a promotion and take his old job as it was. But then, if that was her motive, why would she change her mind about poisoning Kevin?'

'Kevin may have been witness to something,' said Kitt. 'To Margaret's treatment of Leo. Maybe even threats she made. Even if she did like Kevin as more than a friend, somebody capable of killing another person over something as petty as professional jealousy, even if it would result in a lucrative promotion, is not going to risk getting caught for anyone.'

'You think she was worried that Kevin might figure out it was her and report his suspicions?' said Grace.

'I don't think anything yet. I haven't met the woman and I haven't asked her where she was the night we believe Leo to have been poisoned. But, if she can't provide a solid alibi, I suspect her next visit will be from the police.'

'Oh God, I haven't got somebody in trouble unnecessarily, have I?' said Eleanor, her eyes widening. 'I didn't mean to do that, really I didn't. And what I've told you is pure speculation.'

'The most likely person to have stolen that antidote, and the toxin, is somebody who works in that facility,' said Kitt. 'And if somebody who works there has been having trouble with the first victim, and possibly has unrequited feelings towards a second, we need to speak to them further . . . In that statement, I realise I'm making an assumption. Were Margaret's feelings unrequited?'

'Kevin would have told Leo if he had started something up with her and I never heard them mention it. I think, although they are supposed to keep certain things about work under wraps, I would have heard Leo tease Kevin about it at least once if that was the case,' Eleanor said.

'Either way, I think she's definitely somebody we have to speak to,' said Kitt. 'If only to rule her out of the investigation so that the police don't waste any time on her.'

Eleanor nodded. 'It's just all so serious. I've never been in a situation like this before. I want to help Kevin. More than anything. But I can't go around making blind accusations either.'

'I don't think that's what you've done,' said Kitt. 'You've given us something to work with. A hope of saving Kevin's life. And right now, he needs that more than anything else.'

Eleanor offered Kitt a weak smile. 'Please do everything you can for Kevin, will you? He's been a good friend to me. He has been there for me and Leo over the years. And I don't want to lose a friend on top of losing my husband.'

'You have my word that we'll do everything in our power,'

said Kitt. 'I think that's all we need for now . . . unless there's anyone else you can think of, anyone at all, who might have wanted to hurt Leonard?'

Eleanor shook her head. 'I'm afraid not. I've had to really rake my memory to offer you what I have. Leo spoke so little about his work, you see.'

'You've given us plenty to go on,' said Kitt. 'Will it be OK if we give you a call if there's anything we need to clarify? We'll only do that if we absolutely have to. We don't want to bother you needlessly.'

'I think you need to bother me whenever necessary so long as Kevin is alive and has a chance to stay that way. In fact, I think you'll find that it's me bothering you. I'll be endlessly wondering how you are getting on with the case,' said Eleanor, shaking her head. 'I know poisonings have happened in the UK but, even given what he did for a living, this is all so surreal.'

'I know,' said Kitt. 'I hope you won't be too lonely this evening. I would offer to stay a while longer, but I promised Kevin I would work every minute trying to uncover this antidote.'

'Don't worry about me,' said Eleanor, her eyes lowering to the hardwood floors. 'I'm sorry to say there won't be much difference about the evenings around here. It was rare that Leo was home before I went to bed. Of course, anyone else would have suspected their husband of having an affair, maybe even with Margaret, the woman at work he professed to hate, but I knew all along that Leo was married to his job. I was just his mistress.'

Kitt cast a fleeting glance at Grace on hearing this comment. There was no mistaking the bitter tone in which Eleanor's words had been said. Had there been tensions at the office and in the home before Leonard Bell had died? Or was grief just having its way with this woman? In Kitt's experience, people were rarely themselves in times of mourning. All kinds of unpredictable thoughts and feelings could crop up. Still, much as time was of the essence, Kitt knew it was important to do her due diligence. If Kevin Ripley was such good friends with Leo and Eleanor, he could likely shed light on just how happy their marriage was. After all, if they were speculating that Margaret Cryer might have tried to kill Ripley for fear that he'd figure out what she'd done, they couldn't rule out that Eleanor would be capable of just the same. On the surface, Eleanor Meadows seemed all you would expect of a grieving widow. But before Kitt started looking further afield, she needed to know those who had been closest to Leonard Bell could be trusted.

CHAPTER SIXTEEN

It was past eleven that evening before Joe Golding checked in at the offices of Hartley and Edwards Investigations. Kitt had not long since got off the phone with Kevin Ripley when the man she hadn't seen for a good few months now entered in his long, black winter coat and a blue chequered scarf. Along with him, a large Alsatian bounded into the office, looked at Kitt momentarily before charging towards Grace. Although he was too big for such shenanigans, the hound followed up this manoeuvre by leaping onto Grace's knee.

The dog, who went by the name of Rolo, had proven himself fond of Kitt but she suspected he could smell Iago's scent on her and thus always gave Grace the most excitable welcome.

Grace laughed uncontrollably as she tried to get the dog into a position on her knee that was comfortable. A position that also prevented the mutt from insatiably licking Grace's face.

'Way to play it cool, Rolo,' said Joe, rolling his eyes at the dog's antics. He then added, 'It's a lot colder here than it is in Manchester.' He shook off his coat and hung it on the pegs near the door. Though they'd kept in touch since, it had been a couple of years now since Kitt and Grace had first made their acquaintance with Joe. He had completed his work experience at the agency, and what a case they had worked together! Brushing shoulders with a government spy by the name of Agent Smith. Despite the many months that had passed since he had worked as a full-time member of their agency, he still treated the place a bit like a second home, which Kitt found rather touching. So far as she could tell, the time he'd spent with them had helped him navigate a particularly difficult period in his life.

He'd been newly widowed when he'd helped them solve a mysterious murder case on the Scottish border, and although the sorrow hadn't completely left his deep brown eyes, he was looking healthier in himself. He had colour in his face that was, Kitt felt, more than just a flush from the late December chill. Perhaps setting up his own investigative agency had been just the distraction he needed from the pain of losing his wife so young. Perhaps also, the reward of righting wrongs in the lives of other people somewhat made up for not always being able to right the wrongs in your own.

'Oh, it's been snowing on and off for days,' said Kitt. 'Coldest December on record for some years apparently.'

'I'm ... assuming Grace did the Christmas decorations,' Joe said, casting his eyes around the room and then shooting a knowing smirk at Grace.

'What gave it away?' Kitt said, her tone arid.

'Before you insinuate that it's all a bit much—' Grace said.

'A bit much?' Joe said. 'It's like *National Lampoon's Christmas Vacation* in here. I'm surprised nobody's mistaken you for Santa's Grotto.'

'It was out of my hands,' said Grace. 'I was operating under the orders of Tatiana, the Tyrannical Archangel. She is not a taskmaster to be trifled with.'

Joe raised his eyebrows in a quizzical manner and looked to Kitt for some clue as to what Grace was talking about. Not an uncommon gesture when he came to visit them.

'You'll be happier not knowing,' Kitt said, closing her eyes for a moment and shaking her head. 'I know I would be.'

'I'll take your word for it,' said Joe. 'I know time is very much of the essence. Is there anything that can be done tonight on this case?'

'After talking to both Ripley and Leonard Bell's wife, there are a few things on our agenda,' said Kitt. 'Unfortunately, not all of them can be worked on tonight. On that score, we were thinking of doing a drive-by of the facility Ripley works at. Halloran was pretty convinced from the outset that the stealing of the toxin and the antidote was an inside job, which of course would in turn mean the poisonings were likely carried out by somebody who worked there. I'm pretty sure he's right but . . .'

'You don't want to rule anything out,' Joe finished.

'Exactly. Someone who volunteered at the book fair had a run-in with Leonard Bell on the day he was poisoned, and apparently a few times before that. I want to know if there's any way he could have got inside without help from someone who works there. So, we want to take a look at the facility from afar first and then have a go at trying to get some information out of the security guard on the gate.'

'Kitt, you know I've always admired your natural ability in this job,' said Joe. 'But do you really think you can get information out of a security guard who works for the military?'

Kitt smiled. 'I don't know if I can. But Ripley says that all information about the stolen antidote has been compart-mentalised to security staff. So, talking to a member directly is really our only hope of learning something about that break-in. Halloran has to go through official channels and, from the brief call I had with him on the way here, seems to have been stonewalled at every turn. I do not have to go through official channels so I'm going to try a different approach.'

'Well, I'm sure I don't have to remind you to be careful, but I'm going to anyway,' said Joe. 'I'm not sure what being questioned by a military defence agency looks like, but I can tell you I'm not keen to find out.'

'That makes two of us,' said Kitt. 'But doing a little bit of recon on the facility itself might give us a sense of how difficult it would be for a third party to break in there.'

'From what you told me on the phone,' said Joe, 'my money is on this couple, Margaret and Tyler. They sound a bit Bonnie and Clyde. And if it is them, with Margaret still working there, she'd be in a prime position to steal the toxin and the antidote.'

'I agree that we need to talk to both of them as soon as possible but following that up is a bit of a waiting game until morning. Ripley described Tyler as aggressive, so it seems more sensible to start with Margaret. Grace is in the process of cyberstalking her right now to see where the best place might be to bump into her and ask her a few questions, or follow her if she looks like she's up to something untoward.'

'What about this guy who worked at the book fair?'

'Jordan,' said Kitt. 'He's dead set against the Defence Medical Agency's agenda.'

'And . . . you think he poisoned Bell in an act of misguided activism?' said Joe.

'Not impossible,' said Kitt. 'Especially since he also administered CPR when Bell collapsed. He stopped after a very short period of time because he said there was something untoward about the body. Which, of course, there was. But if you wanted to avoid suspicion, making sure you were there to administer CPR is a good way of doing it. Nobody's going to be looking at you as a potential suspect if you were the person who tried to resuscitate the deceased.'

'And I guess we can't go knocking on this guy's door at this time of night without due cause?' said Joe.

'Actually,' said Grace, 'maybe we do have something else we can do this evening besides questioning the guard at a military facility. Jordan has just posted to X about wanting to go out and blow off some steam. His full name is Jordan Ascher. He's not difficult to find through the website for the Christmas Book Fair.'

'Did he say where he's going?' said Kitt.

'Yeah, but you're not going to like it,' said Grace.

'Why, where is it?'

'He's heading out clubbing to Bluetooth,' said Grace.

'It couldn't have been Pop World,' said Kitt, instinctively rubbing her temple.

'Is that the Viking-themed nightclub near Clifford's Tower?' said Joe.

'Yes,' said Grace. 'It plays heavy rock. You know the kind where the baseline feels like thunder? We've had to surveil a couple of people there in the past and Kitt's not a fan. She'd rather question suspicious characters with backing from the Spice Girls than Stone Gods.'

'Every time I leave that place I do so with my head pounding,' said Kitt. 'Still, with Ripley's life hanging in the balance every minute counts so we can't leave it till morning. We've got to at least try and catch Jordan there.

Then, assuming Jordan doesn't offer us a full-blown con-
fession on the spot and can provide an alibi for where he
was the night Leonard was poisoned, we can go on to the
Defence Medical Agency afterwards.'

'I suppose at least we've got a couple of leads between
this Jordan bloke and Bell's work colleagues,' said Joe.

'Yes,' said Kitt. 'I was concerned that the wife herself
might be a suspect earlier this evening. She made an embit-
tered comment about him being married to the job and of
course hell hath no fury and all that.'

'If she managed to find a way to poison him with the
agent he was working on that would be the ultimate way of
offing someone you felt had always put their career before
you,' Joe admitted.

'Agreed,' said Kitt. 'But I spoke to Ripley on the phone
as soon as we got back here, he was close friends with
Leonard and Eleanor – well, he still is with her – and he
said that he wouldn't read anything into that comment.
Eleanor never loved the long hours they worked but she
did understand it was a necessary part of the job. He put
her comment down to her mourning the fact that Leonard's work had got in the way of them spending more
time together when he was alive. That if they'd known
his life would be cut brutally short, he might have made
different priorities.'

'And . . . are you satisfied with his conclusions?' said Joe.

'For now,' said Kitt. 'I don't know how Eleanor would get

access to the lab to steal the agent for one thing. She'd have to hire somebody who was in the know.'

'Or make a deal with somebody who already worked there,' said Grace.

'Yes, but the more people in on the plot the riskier it is,' said Kitt. 'And for another, Ripley knows every minute counts to save his life. If he had even a sneaking suspicion that Eleanor might have that antidote, I doubt he'd waste a second in making his suspicions known. Being loyal to your friends is all well and good, but right now, Ripley can't afford such luxuries.'

'So, for now, we're operating on the understanding that the information given to us by the victim's wife is reliable?' said Joe.

'That's right,' said Kitt. 'We've already visited her at her home address and checked out the business she runs online. There are no immediate red flags there. As I mentioned, I also managed to have a conversation with Halloran on my mobile on the way here. I tried Ripley first, of course, but he didn't pick up the first time I called so I thought I'd try Halloran. I've relayed all of the information Eleanor gave us, some of which she didn't offer up to them because it slipped her mind.'

'Did he have any insights?' said Joe.

'He's made a note of the things that weren't mentioned in the initial interview. He's not shocked that every t wasn't crossed when Eleanor was first spoken to as he had to send another officer, DS Redmond. I've crossed paths with him a few times and, although he's a nice enough guy, his eye isn't always on the ball. Halloran is being stonewalled by the Defence Medical Agency so is spending all of his time trying to get Ripley's superior, Nathan Greene, to answer questions. He's not getting very far and it's stagnating the investigation. They are also looking into the people at the book fair, particularly those who crossed paths with him at the rehearsal in which they think Leonard was poisoned. I assume that Jordan is on that list, but I don't know how quickly he'll get to him with all that's going on with the stonewalling at the agency.'

'I assume he's happy for us to take the reins on these other leads, then,' said Grace.

'You know what the resources are like at that station. Cut to the bone, and the pressure to solve this case is high after the bulletins on the evening news. If we learn something pivotal, he'll perhaps divert his attentions to one of the people Eleanor has named. But until that happens, he's got to focus on the most likely source of the poisoning, which is the place that Ripley and Bell are and were employed. Even if the agency are not themselves responsible for what happened to Bell, it's likely they have some idea who stole that antidote by now and if that is the case, there must be a good reason why they're not handing that information over, given it could save Ripley's life.'

'If you're sure the spouse has been ruled out then, yes,

Bell's employer seems like the next best suspect,' said Joe. 'Especially as they're unlikely to have let the deceased's wife wander in and walk away with a lethal toxin.'

'Halloran said they had already looked into Eleanor's financial and phone records and there was no evidence that she had paid for or organised a break-in of the facility,' Kitt confirmed. 'He said he would look into Jordan's records as soon as possible to give them something to work with when they inevitably bring him in for further questioning. He did think it was a suspicious coincidence that Jordan had that confrontation with Bell and then just happened to be the person performing his CPR. But he doesn't know when the small team he's got will get done with that task with everything else to deal with.'

'Well,' said Joe, 'I say, let's try and save Halloran and his team a job and find out once and for all whether Jordan really is the innocent bystander he's claiming to be.'

CHAPTER SEVENTEEN

'Any sign of the subject?' Kitt said over comms, uncertain whether either Grace or Joe could hear her over the pounding din of heavy rock now that they had split off into different sections of the Bluetooth nightclub in search of Jordan Ascher.

'Nothing here,' Joe said over comms, his voice barely audible even though it was being transmitted directly into Kitt's ear. The temptation was to press a hand against the side of her head in an attempt to hear her colleagues better but that was a bad habit to get into. Nobody in this club might suspect that she was on comms, but if she did it instinctually in the wrong situation, it could mean a lot of trouble. Best to refrain from such actions altogether and avoid building any muscle memory in that department at all. Straining to hear what was being said was by far the safer option.

'Nothing in the cocktail lounge,' said Grace.

'This place has a cocktail lounge?' Kitt said, looking

around the main dance area of the club. Somehow, a Viking-themed heavy rock venue wasn't the kind of establishment she expected to be serving up mojitos. The whole place had black fittings, and lights with cut-out filters projected the faces of mean-looking Viking men in profile. What Kitt presumed to be a faux bear fur hung like a canopy above the bar area and the few tables in the corner of the room were carved like Viking galleons, complete with hideous creatures chiselled into either end. The place also smelled a lot like Kitt would imagine a Viking galleon to smell, although maybe that was being a bit unfair to Viking galleons. The closest thing she could really compare the smell to was PE changing rooms at school. An unsavoury blend of fresh sweat and unwashed socks.

'Aye,' said Grace. 'The glasses are the shape of the horns you see on the side of Viking helmets. But the cocktails are only mixed from the hardest spirits. I'm not sure there's anything for our delicate palates.'

'Actually, there's no historical evidence that Vikings ever wore horned helmets,' said Kitt. 'And when you think about it, they are not very practical in battle. Catch one of those horns on the wrong side of an axe and it's likely to be a clumsy moment you're never going to recover from.'

'I knew I could count on you to take the fun out of this place,' said Grace. 'Any road, I think the people who run Bluetooth are probably less interested in historical accuracy and more interested in charging twelve quid a cocktail.'

'Wait a minute,' said Kitt.

'I know, talk about daylight robbery,' said Grace. 'It's out-rageous.'

'No, not that,' said Kitt, ignoring Grace's patter about the cocktails. 'I think I can see him on the dance floor.' She paused and then looked again at the figure she thought she recognised. 'Yes, yes, it's definitely him. I'll lure him over to the cloakroom area where it's marginally quieter, you two meet me there.'

'What if he puts up a struggle, or tries to run?' said Grace.

'Well, then we'll know we've got the right guy and Hal-loran can track him down using police resources.'

'Alright, received,' said Joe, 'but be careful.'

A few seconds later, Grace also confirmed that she'd heard Kitt's message.

Kitt, who had been standing on a balcony in order to procure a better vantage point, walked quickly down a set of translucent steps and strode over to the far corner of the dance floor where she had spotted Jordan. Recognising a fish out of water when they saw one, the crowd parted with relative ease as Kitt walked through the small throng of people gyrating to a song she did not recognise. They were probably wondering what someone dressed in what essentially amounted to office attire was doing in a rock club. Either that or they were concerned that being smartly dressed was contagious and wanted to keep their distance. As Kitt was having quite the same effect on this crowd as

Moses did the Red Sea, Jordan spotted her long before she reached him.

The moment Jordan's brown eyes met with Kitt's, his eyes widened. Though it was obvious to anyone he was unnerved by her presence, he didn't run. Instead, he stood perfectly still, rooted to the spot until she was practically toe-to-toe with him.

'We need to talk,' she said loudly enough for him to hear over the drill of the bassline.

Kitt noticed Jordan swallow hard at these words, but he offered a tentative nod when Kitt gestured him to follow her.

Manoeuvring her way through the crowds, Kitt made a point of checking Jordan was still behind her every few seconds. If he was smart enough to somehow orchestrate the poisoning of Leonard Bell, he was smart enough to know that running from her would cast immediate suspicion on him – but that didn't mean that fear wouldn't overtake any calculating instincts. Even killers were human and, in most cases, as susceptible to fear as the next person. In Kitt's experience there was nothing they were more afraid of than getting caught.

Mercifully, Jordan was still just a couple of steps behind her when she reached the cloakroom area where both Grace and Joe were already waiting for them.

'Who are they?' Jordan said, pointing a finger first at Joe and then at Grace.

'They're my associates,' said Kitt. 'I work with them. Jordan, there was never any need to tell you this before, but I work as a private investigator and these are my colleagues.'

'Why is there a need to tell me what you do for a living now?' Jordan said, narrowing his eyes.

'As you can probably imagine, the police are under tremendous pressure to solve the murder we witnessed. You've probably seen that it's national news now.'

'Well, they're saying the guy was poisoned with an unknown substance, so that's not a surprise,' said Jordan. 'What's any of that got to do with me?'

Kitt paused, just for a moment. Just long enough to be sure she was choosing her next words carefully. 'A friend of the deceased has asked me to look into some of the less pressing avenues of investigation to make sure that all leads, not just those the police have time for, are followed up.'

'OK . . .' Jordan said, looking between Kitt, Joe and Grace as though their facial expressions alone might provide him with some clue about where this conversation was heading. 'So, what do you want from me? I already told the police everything.'

'Everything?' said Kitt. 'Are you sure?'

'Yeah,' said Jordan, but he looked off to the left as he spoke in a manner that told Kitt at once he knew he hadn't been as up front as he should have been.

'Really?' said Kitt. Jordan was sinking in her estimation

by the second. She had thought him a good Samaritan on the night that Leonard Bell was murdered. Now she couldn't help but wonder if that was just what he wanted them all to think. 'During our enquiries, it's come to light that you and Leonard had several disagreements.'

Jordan didn't say anything but the muscles around his mouth seemed to tighten.

'We have learned that one of these disputes took place on the night Leonard was poisoned. Reportedly, it got quite heated. As far as we know, you didn't mention any of these incidents to the police when you spoke to them,' Kitt added. 'Would you say that equated to telling the police everything?'

There was a pause before Jordan spoke again. It seemed to Kitt that he was weighing his options. Figuring out how to respond.

'You know, when I saw you out on the dance floor, I thought you'd come here to tell me that my life was in danger after all. That the blood test Inspector Halloran ran hadn't told the whole story. That the doctors had got it wrong. Training with the ambulance service I'm no stranger to the fact that that happens more than anyone would like to admit. But, instead, you've come here to insinuate something, haven't you?' Jordan said, folding his arms across his chest.

'Quite the opposite,' Kitt said, noting that he hadn't answered her question. She adjusted her voice so it was lighter and easier in the hope of convincing Jordan she was on his side. If past experience was anything to go by, meeting antagonism with antagonism head on rarely yielded the desired results. 'I'm here to make sure the police don't come knocking on your door and waste their time in what is a very difficult investigation.'

'I don't follow,' said Jordan.

'The police believe whatever was done to Leonard was done on the Friday before he died. Between six p.m. and ten p.m. If you could just tell me where you were at that time, we could verify it and make sure that you aren't bothered by this business again.'

'You're telling me, that just because I had a disagreement with this guy, I'm on the suspect list? I'm the one who tried to save his life,' said Jordan.

'Which would be a very clever way for a killer to disguise themselves as an innocent in a sea of suspects,' said Joe. 'We don't think that's the case with you, we just have to get the information from you about where you were last Friday night. If you've got nothing to hide then telling us where you were really shouldn't be a problem.'

Jordan sighed. He looked down to the black polished tiles of the nightclub. 'I was at the rehearsal for the Christmas Book Fair that night, just like Leonard Bell and everyone else who is – or was – taking part. Obviously, the rest of the book fair was cancelled after what happened.'

'Yes,' Kitt said, trying not to get drawn into that particular subject. There had been several events she had been looking forward to at the book fair. The Narnia-themed Christmas parade had been quite high on the list. The special performance of *The Nutcracker* ballet came in close behind that. Not to mention all the book-browsing she had planned. In light of a cold and calculated murder, and the prospect of a second victim being claimed, such things paled into insignificance, but Kitt couldn't help but feel sad that the York Christmas Book Fair had ground to a halt in such grisly circumstances.

'And this run-in you had with Leonard at the rehearsal. When did that happen?' said Kitt.

'Probably about quarter past six, just as the rehearsal was getting going,' said Jordan.

'And what was said, exactly?' asked Kitt.

Jordan waited for a minute before answering. Possibly weighing up how much of the truth to tell Kitt. After all, Leonard was dead. He could tell her pretty much whatever he wanted.

'I told him that if I had my way, people like him wouldn't take part in community events,' Jordan said at last. 'Glorified murderers, that's all the employees in that place are. I told him that if I had my way, he'd have to look into the eyes of every mum and dad who'd lost a child because of the work he's done. There was someone else there when I said this to him. Shawna McCoy. She was on lights for Leonard's performance and I was on sound. So she was there with me the whole time. It was only a few hours so we were side by side working on the tech for the duration.'

'According to our information though,' Kitt said, remembering what Eleanor had told them. About the fact that she thought someone could have poisoned Leonard's drink in the Book and Candle Bar. 'All volunteers at the book fair were dismissed by quarter to nine. So, where were you between eight forty-five and ten p.m. that evening?'

'I was . . .' Jordan paused; his mouth was open but it took a few moments for the words to come out. 'Round at a friend's house.'

'We're going to need a name, and contact details,' said Kitt.

Jordan shook his head. 'I can't give you that.'

'Why not?' said Kitt.

Jordan again just shook his head.

'Somebody else has been poisoned, you know?' said Kitt, while examining his face for any sign that he did know, and thus had something to do with what happened to Bell and what was about to happen to Ripley.

'What?' Jordan said, frowning as he digested what Kitt had said. 'You mean, it wasn't an isolated incident? Who else has been poisoned?'

'The who isn't important, and I'm not allowed to release any information anyway. What is important is that the person who has been poisoned has days, possibly hours, left to live. Whoever is behind it has the antidote to the poison and every second we spend talking to you is one second less we have to hunt down the real culprit of the crime. We have to go through this process of elimination and you're not making it any easier on us. If the person who has been poisoned dies while we're wasting time trying to get your alibi out of you, well, it's not an exaggeration to say that you'll bear some responsibility for his death.'

'If you've trained with the ambulance service, can you really live with yourself if you know you could have helped to save someone and didn't?' said Grace.

'This person could literally die at any moment,' said Joe, seemingly determined to have his go at piling the pressure on Jordan to cave and spill his alibi. 'Imagine if that were you, or someone you loved. You would want someone in your position to just give us the information we need. You seem like a good person, so stop beating about the bush and just tell us where you were.'

'Alright,' Jordan shouted, and then, more quietly, repeated himself. 'Alright. The guy I was with, he wasn't exactly a friend. More of an acquaintance. I was . . . buying something off him.'

'Something . . .' Kitt frowned and then realised what Jordan was hinting at. 'Drugs?'

Jordan nodded. 'It's sort of common knowledge that some medical staff end up taking something to get them through the long shifts. People who've never done the job don't understand how demanding it can be. It's not just the long hours, it's what you see on the job. It takes its toll. But, for some of us, taking substances, it doesn't stop there. It becomes an addiction. I am getting help but I'm still having lapses. I had one that Friday night that you're talking about.'

Kitt sighed. 'Well, I'm not here to pass judgement on something that you rightly point out I have no experience of. Addiction is a disease that has claimed many lives. I'm glad you're getting help. But Jordan, it is not my intention to make a citizen's arrest on a drug dealer. I'm trying to save somebody's life. If I can just verify where you were last Friday, then none of this needs to come to the police's attention.'

Kitt knew that she wasn't entirely being honest here. She had already told Halloran about Jordan and she would end up telling him who he had given as his alibi. But she had to be sure Jordan didn't have anything to do with Bell's murder and the subsequent poisoning of Kevin Ripley.

'I'll give you the contact details and protocol for meeting this guy,' said Jordan. 'But I can't guarantee that he'll admit he was with me. Admitting that is akin to admitting that he sells drugs. He's not going to volunteer that information.'

'You'd better hope we can persuade him to do just that, Jordan,' said Kitt. 'Because if the current leads the police have don't pan out, given your disagreement and the fact you were at the scene when the victim died, they are probably going to start looking at you next.'

'Well, if they're going to go to everyone at the book fair who had a problem Leonard Bell, I hope they're not under the impression that I'm the only person on that list?'

'What do you mean by that remark?' said Kitt.

'I don't think they had any arguments, but there was someone else on the volunteer crew who had it in for Leonard,' said Jordan.

'I'm going to need a name,' said Kitt, wondering if this was a genuine accusation or if Jordan was just trying to take the heat off himself.

'Donald Sanders,' said Jordan. 'He was in charge of ticketing.'

'And what was his problem with Leonard Bell?' asked Grace.

'He talked a lot behind his back about how Leonard stole his job at the Defence Medical Agency. They both went for the position when it was advertised, but Leonard got it and Donald didn't. He said Leonard knew one of the superiors from the golf club, and that's why he got the job.'

Kitt and Grace exchanged a brief look at this revelation. When Grace had looked up Nathan Greene, the only place she'd found an online presence was on the website for the local golfing club.

'Did he mention the name of this superior?' said Kitt.

Jordan shook his head. 'No, but he never stopped talking about it. It happened over a decade ago and he was still ranting and raving whenever he got a chance.'

'Alright,' said Kitt. 'Thank you for letting us know. We're still going to try and confirm your alibi to rule you out completely, but we'll also check out Donald Sanders. See if his grudge against Leonard Bell stopped at sounding off.'

Jordan nodded, but didn't look particularly reassured, and Kitt couldn't blame him. A shaky alibi and numerous altercations with the deceased was not a good look under these circumstances.

His comments about Donald Sanders had, however, sparked Kitt's curiosity. In particular, the mentioning of the golf club.

It was possible that Sanders had made up a story about Bell having friends in high places just to make it seem as though he unfairly lost out on the job. But what if there was something to it? And what if the person Bell knew from the golf club was Nathan Greene? Thus far, Kitt had assumed that the pair had strictly been work colleagues. But what if there was more to their relationship than she'd thought?

CHAPTER EIGHTEEN

'How long do we have to sit here, exactly?' said Evie, yawning into a flask of hot chocolate she'd brought with her before pouring herself a cup.

'Not too much longer,' said Kitt, trying to ignore how much her eyes were stinging in protest at how many hours they had now gone without any sleep. 'I just want to wait long enough for the guard on duty at the gate to get really, really cold.'

Since just after midnight was about the time that most drug dealers likely started work, Kitt had suggested Grace and Joe pay a visit to Jordan's 'friend', a man who went by the name of Tank O'Neal.

If that was the bloke's real name, Kitt would eat her hat.

She'd worn the same maroon trilby for years now and was quite attached to it, so she didn't make such a statement lightly.

Still, all they needed was confirmation of who he was

with last Friday night after the rehearsal for the book fair events had packed up. If he voluntarily named Jordan as his companion, that would at least, to an extent, eliminate him from their enquiries. It was still possible that Jordan might have poisoned Leonard at the rehearsal, of course, but looking into that was Halloran's domain. He was handling Leonard's movements on the night of the poisoning and would likely soon be able to narrow down Jordan's movements too with some basic investigation.

The best they could do was ensure that Jordan hadn't followed Bell to the Book and Candle Bar after the rehearsal was done, and slipped something into Bell's drink when his party were up and dancing, as Eleanor had described.

Since she couldn't let either Grace or Joe walk into a meeting with a known felon alone, that had left Kitt without a partner to stake out the Defence Medical Agency. She had texted Evie on the off-chance that she'd still be awake with Banks working late. Though not an official part of the investigative team, Evie had helped out on quite a few cases here and there when Kitt needed additional back-up.

Luckily, Evie had still been awake and agreed to drive Kitt to the facility in her car – a 1968 Morris Minor that she had christened 'Jacob'. Kitt couldn't think of a vehicle that would stand out more than a yellow vintage classic, but their presence would become known to the guard on the gate sooner or later, and anyway, it was the only vehicle they had.

'Do you want some hot chocolate?' Evie asked.

'That depends, did you bring the mini marshmallows like I asked?'

'What do you take me for? Some kind of amateur?' Evie said with a grin while pouring her friend a hot chocolate and adding about three times the number of marshmallows Kitt would have used.

'Thanks,' Kitt said, after taking her first big slurp from the mug.

'Do you really think this guy's employer has poisoned him?' said Evie, looking out of the car window at the facility beyond. Though it was well and truly dark this time in the morning. There were some lights on in the facility itself, enough to get at least a vague impression about what the Defence Medical Agency must look like on the inside. Kitt followed her friend's gaze. From this distance she could just make out a guard in uniform standing in a small hut next to a traffic barrier. She had already given the guard a closer look through a set of binoculars and ascertained that the man in question was quite young. Not much older than twenty by the look of him. Beyond the guard's hut was a large set of black steel gates and beyond that, well, according to the brief description Ripley had given them and what she had ascertained from his lab notes, there were several banks of offices and laboratories. The only thing Kitt could make out right now were some buildings made of red brick.

'The suspects are piling up,' said Kitt, in answer to Evie's question. 'But Ripley seems to think that he and Bell were targeted because they didn't want the agency to use the toxin they'd produced. The running theory regarding the agency is that they might have been afraid Ripley and Bell would go to the press about them using an inhumane chemical agent if they continued their research in that area.'

'Seems a bit . . . severe,' said Evie. 'I would have thought an agency as powerful as that could just dismiss them and coerce them into signing non-disclosure agreements.'

'It's definitely an extreme measure; the whole thing is a conspiracy theorist's fantasy. But, unfortunately, the pair did hint that they would go to the press if the agency continued researching the toxin. There's a chance that the agency may not have believed the pair would honour an NDA, so sought other means of . . . solving the problem.'

'Crikey,' said Evie. 'Imagine working for a place like that. Where it was actually within the realms of believability that they might try to bump you off.'

'I'd sooner not imagine it,' said Kitt. 'But I think Ripley's being distrustful of the agency in general because he simply doesn't know who specifically in their employ has targeted him. The odds are it's not the agency itself but someone who has gone rogue within their operation. Someone who perhaps intends to sell the toxin to some unknown third party. And who knows what they might do with it? They might find a way of making it even more potent.'

'Is there a way it could be more potent? I'm never going to forget how Leonard Bell's body looked, I can tell you,' said Evie.

'At present the toxin takes five days to overtake the nervous system,' said Kitt. 'Perhaps somebody is looking to make the effects instantaneous.'

Evie looked across the car at Kitt. 'You know, I don't think you would have even been able to come up with a theory that morbid ten years ago.'

Kitt lowered her eyes. 'I know. Actually, that particular idea cropped up in Ripley's lab notes. But, this work, it hardens you. I mean, if we're honest, the world we live in hardens you. But before I started investigating, I felt like I could . . . stay a little bit soft, if you know what I mean? I don't feel like I've got that luxury anymore and, much as I love him, living with Halloran doesn't help. He was at the place I'm at now when we met.'

'I remember,' said Evie. 'It feels like a million years ago, that first case. So much has happened since then. For both of us.'

'Yes, you got both kidnapped and married in that time,' Kitt said with a wry smile. She didn't make a habit of cracking jokes about the time she thought she'd lost Evie for good, but sometimes it was the only way of digesting the fact that such things had really happened and making your peace with them, so far as anyone could.

'The latter has turned out to be a lot more fun than the

former, I can tell you. Except for the paperwork involved in buying your first house. I've never been asked for so much identification. I've entered other countries more easily than I have buying a house in the country I already live in.'

Kitt chuckled. 'It will be worth it when you and Banks finally have a place that's your own. If I wasn't so attached to my cottage I'm sure me and Halloran would have done the same by now. Goodness knows I could use more space for bookshelves.'

Evie shrugged. 'Fond as you are of the cottage, it might not be such a bad idea.'

'Moving house?' said Kitt.

'Yes. Or maybe even making a fresh start in general,' Evie said, slowly looking at Kitt out of the corner of her eye.

Kitt met her friend's sidelong gaze for a moment. 'You're worried about me.'

'A bit,' Evie said with a nod. 'I knew you before, remember? Before you met Halloran. Before you started investigating murders. I'm not saying you should go back to who you were back then, even if that were possible. But maybe it's time to move forward in some way. Evolve. Because I can see, old chum, the toll it's taking on you. Being suspicious of everyone all the time, prudent as it might be, just isn't good for you.'

'I know,' said Kitt doing her best to keep her breathing steady.

'If you know, are you . . . I mean, what are you going to do about it?' said Evie.

Kitt knew what her friend was hinting at but she simply wasn't ready to hang up her trilby and go back to the library full-time. Or to do something else entirely for that matter. Not just yet. Investigation wasn't just something she did anymore. Being an investigator was who she *was*. And if she gave that up, who would she be then? There weren't many questions in the world that could scare a woman like Kitt, but that one definitely stirred a tightness in her stomach. Perhaps in part because she was beginning to wonder if even she knew who she was anymore without an investigation on the go.

'Let's save the big questions for when we've got to the bottom of this case, shall we?' said Kitt, knowing that Evie would likely not be happy with her side-stepping the issue but unable to forget that she'd made a promise to see this case through. 'Once we've saved Kevin Ripley's life, I can indulge in all the introspection I like.'

Evie offered her a weak smile through pursed lips before moving the conversation on. 'The thing I don't understand about your Defence Medical Agency employee gone rogue theory is why the person who wants to sell it to a third party would need to poison Bell and Ripley to do it. Couldn't they just steal the toxin and the antidote and make off with it?'

'Yes, that's the part that's taken some working out for me too,' said Kitt. 'But I think the answer is simply that the person in question thinks that Bell and Ripley would ultimately have figured out who had stolen the toxin and decided to poison them to make sure that didn't happen.'

Privately Kitt mused again on how strange it was that Bell and Ripley hadn't been poisoned at the same time given that the killer likely had opportunity. The most concrete theory she could muster was that whoever did the poisoning must have been disturbed from their task that Friday night. For whatever reason, poisoning Ripley's glass on top of poisoning Bell's simply seemed like too big a risk to them.

'You know, one day I'd love it if you just got dragged into an investigation to uncover somebody's missing cat. Something low-octane,' said Evie.

Kitt chuckled. 'If the missing cat was Iago I doubt Halloran would let me take the case.'

Evie joined in with Kitt's laughing and Kitt was glad the mood was lightening between them again after their earlier conversation. 'Ah, so the inspector still hasn't improved his relations with your resident feline.'

'It's been ten years, Iago's pushing sixteen and getting more cantankerous by the day, though I admit I didn't think that was possible,' said Kitt. 'I don't hold out much hope that the two are going to call a truce anytime soon. Halloran keeps commenting on the fact that Iago's getting on now and might not be with us for too much longer.'

'He hasn't? The cheeky bugger,' Evie said, with a small laugh of disbelief.

'It's alright,' said Kitt. 'I just remind Halloran that, unlike him, that cat isn't charging into dangerous situations on a weekly basis and may well outlive him. He particularly dislikes it when I tell him that the oldest cat to have ever lived reached the grand age of thirty-eight.'

Evie chuckled and shook her head, while Kitt directed her attentions back over to the facility. It had just started to snow and, through her binoculars, Kitt could see the guard patting his arms and jogging up and down on the spot to stay warm.

'Alright,' Kitt said. 'I think I've got this bloke right where I want him. Pull that pile of maps out of the back seat for me, will you?'

'Your grand plan involves maps?' Evie said, handing Kitt the big bunch of crumpled maps she had bundled into the back seat on entering the vehicle.

'That's right, our cover story is, we're tourists visiting the city to enjoy the Christmas market. We've got lost and we're looking for our hotel,' said Kitt.

'Out here? Which hotel are we looking for? The one in *The Shining*? Civilisation, along with the Christmas market, is very obviously thataway,' Evie said, pointing a thumb over her shoulder.

'I know, I know, but you know how turned about some of the tourists get when they come here, we're just going to have to play the part of particularly ditsy tourists. We're going to pretend we're lost and need directions. See what information we can get out of this guy in the interim. And hand me that pack of Jammie Dodgers, will you?'

'Won't he wonder why we aren't using Google Maps?' said Evie.

'Not if we make it clear we are very confused tourists who also happen to be technology-phobic troglodytes.'

'Alright,' said Evie. 'You're really fleshing out my character now, I'll give it my best shot.'

'That's the spirit,' said Kitt. 'Now, drive towards that man in the hut and try to make it look like you don't know where you're going.'

With a nod, Evie started up the car and headed towards the entrance. Instead of driving in a hesitant fashion as Kitt had intended, however, Evie began gently swerving the car this way and that.

'What are you doing?' said Kitt

'You said to make it look like I didn't know where we were going?'

'Yes, but we don't want him to think you're under the influence,' said Kitt. 'Just drive slowly. Stop a couple of times and then approach the hut.'

'Oh, right, OK. Yeah, I can do that. In my defence your earlier instruction was open to a lot of interpretation.'

'Yes, alright,' said Kitt. 'Of course, it's my fault you're swerving all over the road as if you've never been behind the wheel of a car before. See if you can stall the engine when we pull up to the hut, will you?'

Evie did as instructed but the man sitting in his little hut was out and holding his hands up to them to stop before they even got to the traffic barrier.

'You can't be here, madam, this is military property,' said the guard once Kitt had lowered the passenger window. His uniform was cut of deep khaki fabric and a blue beret rested on his head. He held a small torch so he could see clearly into the car. The beam from the torch rested on the tangle of maps strewn across Kitt's lap for a moment and then flitted from Evie's face to Kitt's.

'Military property! Oh, I am so very sorry, officer. I'm afraid we're desperately lost. Trying to find our hotel, you see, and it's so late. We thought we were on the right track but we've had such a long journey. Oh, listen to me rambling on, keeping you out here in the cold,' said Kitt. 'Although I suppose you must be used to it, if this is your job. Standing out in the cold all night, every night, for . . . well how many years have you done it?'

'Mercifully I've only been in this post for just over a week, madam, but it's set to be a cold winter for me by the look of it.'

'I'll say,' said Kitt, secretly already happy to have got some useful information out of this man. He said he had been in post just over a week. Ripley had said the break-in was about ten days ago. Two possibilities about the break-in at the Defence Medical Agency sprung to mind. Either, the guard who used to work this job was injured, possibly killed when the burglars made their entrance. Or, the agency suspected the guard of being in on the job, fired him and replaced him. Either way, it was good news for Kitt that this bloke had only been on the job a week or so. It made it more likely that he might be a bit green.

'Well, we certainly mustn't keep you,' Kitt continued. 'I'm so sorry to have pulled you out of your shelter. Here, take a Jammie Dodger or two for your troubles. You must be famished sitting out there in the cold.'

'Well,' the guard said, looking longingly at the biscuits. 'We're not really supposed to . . .'

'Oh, we won't tell, your secret is safe with us,' said Kitt. 'Can't have a young lad like you going hungry. You're still a growing boy.'

The guard needed no more coaxing. He dug his big hand into the packet, pulled out three Jammie Dodgers and began munching at once.

'Oh, Evie, look at this poor man, he's starving. I don't know how you do it, the long nights out here all alone. We have a spare mug and some hot chocolate in the flask. I must pour you a hot drink to wash those biscuits down.'

'I really shouldn't, madam,' said the guard though his tone was not at all convincing.

'Nonsense,' said Kitt. 'We've got some mini marshmallows to throw in there.'

Again the guard hesitated, looked over his shoulder and then offered Kitt a nod, coupled with a cheeky grin.

Before he could change his mind, Kitt promptly poured him a mug of hot chocolate, threw in the marshmallows and handed the beverage out through the window.

'I must admit,' said Kitt as the guard gulped at the hot chocolate, 'I've always thought that working in the military must be so very exciting. I mean, take this place, for example. It's all locked up with a guard at the front gate. Who knows what exciting adventures are taking place, or about to take place, behind those gates?'

'I think you might have a bit of a romanticised view, madam,' said the guard. 'Nobody behind those gates is going off to war. Just pushing the papers around for those that do.'

'Still,' Kitt said. 'It must be a matter of great pride to be of service to your country. A lot of people don't want to know about a line of work like that, you know? They're only interested in themselves. You are of a different breed entirely,' she said. 'And though I'm sure we've been nothing but a nuisance to you I'm glad to have crossed paths with you ... I'm sorry, what did you say your name was?'

'Peter, madam.'

'You have my gratitude for all you do to keep our country safe. This looks like a very secure facility. I'm sure it's only made more secure by your vigilance.'

'Can't do any worse than the last guy who had my job,' Peter said, his eyes widening the moment he realised the words were out of his mouth. 'I mean, I strive to always do my best, madam.'

'I've no doubt,' Kitt said. 'I bet the guy who did the job before wasn't a patch on you.'

In spite of himself, Kitt noticed a satisfied smirk creep over Peter's face that he couldn't hide.

'Let's just say,' Peter said, giving Kitt a wink, 'there'll be nobody sneaking in here undetected on my watch.'

'Would anybody dare?' Kitt said with a gentle chuckle. 'I imagine this place has state-of-the-art security systems too. Oh, you live in a much more exciting world than I do, Peter. A woman like me will never know the startling highs of the job you do. A hot mug of cocoa and a book before bedtime, that's my biggest excitement. Whereas you get to live these grand stories for real. And don't be telling me nothing exciting ever happens around here. I bet it's much more gripping than the bestselling thriller novels at times.'

'Well,' Peter said, 'there may be one or two stories about this place that would get your adrenaline pumping.'

'Oh, I'm all ears,' said Kitt.

'Well, er.' Peter looked over both shoulders again. 'This isn't about this facility, you understand, it's about a facility far, far away from here that I cannot name.'

'Right . . .' Kitt said, wondering exactly what was going to come out of Peter's mouth next.

'And in this facility, they had some very dangerous weapons. Top secret. Classified stuff. The kind of thing you'd expect to see in a James Bond movie.'

'Oh my goodness,' Kitt said, confident that Peter was

in fact talking about the facility he was standing outside of right now and just didn't want to get into trouble for regaling lost tourists with its most closely guarded secrets.

'And one night, this facility was robbed. Whoever did it must have been the master of all crime, because nobody saw them go in and nobody saw them go out. They couldn't be detected by any of the security measures. And yet, one of the most prized weapons in the facility went missing.'

'Did this really happen?' said Kitt. 'You're not telling an old woman tall tales, are you?'

'Well, maybe I am having you on,' said Peter. Kitt could tell by the way his eyes were darting about that he was conflicted. He wanted to show off but he also wanted to keep his job and maintain his cover.

'I thought so,' Kitt said, wagging a finger at Peter. 'I won't be able to sleep, however, unless I hear the end of the story. How does this tall tale end? Do the military catch the people who stole their weapon?'

Peter shook his head. 'No, they have no choice but to do a big cover-up. Pretend the weapon never went missing in the first place. The person who did it is left to roam free, nobody can track them down!'

'That doesn't sound like a very happy ending to the story,' Kitt said, catching Peter's blue eyes for the first time since he started his hypothetical tale.

He cleared his throat and looked over his shoulder at the facility for a moment, as if remembering himself and why he had been posted here in the first place. 'No, madam. Not a very happy ending. You'll have to excuse me, I'm not very good at telling stories. The ending is always a let-down. All my friends say so.'

'Well, I enjoyed the story, Peter,' said Kitt.

'Very nice of you to say, madam. But I'm afraid I must get back to my post and ask you to move along now.'

'Of course,' said Kitt. 'But here, take these to get you through the night.' She handed the rest of the Jammie Dodgers through the window to him and the stern look that had crossed his face softened once again.

'Thank you,' he said.

'Merry Christmas, Peter,' said Kitt.

'Merry Christmas to you, madam,' Peter said. 'If you're looking for a hotel in the centre of town, you want to be heading in that direction.'

'Thank you so very much,' said Kitt, before Evie made a hasty U-turn and drove them in the direction Peter was pointing.

'I'm a bit concerned about national security if he's the one on guard,' Evie said, once they'd driven a minute down the road.

Kitt chuckled. 'He was just a young lad, trying to make his way in the world.'

'Who's willing to accept a drink off a total stranger when he knows a top-secret neurotoxin has been stolen,' said Evie. 'Do you think he wanted you to understand that the story he was telling wasn't fictional but a broad recount of what happened at that facility just ten days ago?'

'No,' said Kitt. 'I think he thought we were lost tourists and he was just passing the time. But his choice of words when telling the story was interesting. He suggested the people who took the antidote had sneaked in rather than used force. So, whoever had Peter's job before him was probably fired for incompetence.'

At this juncture, Kitt's phone beeped and she looked down to see a message from Grace:

Tank O'Neal (if that is his real name) confirms he did see Jordan that evening but is being sketchy about the timings. Can't confirm categorically that they were together directly after the book fair rehearsal.

'Oh God,' said Kitt. 'Jordan's alibi is shaky.'

'Yeah, well, I didn't really think a drug dealer would be keen to paint a vivid picture of what he was up to that night,' said Evie.

Kitt sighed and rubbed her eyes. 'Forget your idea about investigating a missing cat, I won't even ask for life to be that easy, but one day I'm going to work a murder case that is open-and-shut. It will be obvious who the killer is from the get-go, and I'll have all the paperwork squared away in a couple of hours . . . I guess that day just isn't today.'

'Obviously the investigative work isn't my strong suit, but is it really likely that Jordan is mixed up in all this?' said Evie. 'From what I've heard, it's not very convincing. A few disagreements with someone who subsequently passes away isn't exactly a smoking gun. Especially since sneaking into a facility like that looks like a job for a professional.'

'I know he's not the most likely of suspects,' said Kitt. 'But we just keep uncovering things about him that don't cast him a particularly positive light. First the disagreements, then the admission that his alibi after the rehearsal is a drug dealer, and then said alibi not being particularly concrete. Added to that is the fact that he chose to give up the CPR as well, and I think it's easy to tell why my suspicions are raised when it comes to him.'

'But I heard that crack from Leonard's body just as clearly as you did. I've not been around anybody when they've been given CPR before but it didn't sound natural to me,' said Evie. 'I think sounds like that would stop most people in their tracks.'

'I know,' said Kitt. 'I haven't forgotten the sounds and sights of that day any more than you have. I'm just not a big believer in coincidences when it comes to a person's name cropping up more than once in a murder investigation. It would be such a good way of avoiding any attention from the police: being the one who tried to revive the victim at the scene. But maybe this is the exception, and it was just coincidence after all.'

'Didn't you say Halloran's team were checking into Jordan's financial and phone records?' said Evie. 'That might settle the matter once and for all.'

'Yes, I think it will. We've certainly done pretty much all that we can in terms of getting the investigation into Jordan started, though I will have to get Grace to look into whether or not Bell and Jordan have any prior connections. I do hear what you're saying, we could just be clutching at straws as far as he's concerned, and I definitely don't have time to waste on things like that if I'm to find that antidote.'

'Again, I tend to leave the sleuthing to you, but I'd be tempted to say that there might be a bit of straw-clutching going on where Jordan is concerned,' said Evie.

'You seem very sure of yourself,' said Kitt. 'More sure than I am about anything at the minute and I'm supposed to be leading this investigation.'

'Well, having seen that facility for myself is it really possible for a civilian to get inside a place like that without being noticed? Even with the security cameras down? And what about the fact that the security cameras *were* down? Hacked, I think you said.'

Kitt nodded. 'That's the way Kevin Ripley described it.'

'Then that was surely most likely done by someone who knows their system,' said Evie. 'They have security personnel and anyone they don't recognise is going to get questioned. If someone was in there doing sneaky things, they likely got past security because they already had clearance.'

Kitt took in a deep breath before slowly letting it out again. 'You're right. If you're nothing more than the average citizen, as opposed to some kind of special forces professional,

I'm not convinced it is possible to get in there unless they let you in. Halloran was on the right track from the outset and you've made the point very well. The security guard that Peter has replaced was probably fired simply because this incident happened on their watch and they likely had no answers about how. I'm even more resolved than I was before that the person who did this was already in there when they committed the crime.'

'So, what are you going to do?' asked Evie.

'Anything I can to cross paths with a certain Margaret Cryer,' Kitt replied.

CHAPTER NINETEEN

Kitt sat on a wooden bench in St Helen's Square in the heart of York city centre. The surrounding buildings, including the church after which the square was named, were illuminated only by the yellow glow of Victorian lampposts and the fairy lights on the Christmas tree that stood in the middle of what was, in the daytime, one of the city's busiest thoroughfares.

Snowflakes scratched against Kitt's cheeks. Even bundled up in her winter coat, hat and gloves she should be freezing to be out in the elements at this ungodly hour. What must it be? Five in the morning by now for sure. And yet, the cold didn't touch her. And, in fact, she was struggling to recall how she had even come to be at the square in the first place . . . It was then that the thought struck her that this space, now occupied by shops fronted by festive displays boasting every Christmas character from nutcrackers to elves, used to be a graveyard.

No sooner had it dawned on her that she was sitting in a repurposed cemetery than Kitt noticed a figure standing . . . perhaps even lurking? Next to the Christmas tree. Though the lights from the tree were fierce, the figure, whoever they were, kept to the shadows in such a manner that it sent goosebumps running up Kitt's arms.

'Who's there?' Kitt called out.

Her voice echoed around the square which was, aside from herself and the yet-to-be identified figure, empty. An odd detail in itself. Even in the early hours she would have expected a few people who worked the night shift to be milling about.

When the figure did not respond to her query, Kitt felt the fire in her chest, which always flared when something frustrated or angered her, begin to kindle. Ordinarily, Kitt might have travelled through the realms of fear or frustration before reaching aggravation. But she'd had her fill of fear and frustration in the last sixteen hours or so and she was all out of patience with it.

'I said, who's there?' she called out again. This time standing from the bench. 'For heaven's sake,' she muttered to herself when she again got no response. With no patience left, and no regard for her own safety, Kitt strode towards the Christmas tree full pelt, stopping only when she had a clear view of the figure that still hid in its shadow.

Kitt took a step backwards as she digested the rather striking sight before her. The figure turned out to be a man dressed in a dark vintage suit. Thin, wiry spectacles were perched on his nose, and he boasted a bushy white beard. Kitt paused for a moment and frowned but then continued to walk slowly towards the man she recognised from the dustjacket on a book in her own library.

'This is the story of what a woman's patience can endure . . .' Kitt began to recite.

'And what a man's resolution can achieve,' the man finished.

'Wilkie Collins . . . ?' Kitt said, her tone more weary than it was laced with surprise. 'I see I'm dreaming again. No wonder I've dropped off really. I've worked some long days in the past but staying awake for over twenty hours is pushing the limit even for me.'

'Charles said you were a sceptic,' said Collins. 'Too bad. You'd make so much more progress on the case you're working if you were more open-minded.'

'There's open-minded, and then there's believing that long-dead authors visiting you in your dreams have some bearing and influence on the real world.'

'Touché,' said Collins, 'when you put it that way it is a bit of a stretch. But you've already had that debate with Charles once and my visit is to be even briefer than his. Us spirits do not get long on this side, you know?'

'Very well,' Kitt said, sighing and only just managing not to roll her eyes. 'I'm listening to whatever you have to say.'

'You've made a fine start to the investigation considering

your limitations, but with time being so against you, it is imperative you get to the heart of this situation and fast,' said Collins.

'Oh really?' said Kitt, slapping her forehead. 'Is that what we've got to do? Well thank you so much for informing me, I don't know what I would have done if you hadn't conveyed this vital piece of information.'

'I know, I know, I see what you're doing. But I'm not critiquing. I'm just here to give you a helping hand. To try and move things along a bit.'

'That remains to be seen,' said Kitt.

Collins cast a stern glance at Kitt before speaking again. It was enough to make her stand up a little straighter, even though she knew she couldn't really be standing at all and had most likely fallen asleep in her chair at the agency. Again.

'I've written a mystery or two in my time. No easy task, you know? People commit terrible deeds every day, far worse than I ever wrote about. But in a mystery story, you actually have to do what real-life criminals never have to do. You have to justify the most heinous acts a person might commit. Explain *why* a person might do these things. When I was writing *The Woman in White* I had to ask myself, why would Glyde go this far? Why would he enact this despicable plot against his wife? What motivations did Count Fosco have for assisting him? All of this had to be carefully considered.'

'I'm well aware that working out why a murder might have happened is often the key to unlocking who's behind it,' said Kitt. 'But we're still trying to establish a motive for the poisoning of Bell and Ripley.'

'You'll get there a lot quicker if you ask yourself who had the most to gain from Leonard Bell's death,' said Collins. 'People will do unthinkable things for their own gain in this world. At least, that's the world as I experienced it.'

'It's difficult to think that the Defence Medical Agency would have that much to gain from killing off Bell and Ripley,' said Kitt. 'Killing them off just draws unwanted attention to an already controversial bioweapons project.'

'Individual murders are routinely carried out by people acting alone, even if they are sanctioned by a bigger group.' Collins pointed over to his left and Kitt followed the trail marked out by his finger until she clapped eyes on the Book and Candle Bar, the place Bell, Ripley and Eleanor had been drinking the night Bell was poisoned. 'The wife of the deceased told you herself where she thought the poisoning had happened. In all likelihood, last Friday night an individual went into those premises and poisoned Bell's drink. Rather than chasing grand conspiracies that circle around a military organisation, it is the individual you need to focus on. That person is the key to all you want to know.'

'It's all got so confused so quickly,' Kitt said, thinking out loud. 'With the agency stonewalling Halloran and the information about the theft being so compartmentalised . . .

You're right. We need to forget the conspiracy theories and boil it down to a single act. Last Friday night somebody put something into Leonard Bell's drink. Something they knew would kill him. If we can find out who did that, regardless of who put them up to it, we might be able to unravel this whole mystery. And, as you say, the person most likely to have done it is the person with most to gain. There must be some clue in the fact that there are two victims. We just have to figure out who had the most to gain from both Leonard Bell and Kevin Ripley dying ... Thank you,' Kitt said, turning back around to Collins.

But Collins was no longer there.

Only she remained as the snow settled on the damp paving stones and the bells of St Helen's tolled five.

CHAPTER TWENTY

'Aren't those the same clothes you were wearing yesterday?' said Grace as Kitt joined her under the small canopy outside Clifton Bingo Hall. The venue itself was not open right now, but the sleet had started to fall early this morning and Kitt could do without being sodden and frozen to the bone before she confronted Margaret Cryer about her relationship with the deceased.

'I fell asleep at the office,' Kitt said, deciding against mentioning the strange dream she'd had featuring Wilkie Collins. Grace was prone to teasing Kitt about nothing at the best of times, she didn't need to give her obvious ammunition. 'I didn't have time to go home to change if we wanted to catch Margaret on her way to work.' With that, Kitt flicked on the transmitter in her coat pocket. Following her lead, Grace did the same. 'Joe, are you in position?'

'Me and Rolo are in place,' Joe confirmed. 'We'll wait for the signal.'

'Great stuff, thanks for confirming,' said Kitt. Ripley had assured her that rain, sleet or shine, Margaret always walked to work, passing Clifton Bingo Hall on her way to the facility. She was due to arrive at the agency at nine and it was currently twenty past eight in the morning. It couldn't be more than a thirty-minute walk between the bingo hall and the facility. so Kitt was confident they would catch her and that she, Grace and Joe would be able to execute their plan to get Margaret to part with at least some information about that missing toxin, not to mention the antidote. Assuming, of course, that she knew more about it than the average employee at the Defence Medical Agency.

Kitt thought again about what Ripley had said about there being some kind of romantic connection between Cryer and Tyler Simmons. Simmons had reason to be angry at the agency and Cryer still had a place on the inside. Could it be possible that the pair had orchestrated this whole affair between them in order to disgrace the agency? Kitt would be looking very carefully for any signs that indicated that might be the case.

'Did you look up this Donald Sanders person Jordan was talking about?' said Kitt.

'Yes, here's a screenshot of his Facebook profile picture,' said Grace, turning her phone so that Kitt could see it.

Donald Sanders had a full head of snow white hair that seemed to sort of stand on end even though it was cut very short. He was posing in the picture with a Golden Retriever that was pawing at his moss green cardigan. If there was a portrait in somebody's mind of what a murderer looked like, this man couldn't be further from that. But then, looks could be deceiving.

'What do we know about him?' Kitt asked.

'He's retired now but he had his own business as a chemist on Bishy Road. He was there about thirty years. He's married with three children and eight grandchildren. There are no immediate red flags on his social media profiles, the electoral roll records or court records.'

'Well, we'll have to speak to him at some point, but Margaret Cryer and Tyler Simmons have to be the focus for now. Unless you had any luck finding any previous connections between Jordan, Bell and Ripley?' Kitt said. Before, she'd decided definitively in her own head that Cryer and Simmons were the most likely culprits. Jordan had never seemed that likely a murderer but she had to keep an open mind.

'Nothing has popped up yet,' said Grace. 'He probably was telling the truth about where he was, even if O'Neal was sketchy about the time frame. I know that doesn't mean that he couldn't have poisoned Bell at the rehearsal he attended earlier on, but I do think that's a big risk. So many people are milling about and if you get spotted doing something like that, it's game over.'

'The Book and Candle Bar will have been just as busy that night,' said Kitt. 'It would have been just as easy to get spotted there.'

'Yes, but the people at the rehearsal might have had cause to talk to Jordan. To come to him and ask him something at any moment. If you're in a bar full of strangers, it's unlikely you'll get noticed by anyone let alone stopped for a conversation. So, on that basis, I think if he was going to do it he'd probably follow Bell after the rehearsal rather than risk poisoning him during.'

'What if he handed him a drink with the poison already in it?' said Kitt.

Grace nodded. 'It's a possibility. But again, I'm assuming that when Halloran talks to Shawna McCoy who, Jordan says, was with him for the duration of the rehearsal, she would tell the police about that if she saw it.'

'I know,' said Kitt. 'I just wish his alibi for the whole window could have been clear cut. What we've got on him is not enough to pass the threshold of evidence Halloran needs, anyway. I suppose we're just going to have to see what turns up next in the investigation. Speaking with Evie last night I'm more convinced than ever that this was an inside job. Which means that there are two, or perhaps three, people at the top of the suspect list. Nathan Greene, who Halloran is already talking to ... even if he's not getting very far with that. But if it's not him, then it could well be Margaret Cryer, with some involvement from this Tyler Simmons person,' said Kitt.

'Yes, I don't know how many thousands would be added to Cryer's pay packet if Bell and Ripley were out of the picture,' said Grace. 'But from the way Ripley was talking, I imagine it is quite a princely sum. Not to mention the prestige of climbing the ranks at such a young age.'

'And add to that the possible revenge for the agency letting her boyfriend go on less than amicable terms, and I'd say you've got a significant amount of motive building. She'd definitely have quite a lot to gain by their absence,' said Kitt, thinking back to her dream conversation with Wilkie Collins the night before. 'And maybe it would explain why the two victims were poisoned individually. Ripley said if he'd seen Simmons in the bar he would have mentioned it. The same may be true of Cryer but maybe she's better at blending in than he is. If she actually poisoned them herself, then she may have only had the opportunity to poison one glass. She wouldn't have wanted to be hovering about in case Bell and Ripley recognised her.'

'So she took her opportunity at the bar on that Friday night, and then, to play it safe, found another opportunity to poison Ripley,' said Grace.

'That would be my guess,' said Kitt.

'But isn't it just as quick to poison two glasses as it is one? Pouring something into somebody's drink takes a split second,' said Grace.

'Yes, but it's also a highly suspicious thing to be caught doing,' said Kitt. 'If someone thought they'd seen you doing it, out of the corner of their eye, they might turn to watch you very fiercely to see if you did it again. And if you're up to no good, you're going to be frustrated but you're probably not going to take the risk. Eleanor said that she, Bell and Ripley were up and down from their table all night. Maybe once interrupted, the killer saw them coming back to the table and fled before they could be recognised or, if not recognised, at least seen.'

'If they were up and down all night, couldn't the killer just wait until they left the table again?' said Grace. 'If someone had clocked them the first time, the odds are they will have stopped paying any attention once that person left the area.'

'Right now, we've got little choice but to assume that for some reason it was too risky. For example, maybe the person who thought they saw them do something the first time didn't have to turn their head to have a clear view of Bell's table. Maybe it was right in their field of vision and the killer knew if they returned a second time, and that person noticed them doing something to a drink, they would likely be reported to staff at the very least. This isn't like committing a robbery. The person won't have been able to wear a mask. Maybe a hat, if they were lucky. Maybe they might have worn some kind of vague disguise, but my guess is, they'll have wanted to remain as inconspicuous as possible and would not have wanted to take many – if any – risks.'

'Maybe something else will come to light about the separate poisonings as we continue the investigation,' said

Grace, clearly still not quite satisfied with Kitt's explanation. And deep down, neither was Kitt.

'Maybe it's as simple as Ripley getting to a point in the evening where he stopped drinking for one reason or another and the killer didn't have another drink to poison.'

'Maybe,' said Grace. 'But while we're on the subject of things that don't quite add up, what I don't get about Margaret as a suspect is why she would have had to go to the lengths we suspect her of. If she literally had a catalogue of complaints against them on a professional level, why not take it to Greene and have them dismissed over their poor conduct? Even if you take into account the revenge she may or may not want for the dismissal of her boyfriend, which maybe Cryer part blamed Bell and Ripley for, that's a more proportionate punishment.'

'Perhaps she did take her complaints to her superiors,' said Kitt. 'And perhaps she was ignored. Eleanor said the agency ran a tight ship but we both know how male privilege can colour a workplace experience. Especially in a science environment. Eleanor also made it clear that Margaret hadn't worked at the agency as long as Bell and Ripley. She was a relatively new girl whereas they had been there long enough to earn trust and respect. In which case, Margaret may have just been dismissed as nothing more than a troublemaker and, consequently, she felt she had to take matters into her own hands.'

'It's plausible,' said Grace. 'But my money's on Greene. Or

someone working for him. To be high up in a place of work like that, well, I think you start to see human casualties as collateral damage. Nothing more. If it's not Greene himself, it might be someone even higher up. Whoever it was, they were likely afraid Bell and Ripley would go public about the continued research into an inhumane toxin and ordered Greene to ensure that would never happen.'

'Have you been binge watching *The X Files* on Netflix again?' asked Kitt.

'No . . .' Grace said. 'Well, not much. Anyway it was a really good show. And just because you're paranoid doesn't mean *They're* not out to get you.'

'Well, I suppose that's true,' Kitt said, wondering for a moment if she should tell Grace about the strange literary visitations she'd been having in her dreams, after all. No doubt Grace would have an absolute field day with such information and tease her for the rest of time about the fact that she'd started to imagine dead authors were following her about. But maybe Grace would see something in the words of her unexpected visitors that she hadn't because she was too busy writing them off as silly hallucinations. Likely caused by a mixture of stress and the after-effects of Ruby's mulled wine. But if what Dickens had said was right, if they did represent her subconscious speaking to her, then perhaps they were trying to tell her something really important.

Before Kitt had time to open her mouth, however, Grace

interjected. 'Here she comes now. That's definitely her, right?'

Kitt glanced along the street to see a red-haired woman with sparkling green eyes walking towards them. Kitt immediately recognised her from the Facebook profile picture Grace had pulled up when they got back from visiting Eleanor the night before. It was Margaret Cryer alright and she looked to be in a hurry. Her step was light and quick, despite how slippery the pavement had become because of the sleet.

As Cryer drew closer, Kitt realised there was something narrow and hard about those green eyes. They were the eyes of a person who spent their life suspicious of other people. Kitt noticed that in her determination to keep up a fast pace, she knocked into a young mum holding a baby on her hip. Instead of apologising, Margaret tutted and glared at the young mum until she was the one in receipt of an apology.

Is there anyone this woman won't barge out of the way for her own gain? Kitt wondered, while remembering Collins's words in the strange dream she'd had the night before. An individual had taken the opportunity to poison Leonard Bell's drink last Friday. And whoever they were, they had something to gain from his passing. Grace was right that a promotion in the defence industry, especially in the bio-chemical arm, was likely to be lucrative. And who knew what other opportunities would be pushed Margaret's way once she had usurped Bell and Ripley? Kitt had never worked a case in which somebody had killed for a promotion before, but she was becoming more and more convinced that she might be working her first one right now.

The original plan was to find a way of stopping Margaret in the street to talk to her. Bumping into her, seemingly by accident, had been Kitt's primary plan, but considering the way she treated that young mum, Kitt wondered if that would do anything to slow this woman down. Looking around, Kitt noticed a fresh bank of snow that had been shovelled off the pavement to make it walkable for pedestrians.

'Yes,' Kitt said under her breath. 'That will make for quite the soft landing. No real damage likely to be caused if I aim for that.'

'What was that?' said Grace.

'Nothing, don't worry, just follow my lead,' said Kitt.

And for a moment, the pair stood there in the inclement weather, waiting for Margaret Cryer to pass them by. The moment the woman was parallel with her, Kitt stuck out her right leg, tripped her, grabbed her and threw her into the soft bank of snow at the side of the pavement. It all happened so quickly that the only sound that Margaret Cryer emitted was a shriek, along with an 'Oof' as she landed face down in the snow.

Kitt was well-versed with the Margarets of the world. Everything was always somebody else's fault. She knew full well she'd be in for a mouthful if she didn't act quickly.

'My goodness,' Kitt said, bustling over to where the woman was still stretched out on a heap of snow. 'Are you quite alright? I'm sorry but when you tripped so suddenly the only thing I could think to do was manoeuvre you so you didn't go down on the pavement. That would have been a hard bang to the bones if you had.'

Those narrow green eyes looked upward and fixed on Kitt.

'How stupid do you think I am?' said Margaret. 'You tripped me deliberately.'

'Oh, I assure you I didn't,' said Kitt, dusting the snow off Margaret's coat in a bid to look concerned. 'Why on earth would I do a thing like that? Here, let me help you up and I'll show you, there's an uneven paving slab on the pavement. You went right over it, see.'

Kitt pointed down to a paving slab that jutted up at an unfortunate angle. Unfortunate for Margaret Cryer as it meant she would never be able to prove that Kitt had tripped her on purpose. It was quite the fortunate angle for Kitt and she was glad to have noticed it before Margaret was in range.

'Hmmmm,' Margaret said. Kitt was sure she could almost see steam coming out of the woman's nose the way it did from cattle when they were about to charge. 'I pick my feet too far off the ground for that to have tripped me if you ask me.'

'I can only tell you what happened,' Kitt said. 'What you do with that information is quite beyond my control.'

Margaret glowered at Kitt, and rubbed her elbow, which

must have taken quite a jolt when she fell, even though she landed in the snow. Margaret was making a move to storm off without another word but before she could Kitt laid what continued to be her royal flush on the proverbial table.

'You did give me a terrible fright when you went down like that. I witnessed a death on Wednesday evening just gone at the Christmas Book Fair. I was just telling my friend Grace here all about it. A man went down right in front of me just as you did there.'

There was no mistaking that this caught Margaret's attention. She had been about to stride off but this stopped her. Slowly, she turned her head first towards Grace, then in the direction of Kitt and further narrowed her eyes. 'The Christmas Book Fair . . . You're not talking about the death of Leonard Bell, are you?'

'Why . . . yes,' Kitt said. 'I was at the reading he was giving when it happened. The most tragic thing, it really was. I'm so sorry, did you know Mr Bell?'

'Yes, I did,' she said. But she did not volunteer how she knew him. Kitt sighed inwardly. Maybe she wasn't going to have any more luck getting information out of Margaret Cryer than Halloran was out of Nathan Greene. Still, there was another arm to this plan if she really insisted on staying tight-lipped. 'Did you two know Leonard Bell?' Margaret fired back.

'No, I don't know him personally,' said Grace. 'I just read about what happened to him online, you know.'

'I didn't know Leonard specifically,' said Kitt. 'But I am acquainted with his widow, Eleanor.'

A bit of a sly answer, but not a complete untruth.

'Oh . . .' said Margaret, and her hard narrow eyes became more almond shaped at the mention of Bell's wife. Was that a sign of guilt? Or merely sympathy? 'And you say you saw him . . . die, Leonard?'

'Yes, as I say, I was at the book fair watching his performance of A Christmas Carol. On the front row, no less. It was the most distressing thing I've ever witnessed,' said Kitt. This wasn't strictly true. She'd actually be hard pressed to choose the most distressing thing she'd ever witnessed, especially since she'd started in the private investigation business. And some of Grace's spontaneous renditions of 'The Thong Song' were definitely up there. But she seemed to be getting Margaret on side and she needed to do whatever she could to get her to open up. Even if that required a little bit of exaggeration.

'I . . . I can imagine,' said Margaret, those hard green eyes lowered momentarily to the pavement.

'Yes, I can't really understand what Eleanor's going through, of course,' said Kitt. 'I don't know if you are in a romantic relationship yourself—'

'What business is it of yours if I am or not?' Margaret snapped, her eyes narrowing again as Kitt chided herself for getting overzealous and too personal too quickly with someone who was obviously of a cagey disposition.

'Oh, it certainly isn't any of my business,' Kitt said, hoping her simpering would placate Margaret somewhat. 'I was just saying that even if you do have a partner, as I do, it's difficult to imagine what it would be like to lose them under any circumstances, but particularly in the way that Eleanor has.'

'Oh, I see,' was all that Margaret offered.

'The sad thing about it all,' said Kitt, trying to keep the natural momentum of the conversation going, 'is that he wasn't very happy before he died. Apparently he'd been experiencing a lot of stress at work. His superiors were angry with him about something – not sure what as he worked for that military agency beyond the Clifton edge of town, you know? So the whole thing is probably top secret. But there was some big skirmish according to Eleanor. And apparently someone in the workplace had been making his life a misery.'

'What a terrible situation,' Grace said, shaking her head a bit too vigorously for Kitt's liking. Hopefully Margaret wouldn't notice that Grace's acting skills were subpar, to put it politely.

'Wh-what do you mean?' said Margaret. 'I mean, how? How had they been making his life a misery, exactly?'

'I . . . I'm afraid I don't know all the ins and outs,' said Kitt. 'I don't want to gossip about things that I don't have a good grasp of. But from what Eleanor could get out of Leonard, it was someone younger than him. Making threats, I think. Because they wanted his job or something. Or felt like they deserved more recognition. Apparently, it had been going on for some time and Leonard had very much taken it to heart.'

'He ... he had?' Margaret said, an unmistakable crack creeping into her voice now.

'Oh yes, from what Eleanor said, he came home miserable night after night. Nothing she said could console him. In light of how short Leonard's life turned out to be, she can't help but feel robbed that his last months were spent fretting over a problem at work that she couldn't even help him with. According to her, he would sit up late at night, alone, worrying about it all. There were even times when he wouldn't eat. Poor man. It's such a shame that the last few months he had here weren't happier for him. Such a terrible waste.'

Margaret had gone distinctly pale and was beginning to look somewhat unsteady on her feet.

'Oh God,' she said, clutching her stomach. 'I think I'm going to be sick.'

Just a few moments later, Margaret went stumbling towards some bushes at the back of the bingo hall while Kitt and Grace shot a look at each other. They could hear her retching between little stifled sobs.

Although Kitt had not quite expected such a violent physical reaction to what she was saying, even if Margaret was innocent of murder, she didn't have any regrets about laying it on thick. Kitt had seen enough death up close and personal to understand just how precious every experience on this planet was, even if it didn't feel very precious at the time. As Grace had said herself on their way to Eleanor's house, nobody has forever. Kitt was certainly not one for casting moral judgements on others but she had seen enough of Margaret Cryer, and heard enough about her too, to know that a little bit of a Scrooge-like epiphany wouldn't go amiss.

A minute later, Margaret had collected herself and walked back to where Kitt and Grace were standing, but she still looked very pale.

'I'm so sorry if anything I've said caused you to feel unwell,' said Kitt. 'It's just, when you said you knew Leonard I wanted to answer your question as thoroughly as possible. I should know not to talk about such morbid topics. I suppose I'm just still trying to process what happened. While also trying to support Eleanor as best I can.' Kitt paused then, and said the next sentence a little bit louder than necessary. 'I really don't know when to shut up.'

This was the agreed code phrase Kitt had exchanged with Joe before she had left to meet Grace and subsequently Margaret that morning. Like clockwork, he rounded a corner near the bingo hall and strode in a determined fashion in their direction. Rolo was pulling at the very short lead Joe had him on, his sharp ears pointed upward like antennas. From what Joe had told her, Kitt knew that Joe often used Rolo in his investigations as a sort of wing-man . . . or wing-hound, Kitt supposed. According to

Joe, people were certainly a lot less likely to cross Rolo than they were him.

'Ey up,' Kitt said. 'This fella looks like he means business.'

Margaret and Grace both turned in the direction of Joe. While this was a practised gesture from Grace, the frown on Margaret's face betrayed her natural confusion. There was no doubt that this tall, broad, suited man was heading straight for them. Kitt watched Margaret's eyebrows twitch as she tried to work out why.

'Margaret Cryer?' said Joe in a stern voice that wasn't at all like his usual gentle tenor. Rolo was straining at the lead, pulling hard in their direction. Kitt knew that this was Rolo just attempting to get to Grace and enjoy some much-desired fuss off her. But Margaret didn't know that. She took one look at the overly excited Rolo and stepped back two paces.

'I'll leave you to identify yourself before I identify myself,' Margaret said, shooting a scowl at Rolo, who let out a low growl in return. Tearing her eyes away from the dog, she then looked Joe up and down from his head to his toes. Give Margaret her credit, she was a lot more reserved and streetwise than poor Peter had been at the gates. Kitt wasn't sure exactly how long Margaret had worked for the Defence Medical Agency but it seemed she had taken their training on compartmentalising information to heart.

'Joe Golding,' he replied. 'I'm a private investigator consulting with the police on the matter of Leonard Bell's death. And I'm afraid I need to ask you a few questions.'

'Any questions on that matter need to go through my superior at the Defence Medical Agency, a Mr Nathan Greene,' said Margaret.

Damn, thought Kitt.

The plan had been to disorientate Margaret enough, in essence shame her enough, that she offered the information about her whereabouts on the night of Leonard's poisoning willingly. But it looked as though even throwing up in a hedge wasn't enough to make Margaret breach protocol.

'Yes, I'm aware of that, madam,' said Joe. 'But I wanted to come to you first as I was concerned the information I have about you might unnecessarily harm your career if it were shared with your superior.'

You can bet that sentence caught Margaret's attention. She looked at Joe sidelong. 'Harm my career? How?'

'Well madam,' said Joe, 'there have been reports from other employees that you subjected Mr Bell to what amounts to workplace bullying.'

Kitt watched Margaret's face carefully as Joe stretched the truth. Technically that information had come from Eleanor, but she didn't need to know that. If Margaret thought other members of the staff at the agency were mouthing off to officials about her, she might be more minded to do the same in a bid to defend herself.

'Oh dear,' said Kitt. 'You mean, the person who was making poor Leonard's life a misery . . . that was you?'

'That's speculation!' Margaret snapped in Kitt's direction.

Rolo growled again, showing his distaste for Margaret's tone, but this time the growl rumbled louder than it had before.

'You better have that thing under control,' Margaret said, waving a hand at Rolo as she turned back to Joe.

'He's perfectly under control,' said Joe. 'He's just doing his job. You see, some dogs are trained to detect drugs or money. This dog can tell if a person is lying.'

'That's ridiculous,' said Margaret. 'You can't train a dog to do that. I'm a biologist by training, I know that.'

'Then you'll know that when people are being deceitful, it creates physiological changes in their body. This dog is trained to detect those changes in voice, in sweat production, in breathing patterns.'

Margaret looked at Rolo and narrowed her eyes; she clearly wasn't convinced by Joe's completely fictitious story about Rolo's capabilities but she also wasn't looking so sure she could dismiss it anymore either.

'Who are the other employees who have been making accusations about me? I'd bet my hat that Kevin Ripley is one of them. He was always clubbing together with Leonard,' said Margaret.

Kitt did her best not to react to the fact that Margaret had just voluntarily made it clear there was bad blood between her and Ripley.

'I'm afraid all information given to me is confidential,' said Joe. 'As is anything you might tell me. So, I can't reveal the identities of the people who have come forward. And the thing is, we have to investigate anyone who may have had a problematic relationship with the deceased.'

'We had a few workplace disagreements, that's all,' said Margaret, holding her nose in the air in such a manner that it was clear to Kitt she was rewriting history. She was a little too adamant that their interactions were no big deal but Kitt, Grace and Joe knew better.

'I am sure that was all it was,' said Joe. 'And the truth be told, I have a young daughter who wants to get into science and we're keenly aware of some of the barriers she's going to face as a woman in that kind of environment. So, I suppose you might say I'm particularly sensitive to harming a woman's career in the STEM industry.'

'I . . . I . . . see,' Margaret said, softening at the story Kitt, Grace and Joe had cooked up between themselves via text message earlier that morning.

'So, if you wish, I can take this to your superior directly,' Joe went on. 'But I was concerned about sharing some of the things people have said about you, likely out of spite or sheer jealousy, with someone who is going to determine the future of your career, not to mention your pay grade.'

Margaret was quiet for a moment and then in an almost inaudible voice asked: 'What is it you want to know?'

'All I need to put these ridiculous claims to rest is your whereabouts a week ago today between the hours of six p.m. and ten p.m.,' said Joe. 'If you give me that, I can quietly look into it and Nathan Greene never needs to know about any of the things people are saying. I'm sure you were more than justified in anything you said to Leonard Bell. It's not easy being a woman in that kind of a workplace, but I'm concerned that your superiors may view things differently in light of Bell's death.'

Again Margaret thought quietly for a moment before answering. 'I will tell you, but it will need to be over here' – she paused to shoot a stern look at Kitt and Grace – 'in private . . . and without that . . . animal panting in my face.'

'Very well,' Joe said, gesturing over to the grassy area that was still covered in slowly melting snow. 'Would you be so kind as to hold my dog for a moment, madam?' Joe said to Grace.

'Not a problem at all,' Grace returned with a knowing smile.

Before Margaret walked over to talk to Joe, she turned to Kitt and said something that surprised her. 'Please don't tell Eleanor that I had disagreements with her husband before he passed away.'

Kitt cleared her throat and gave Margaret a stern look. 'I see no reason to make Eleanor feel worse about anything right now. Let's just say that it's water under the proverbial bridge on the understanding that you won't do anything like it again.'

Margaret's face twisted into yet another scowl. 'I can't make any promises like that. Who knows who will get in my way? What am I supposed to do, just lie down and let people walk all over me? Best I can do is tell you I'll try.'

With that she followed Joe over to a quiet area on the grass, some twenty feet away from where Kitt and Grace were standing.

'What did you think of that performance?' Grace said when she was sure that Margaret and Joe were well out of earshot.

Kitt gently shook her head and pressed her lips together. 'I don't know,' she said looking at Margaret's pale face. 'I just don't know.'

CHAPTER TWENTY-ONE

'Now then, pet, good to see you're still alive,' Halloran said an hour later as he walked through the door at the agency to find Kitt, Grace and Joe sitting around Kitt's desk. There was one other person that Halloran had not been expecting – Kevin Ripley.

Kitt had to bite her bottom lip to keep from laughing at Halloran's reaction once he realised Ripley was in attendance. His tart comment about how little they'd seen of each other in the last couple of days was a little bit insensitive when there was a man sitting opposite Kitt whose number could be up at any moment. Of course, it wasn't really funny. In fact the whole situation was desperately sad. But Kitt had developed such a dark sense of humour over the time she'd been investigating, merely in order to survive from one case to the next, that she couldn't help but be tickled by just how poor Halloran's choice of words were at this juncture.

'Oh – er,' Halloran said. Kitt wasn't sure she'd seen him this awkward in the whole decade she'd been with him. 'I'm sorry, Kevin, I didn't mean. I didn't know you were . . . I just meant I hadn't seen a lot of Kitt. I really should've thought about the wording there. I'm . . . I'm very sorry.'

Kevin offered Halloran a wry smile. 'I assure you, right now nothing can make me forget that my next moment might be my last. I don't think you should worry too much about censoring yourself.'

'I understand you had a bit of a showdown with Nathan Greene when you were last in at the agency,' said Halloran.

'Yes, since I might soon suffer the same fate as Leo, they've stopped short of firing me for coming to you with all the information about the toxin. But they don't want me any-where near that place. Of course, I told them I couldn't be happier to be out of there. The last thing I want to be doing with what are potentially my last days on this planet is spending them in the very place responsible for my predic-ament. I have instead taken the time to wander the snowy streets of the city and take in all the Christmas cheer. And I've spent some time with a special lady friend of mine.'

'I'm glad you've got someone to be close with at a time like this,' said Kitt. 'But let's not give up hope yet that you'll still be here next Christmas.'

'Does that mean you've got some solid leads?' said Halloran.

'Well,' Kitt said, expertly avoiding Ripley's eye since nothing at this moment was particularly certain. 'We might be onto something with a disgruntled employee who seemed to have it in for Leonard and Ripley. She was with her boyfriend on the night we think Leonard was poisoned.'

'Did her alibi check out?' said Halloran.

'I don't know yet, we're just figuring out how to approach the boyfriend because he's a person of interest too. He was dismissed from the Defence Medical Agency a few months back and he did not leave on good terms. It's possible the two of them could have planned the whole thing between them.'

'I've got a note of their names from what you told me on the phone,' said Halloran. 'I'll get one of the team to look into their financials and phone records whenever they get a chance, see if anything suspicious is going on.'

'You might have a job on your hands with the boyfriend,' said Joe. 'From what Kevin's told us, he's lived largely off-grid since the agency dismissed him.'

'Yes, that's right, I'm afraid,' said Ripley. 'As I've told Kitt, I do know where he lives so I can give you that much. But I suspect he's smart enough not to leave any digital footprints for you to find.'

'This guy is sounding more suspicious by the minute. We'll start with Margaret's records, there may be a red flag in there that gives us leverage to bring one or both of them in for questioning under caution,' said Halloran.

'Thanks Mal,' said Kitt. 'Margaret Cryer was a bit of a funny character. Sort of slippery. I couldn't get a handle on her. And her boyfriend doesn't sound particularly well-balanced.'

'I'm happy to look into it. Everything else we've tried has got us exactly nowhere,' said Halloran.

'The agency aren't playing ball, then,' said Ripley. 'Wish I could say I was surprised.'

'I'm sorry Kevin,' said Halloran. 'I know what's at stake for you but I have to be honest. Every attempt to get information from the Defence Medical Agency has been fruitless. We've tried going to Nathan Greene direct. We've tried going above him and around him to other agencies that have relationships with them. It's a brick wall at every pass. All I've actually asked for, besides preliminary interviews about the toxin, is TTYX8.'

'What's that?' asked Joe.

'It's the report that me and Leo wrote about the toxin,' said Ripley. 'The one we submitted to Nathan Greene the night the toxin was stolen.'

'If that report did spur someone to steal the toxin and the antidote and then go on to poison two people, it's a vital piece of evidence,' said Halloran. 'But Greene is smart. He won't let me near it.'

At this juncture, the door opened and Eleanor bustled in out of the cold and sleet. 'Hello, oh, I hope I'm not interrupting anything,' she said, at once taking note of the fact that there was quite a gathering of people around Kitt's desk.

'We're just discussing the case,' said Kitt. 'Did you think of something else you wanted to tell us?'

'I'm afraid not,' said Eleanor. 'I just came into town for the first time since ... well, you know, and curiosity got the better of me about how you were getting on with everything. I just wondered if you were any closer to finding the antidote for poor Kevin here – hello love.'

Kitt smiled. Eleanor was doing well to think of anything besides her own grief just then. But then, she had underlined that Ripley was a good friend to her so she was likely anxious about whether or not she was about to lose him too.

'The agency have been less than forthcoming, and that's putting it politely,' said Kitt.

Eleanor shook her head and tears rose to her eyes. 'I'm sorry,' she said. 'I don't mean to waste your time when every minute counts but I just had to ask. I really don't know how they do it, those agency bods. How they can be so unfeeling. They know what my Leo went through. That Kevin will suffer the same way if they don't cooperate. Why are they doing this?'

'I don't know,' said Halloran. 'In fact the truth is I don't know exactly what they are *doing*. For all I know they really do have no information about what happened to your husband. But they won't let me at the document that would prove it.'

'Hmmm,' said Ripley.

'That sounded like more than just a casual "Hmmmm",' said Joe. 'What are you thinking?'

'I'm thinking that although they don't want me in that building they may not have had time to revoke my clearance yet, what with all the questions they're likely having to answer about this whole episode. Not to mention any lengths they are going to in order to cover up what they've done, or somebody working for them who has gone rogue has done.'

'You're . . . you're not thinking of going back in there, are you?' said Eleanor, her eyes widening at the thought.

'The way they're stonewalling Inspector Halloran, I don't think I have much choice,' said Ripley. 'If I'd known how crucial the report me and Leo wrote would be at the time, I'd have printed a copy. They may well have destroyed it already, but if it is still in existence, I could try and get a copy of it.'

'You . . . you really think you could?' said Halloran. 'Because right now I don't see any other way of me getting my hands on that report. I can't tell Greene what I suspect, because then he'll know that I might be coming after him. It'll tip off the person who might quickly become a chief suspect.'

'I understand your reservations,' said Ripley. 'When it comes to Greene, I think it's best only to disclose what you have to. It may not be him behind the poisonings. I certainly hope not given how long we've worked together. But he might be subservient to the person who is behind them. I appreciate that it's just my word against the agency's unless we can get a copy of that report. I should have printed that off instead of copying my diaries and lab notes. I wasn't thinking straight.'

'That's understandable given what you're going through,' said Halloran. 'But if yours and Leonard's recommendation to cease research on the toxin, and your veiled threat to go to the press about it, was a factor in what's happened to you both, I need that report to prove what was said and done at certain times. I've got a strong feeling someone in that agency knows something they're not telling us. It's really the only way the toxin and the antidote could have been stolen. None of the council CCTV footage brought up any vehicles heading to or from the facility in the hours you gave us. The exception was a couple of lorries that were using the road to bypass the city. We've tracked down the drivers via their numberplates and they were on the job delivering goods to another part of the country. Their stories check out with their employers.'

'Oh Kevin, are you sure about this?' said Eleanor. 'After what happened to Leo, I don't trust them. What if they hold you there or . . . worse?'

'The truth is, Nell, I'm dead anyway without that report,' Ripley said, though his voice faltered as he did so. 'I can't promise anything but we're running out of time, and options. I can only try. If I can't access it for any reason, then we're no worse off than we were before.'

'I suppose that's true,' said Halloran. 'I also did try and get CCTV footage from the Book and Candle.'

'No dice?' said Joe.

Halloran shook his head. 'They only keep footage for forty-eight hours, so there's no chance of recovering what happened in the bar that Friday night.'

'Well, short of that, we'll go down there ourselves and try and find out who was on shift that night,' said Kitt. 'They might have seen something. Or they might recognise somebody on our suspect list if we show them photos. I want to talk to Tyler Simmons first, but after that we'll definitely pay a visit to the Book and Candle.'

'I would have had an officer down to the Book and Candle myself if I could have spared the resources,' said Halloran. 'I've been up against tough constraints before but this is something else. There are now news crews camped outside the station – it's a battle to get in or out every time.'

'As if things aren't bad enough without having the press on your case,' said Kitt. 'But at least one person knows what happened in the Book and Candle that night, assuming that's where the poisoning took place. And as we both know, nothing much happens in this city without somebody noticing something. So we'll go down to the bar and try our luck while Kevin goes back to the facility and you see about Margaret Cryer's data.'

'It will feel good to be able to try and do something, even if I fail,' said Ripley. 'The worst thing in the world is waiting around helplessly, wondering if when the clock strikes the next hour I'll still be here.'

'Oh Kevin,' Eleanor said. 'I'm so sorry you're going through this.'

Kitt looked at Halloran and they exchanged a pained expression. Over the years they had been investigating they'd both saved their fair share of lives. But there was no denying there had been casualties too. People they couldn't save. Kitt could see the worry in Halloran's eyes, the same worry that was turning her own stomach over and over. The fear that Kevin Ripley might be the next name on that list.

CHAPTER TWENTY-TWO

'No answer at the front door,' Joe said over comms. 'And no sign of anyone. I'm going to try wandering round the back in the spirit of seeming very eager to clear Margaret's name.'

'Be careful, Joe,' Kitt returned. 'We don't know what the hell might be back there.'

'The look of this place is already giving me the creeps,' said Joe. 'From what glimpses I can see through the windows, Simmons has got more taxidermy hanging on his wall than a natural history museum. No reminder to be careful required.'

Before Ripley had left their company, Kitt had been sure to get Tyler Simmons's address from him. The second they'd said their goodbyes to Halloran, Eleanor and Ripley, Joe had driven Kitt and Grace out to Simmons's house on the southerly edge of the city in Fulford. Calling the place a house, however, was a little bit generous.

Shack would be a more appropriate noun, though

admittedly the place did look plumbed and probably did have electrics.

Still, as Grace had so succinctly put it when they had first pulled up, the place looked like a killer's lair if ever she saw one. In truth, Kitt hadn't known there were properties like this one still standing.

After what Ripley had told them about how unpredictable Simmons could be, Kitt was determined to have strength in numbers on her side and insisted they stuck together as a trio. Mercifully, now that Margaret had given Simmons as her alibi, they actually had a legitimate reason to drive out and talk to him.

There was just one problem.

Kitt and Grace had pretended earlier not to have any affiliation with Joe when they were talking with Margaret. There was little doubt that Simmons would tell all about the follow-up visit from Joe and she would be sure to recognise Kitt and Grace from their descriptions. Both Cryer and Simmons worked for a military organisation so it was worth betting that their attention to detail was keen and nothing would be left out. As such, it had seemed prudent to send Joe in solo in the first instance, keeping him on comms the whole time.

That decision seemed less like a good idea, however, when Kitt heard Joe's next utterances.

'Oh my God,' Joe said. 'There are spring traps in the long

grasses out here. You know, the kind with teeth. Are they even legal?'

'Joe, don't take another step,' Kitt said, her breath quickening. 'You might be able to see some of them but there may be others better concealed. Wait there, we'll come and get you.'

'No, it's OK. There are paving stones leading up to the back door. Presumably so Simmons himself doesn't accidentally step on one going in and out of the house. He's cut himself a clear path. I'm going to follow it and at least knock at the door. I did tell Margaret that I'd be following up on her alibi so he's probably expecting a visit.'

'That's what I'm worried about,' said Kitt, glancing over at Grace.

'I didn't think those spring traps even existed anymore, except in horror films,' said Grace. 'Joe's right, they can't be legal, can they?'

'I don't know,' said Kitt.

'You mean, you haven't read the latest non-fiction tome on the history of spring traps? Tut tut, Kitt. You really are falling behind with your reading.'

'Thank you, Grace,' Kitt said. She knew her assistant was only goading her but just how far she'd fallen behind with her reading was a bit of a sore spot. She hadn't even managed to enjoy the Christmas Book Fair without someone being murdered. 'You know, it wouldn't surprise me if there were a way of legally setting those things on your property.

I doubt Simmons is daft enough to be so blatantly on the wrong side of the law.'

Kitt waited for Grace to respond, but she didn't. When she turned to look at her colleague, she noticed that the smile that had previously crossed her lips had faded. She was looking in Kitt's direction but not right at her. Her stare was fixed on something past her. Something out through the window. And her eyes were widening with every second she looked at it.

'What is it?' Kitt said, turning her head in the direction of whatever had caught Grace's attention.

'Someone's there,' Grace said, her voice a sharp whisper.

'Someone's where?' Joe said over comms.

'This side of the property,' Grace said, 'up in what looks like a hide for bird watching.'

Kitt saw what Grace was describing then and her breath caught in her throat.

There was somebody there alright.

From the build, Kitt instantly recognised the figure as a man. Due to the fading daylight, the man appeared as nothing more than a black silhouette against a greying sky. Kitt couldn't be sure, not really, but from the position the man was standing in, it looked to her like he was staring straight at them and had been all along.

Kitt barely dared take another breath as the dark figure began to climb down from the hide which had been heavily camouflaged with foliage. The second he had finished his descent he began to walk slowly towards them.

'Joe, I think you better get back here, right now,' said Kitt, her voice wavering as the unknown man advanced towards the car.

CHAPTER TWENTY-THREE

The man reached the car before Joe did, standing about a foot from the driver's side. Kitt had slid into the front seat after Joe had left to see if anyone was in the house. Now that he was up close, Kitt could see that he matched the description Ripley had given them: a tall, broad man in his mid-thirties with a thick brown moustache and a crop of hair to match. Thus, this man was most likely Simmons.

Rolo was in the boot of the car and was growling at the new potential threat standing outside the vehicle. Looking at Simmons for herself, Kitt couldn't blame Rolo for his immediately defensive reaction.

He stared at her through the window. He wore a pair of camo trousers and a pair of heavy black boots that looked like they could snap a bone with one stomp. Given that they were essentially trespassing on his property, Kitt would have expected a frown or some other facial tic that indicated anger or agitation. But Simmons's face was completely without expression to the point that Kitt felt he was looking through her rather than at her. And somehow, that was worse, far worse than if he had exploded in a fury over their invasion of his privacy.

For a moment, Kitt didn't move. She just stared back at Simmons through the glass. Wondering if the car door was locked or if, should Simmons choose, he could pull the door open and make a grab for her. She didn't really know why she thought that was a likely turn of events. Perhaps simply because Simmons was intimidating to look at. Whatever the reason, she couldn't shake the feeling that it wasn't safe to even crack the window right now, let alone blithely step outside to have a conversation about alibis.

'What should we do?' Grace said in a whisper that Kitt could only just hear even though her assistant was sitting right next to her.

Mercifully, Kitt didn't have to formulate an answer to that question as Joe had finally made it back to the car and made a move on her behalf.

'Mr Simmons?' Joe said, while Kitt wondered if Joe was rueing the decision to leave Rolo in the boot instead of walking him up to the property. The dog was still growling, the low rumble adding to Kitt's sense of increasing dread.

'Who's asking?' Kitt heard Simmons say, his voice muffled by the car window. Though he answered Joe, he did not look at him, but kept his eyes fixed firmly on Kitt.

'Joe Golding, from Golding Associates. I spoke with Margaret Cryer earlier today and—'

'And you weren't the only one, were you?' said Simmons.

'I'm sorry?' Joe said.

'She talked to Margaret too,' Simmons said, nodding at Kitt. He still hadn't looked once at Joe. His eyes had remained on the car. 'And 'er as well,' Simmons added, waving a hand in the direction of Grace.

'They were talking to Margaret when I located her, yes,' Joe said, in what Kitt thought was quite an expert way of skirting around the issue at hand.

'And why are they 'ere now?' said Simmons.

'Well.' Joe paused, clearly weighing up his options. What would make Simmons more angry? If he told him the truth or if he concocted some kind of lie? 'Alright, the truth is these two ladies are my associates.'

'I know,' said Simmons. 'I've 'eard every word you've said to each other since you got 'ere. You 'aven't been very kind about my taste in interior decorating.'

Kitt barely dared take a breath. She noticed then something attached to Simmons's belt that she hadn't seen before. Some kind of radio receiver. He must have found their comms channel and been listening in the whole time. Kitt was trying to go over what information they'd shared without realising someone else was listening in, but she was so tired she couldn't get straight what had been said on the way to the property and what information they'd exchanged since they switched to comms. Thank God Joe had opted to go for the truth. Goodness knew how Simmons would have reacted if he'd caught them in a lie.

'You used these associates to manipulate Margaret earlier today,' Simmons said. By now Kitt was praying this guy would look somewhere, anywhere, instead of at her. But she wasn't going to be the one to break eye contact.

'Not at all,' said Joe. 'My associates approached Margaret informally in the hopes of keeping the conversation quiet and cordial. Everything my colleagues told her this morning is true. They are acquainted with Leonard's widow, Eleanor, and Kitt there did see Leonard Bell die.'

There was a pause then as Simmons seemed to be computing Joe's words.

'Mr Simmons,' Joe said.

It took a second but Simmons at last dragged his eyes off Kitt and turned his head to look at Joe.

'We're really not trying to cause any trouble here,' Joe said. 'We are simply trying to rule Margaret out of the investigation after other people we've spoken to have flagged that her behaviour towards the deceased was less than civil.'

Simmons gritted his teeth. 'Civil? What good is it being civil to anyone who works in that place?'

'What do you mean?' said Joe.

'What I mean,' Simmons said, raising his voice. 'Is that they're all a bunch of charlatans. Pretending to be doing their best for crown and country when really they're just on a sick power trip.'

Kitt wondered if Simmons realised they were actively looking for people who had a negative relationship with the agency and that this particular line of conversation was only increasing the suspicions they already had about both him and Cryer.

'They're not busying themselves in that building by curing cancer,' said Simmons, continuing to speak a lot louder than necessary, though for Kitt and Grace the sound was still somewhat muffled by the car window. 'They think they're gods, the ones who work there. They think that they get to say who lives and who dies. I'm glad I got out when I did.'

Joe flashed the quickest of glances in Kitt's direction. They both knew, from what Ripley had told them, that Simmons had not walked away from his position at the Defence Medical Agency. He'd been dismissed under a black cloud. Was he trying to rewrite history just to save face or was he hiding something? Was he, in essence, trying to make it seem that he wanted nothing to do with the agency when, from what Kitt had heard, he had a dark obsession with them?

'I must admit,' said Joe, 'even the thought of the place gives me the creeps.'

The sharpness to Simmons's face seemed to soften a bit at this and it was enough to embolden Kitt to open the window a crack.

'I have to agree with you both on that,' said Kitt. 'I'm scared of what they might be doing behind those gates.'

'You don't know the 'alf of it,' Simmons said, his body tensing as he said those words. As if he was remembering something that he wished he could forget. 'Anyone who's come into contact with them isn't safe. Just because you get out of the gates without any 'arm coming for you, doesn't mean they won't come for you later.'

Simmons stopped what he was saying then and looked this way and that around the garden. As though he expected to be apprehended by a military employee in that very moment.

'If they're as bad as you say,' said Kitt, 'then they won't think twice about framing Margaret for what happened to Leonard Bell, especially if they're responsible for what happened to him. And they might even try to drag you into it too.'

'I'd put nothing past them,' said Simmons, speaking at a much more reasonable volume.

'Then you must help us,' said Kitt. 'Otherwise, they're going to get away with murder.'

'They already 'ave,' said Simmons in a cool, detached tone that made the hairs on Kitt's arms stand up. 'Many times,' he added.

'Well, it's got to stop,' said Kitt, quite unsure what to believe at this point in the proceedings. It was clear that Simmons marched to the beat of his own drum, but that alone didn't make him a murderer. Perhaps rather than being a murderer, Simmons knew the true, quite sinister, inner workings of the Defence Medical Agency. He wasn't a very credible source, and perhaps the agency relied on the fact that he wouldn't be taken seriously by many, especially after being dismissed under dishonourable circumstances.

Simmons fixed his eyes on Kitt again and for a moment she regretted saying anything. The man's dark brown eyes bore into her and they were filled with a mixture of fury and hopelessness. 'There's no stopping an organisation like that. You're out of your depth,' he said, before adding, 'We're all out of our depth. We just need to steer clear and pray what 'appened to Leonard Bell doesn't 'appen to us.'

There was a brief pause while Kitt, Grace and Joe tried to digest what Simmons was insinuating. From his words, it did seem as though he believed the agency was directly responsible for Leonard Bell's poisoning. Which would mean that they were responsible for poisoning Ripley too. But why? Was it really all because they'd vaguely suggested they might go to the press about the toxin if the higher-ups continued to work on it?

''Ere, what you doing?' Simmons said, when he caught Joe pointing his phone at him. Kitt knew exactly what Joe was doing. He was trying to get a clear photograph of Simmons. They didn't currently have one and a photograph would come in handy to show any potential future interviewees.

'Just bringing up the information Margaret gave me on

my phone,' Joe said, in an easy enough manner that Simmons seemed to believe him. 'I agree with you that the agency seem a threatening bunch but I still have to check Margaret's alibi so she can be eliminated from the investigation.

'Alright, then,' said Simmons. 'It were last Friday, is that right?'

'That's right,' said Joe. He went to ask a question – likely what time Margaret arrived to see him – but he was cut off.

'Margaret was with me all of last Friday night,' said Simmons. 'She came around straight after work, so she was 'ere from about five thirty in the evening. We went to the local chippie to get some tea and then came back 'ere to . . . play chess.'

Kitt strongly suspected that the playing chess part was a euphemism but that wasn't a thread she wanted to tug at any further.

'What time did Margaret leave?' asked Joe.

'She didn't,' Simmons said, and slowly a toothy grin that quickly turned into a leer spread across his face. 'Not till about midday on the Saturday.'

'Well, that matches what Margaret told us, Mr Simmons, thank you, I'm grateful for your help. We shan't trouble you any longer. I'm glad we could clear all that up for Margaret,' said Joe, making his way towards the driver side of the car. Kitt did not relish having to get out of the vehicle to slip once again into the back seat but she did so as quickly as possible and ensured the door lock was enabled once she had.

Simmons didn't say any more but the leer he'd been wearing had settled into a self-satisfied grin in the time it took Joe to start the engine and back out of Simmons's property.

Once they were out of view of the house, Kitt tapped Grace on the shoulder and made a show of turning off her comms. Grace followed suit and when they stopped at the next traffic light, Joe did the same. Only then did anyone dare to speak and it was Grace who first broke the silence.

'Just because Cryer and Simmons have alibis in each other, doesn't mean they aren't in on it together,' she said.

'My thoughts exactly,' said Kitt, while wondering what the police would find on Simmons's property should they have the warrant to search it. From the behaviour she'd just seen and the degree to which he had it out for the Defence Medical Agency, she'd wager they'd find a lot more than a few spring traps.

CHAPTER TWENTY-FOUR

Though Kitt, Joe and Grace were all sufficiently rattled after their strange encounter with Tyler Simmons, there was no time to sit with a soothing cup of tea and collect themselves. Grace, due to her being, to the best of Kitt's knowledge, the most efficient cyberstalker in the county of Yorkshire, returned to the agency to see what else, if anything, she could turn up on Nathan Greene, Margaret Cryer and Tyler Simmons. Meanwhile Kitt and Joe headed straight out to the Book and Candle Bar, the assumed location of Bell's poisoning.

Hunting down information on three individuals who worked for a military agency – one of whom had since been dismissed – would likely be a formidable challenge even for someone as shamelessly social media-orientated as Grace. Still, with the churn in Kitt's stomach only increasing in speed every time she thought about Ripley's watery eyes, she was willing to try anything to find out who had stolen this toxin and antidote. Although her sense of curiosity was legendary among her friends, at this stage in the game, Kitt didn't even much care about finding out why the antidote had been stolen. She just wanted it back to make sure Kevin Ripley lived to see this Christmas and the next.

A little shudder ran through Kitt as she stepped away from the icy paving of St Helen's Square and into the Book and Candle Bar. The strange dream she had had the night before seemed all the more vivid and present as she did so. She remembered again how Wilkie Collins had pointed his old, withered fingers at the large glass frontage. Filled with a Christmas tree that was itself an impressive upcycling project as it was made entirely of stacked books topped with an ornamental star. Kitt resisted the temptation to get a closer look at the book spines. She was here for one reason and one reason only: to find out if anyone on their suspect list had been in that bar last Friday night. And if so, if they had been witnessed doing anything untoward.

'I can see why you've got a soft spot for this place,' said Joe, 'the decor is a librarian's dream.'

'Yes,' said Kitt. 'I didn't want to say anything about it in front of Halloran – I get enough stick about my book habit from him as it is – but I'm quite friendly with the owner here so hopefully it won't take us too long to find out if there's some information to be had.'

Joe smiled. 'Why am I not surprised you're on a first-name basis with the staff here?'

'And it's exactly that kind of comment that makes me keep these things to myself,' Kitt said, returning Joe's smile.

The pair of them walked towards the bar and approached a young woman who was bartending. She wore a Santa hat and a red pinafore dress to celebrate the season and, one of the many reasons Kitt liked to visit this bar, she greeted them with a broad smile that made her feel as though she was actually happy to see them. Not all hospitality staff across the city were quite so welcoming.

'What can I get for you?' said the bartender.

'Actually, I was wondering if Flick's around?' said Kitt.

'Can I ask what it's regarding?' said the bartender. 'She doesn't accept visits from sales reps without an appointment if it's a product you want to show her.'

Kitt chuckled. 'I'm not selling anything. I'm Kitt, a regular customer turned friend.'

'Oh,' said the bartender with a blush in her cheeks. 'Sorry, I'm new so I'm still getting used to recognising the regulars. She's in the back office, I'll just nip and let her know you're here.'

'Not a problem, and thank you,' Kitt said.

A few moments later, Felicity, or Flick to her friends, emerged from the back office and smiled when she saw Kitt on the other side of the bar.

'Ey up lass, haven't seen you in a few weeks,' said Flick, grabbing a fistful of her black hair and pushing it over the shoulders of her thick jumper which was a dazzling shade of cobalt blue. It contrasted beautifully with the thick gold eyeshadow she was wearing, likely applied in a bid to keep herself looking a bit festive in case the bar got busy and she had to serve some drinks.

Flick looked Joe up and down and raised her eyebrows in approval. 'Does Halloran know about your new fella?'

'It's been a busy time at the agency,' said Kitt with a smile. 'This is a colleague of mine, Joe Golding.'

'Pleasure to meet you, Joe,' Flick said, her eyes not leaving his as she flashed a knowing smile.

Joe, never one to invite attention, even if he might want to, smiled and gave her a polite nod in return.

'I'm sorry that I don't have any time for a proper catch-up,' said Kitt. 'I'm sure you're run off your feet anyway on the approach to Christmas. But I'm working on a very sensitive case at the moment, the same one the police have been in touch with you about?'

At this, the smile on Flick's face faded at once. She looked from side to side to make sure nobody could overhear. It wasn't too busy for a Friday afternoon two days before Christmas, but there were a few groups on the surrounding tables and Kitt thought it was more than understandable that Flick didn't want anyone to overhear, given the nature of this dreadful business.

'We've been lucky the media haven't caught on that the poisoning happened here. God knows what it would do to the business. Don't get me wrong, I am absolutely mortified that something like that took place on our premises. But it certainly didn't have anything to do with myself or the staff,' Flick said, fear flaring in her dark hooded eyes.

'Of course it didn't,' said Kitt, understanding completely why Flick was so keen to avoid any negative press. Just because someone had taken it upon themselves to commit a terrible act of cruelty, didn't mean that Flick's business should go under for it.

'You might believe that, but anyone who heard the headlines of what happened here a week ago might think differently. We've had to report the incident to the Food Hygiene Commission and they'll be doing a routine inspection following the incident to make sure everything is above board here. If we keep it quiet we're going to do very well. It's not what I need right now, I can tell you. But then, I feel terrible for even thinking that way when that poor chap lost his life.'

'It's perfectly normal to think like that when something threatens your livelihood. You can guarantee I won't be saying anything to anyone,' said Kitt. 'But I do need to ask you a couple of questions about that Friday night, if you can spare a few minutes?'

Flick nodded. 'What can I do to help? I already told the police that unfortunately we only keep the CCTV for forty-eight hours.'

'I know, that's about the same as most businesses, to be honest,' said Kitt. 'Were you working last Friday night?'

'I was on the bar. It's been very busy on Friday and Saturday nights in the run-up to Christmas so it's all hands on deck,' said Flick. 'I already questioned the other members of staff who were on shift myself to ask if they noticed anything strange, or anyone shifty hanging about, but we were all run off our feet that night so there was no time to notice anything except what the next order was from the next customer.'

Kitt nodded. 'I've done a few shifts behind the bar myself, I know how it can get in busy periods. These are the three people who were sitting at the table where the poisoning took place,' she said, laying out photographs of Leonard Bell, Kevin Ripley and Eleanor Meadows one at a time. 'Do you remember them?'

'I think I served them a couple of times when this guy came to the bar for a round,' Flick said, pointing at the photo of Ripley.

'And you didn't notice anyone else around him, maybe standing behind him?' said Joe. 'Or anyone who seemed to be watching him?'

Flick shook her head. 'I'm sorry, when you're serving a customer in a crowd like that, you're just focused on what they're asking you for and getting it to them as quickly as you can. It's pretty impossible to notice anything else because it's so rowdy in here when it gets busy.'

'I understand. Let me show you some other people,' said Kitt, laying out photographs of first Jordan Ascher, then

Margaret Cryer and then Nathan Greene on the bar. She also asked Joe to show Flick the photo of Tyler Simmons he had taken on his phone.

'Do you recognise anyone? Could they have been in the bar that night?' Kitt said.

Flick looked along the row of photographs and then at the one on Joe's phone. Her eyes then hopped back to the last photograph lying on the bar.

'Him,' she said, pointing at the photograph of Nathan Greene.

'He was . . . in the bar on Friday?' said Kitt.

'I don't know that for sure,' said Flick. 'But he is a regular here. We're not on a first-name basis but I've definitely served him a few times. He's always alone when he comes. Has a particular drink that he likes, just the one every time, and then leaves. I don't remember serving him on that Friday but that doesn't mean he wasn't here. That night was so busy it's really more of a blur than anything else. One of the other bartenders might have served him and I wouldn't have known a thing about it. Why? Who is he?'

'Someone of interest in this case,' Kitt said. It wasn't fair to say anything more than that until she had concrete evidence. Even if this was looking more and more like the Defence Medical Agency, or someone working there, had been behind what happened to Bell and Ripley. 'And you definitely can't remember serving him on the Friday?'

'No,' said Flick, 'I'm afraid not. The most I can say is that he visits us here for a drink on a semi-regular basis.'

'Alright,' said Kitt. 'I mustn't push you anymore or you might start believing you did serve him when you didn't.'

Flick chuckled. 'My mind has been so all over the place since I heard about the poisoning that it's fair to say I'm not really with it right now, so yes, don't give me too much of the third degree if you want reliable information.'

'I'm really very sorry that this horrible thing had to happen here, Flick,' said Kitt. 'We'll be very discreet in our investigation. I think most people are associating the poisoning with the book fair, so you might yet get out of this with your business reputation unscathed.'

'Here's hoping for small mercies,' said Flick.

At this juncture, Kitt's mobile rang and she excused herself from the bar, leaving Joe and Flick to chat between themselves. A turn of events that saw the smile return to Flick's face.

Kitt could see by the name on the phone's display that it was Ripley putting in a call. She quickly hit the answer button before her mobile had a chance to divert him to voicemail.

'Kevin? It's Kitt speaking,' she said.

'Kitt,' Ripley's voice said in return. His voice sounded weak. Was the toxin starting to take effect on him or was it just a bad signal?'

'Are you ... alright?' Kitt asked, not sure if she really wanted the answer.

'I'm not sure I could really describe myself as alright at present,' said Ripley. 'I managed to get into the facility. Made some excuse about having left some personal effects in my desk drawer. As I assumed, they haven't had time to revoke my clearance but it's no good anyway.'

'Why not?' said Kitt, her heart sinking at the prospect of them hitting yet another dead end in the case.

'My own report has been classified to a level where even I can't access it,' said Ripley. 'Do you know how rare that is? I wrote the document and despite having my normal clearance I can't get it . . . I will give you three guesses as to who has changed the status of the document to classified.'

'Nathan Greene,' Kitt said without missing a beat.

CHAPTER TWENTY-FIVE

Kitt had to admit that, despite the amount of anguish it could cause on a personal level, there were perks to having a romantic relationship with a police officer when you were a private investigator. All of those worries about whether your partner would come home on any given night, or whether they might return home battered and bruised from some violent incident that had escalated beyond their control, were offset when they could help you track down a person of interest on a case. Even if only because that particular individual was of great interest to them too.

Kitt and Halloran sat in Halloran's car which was parked outside Greene's home address on the outskirts of the city near Holgate Windmill, a five-sailed tower mill lovingly restored by a local preservation society. The pair had already waited twenty minutes for Greene to emerge, so by their calculations it really couldn't be much longer before the man in question showed himself. Halloran had already ascertained, from the hours Greene was available to speak to him on the phone, that he didn't leave for the facility until after midday and worked into the early evening. Since he had point blank refused to hold an interview with Halloran in person and Halloran had no concrete grounds on which to arrest him, catching him off-guard and trying to persuade him to cooperate was the only card they really had left to play.

After Kitt had relayed to Halloran that Nathan Greene was a regular at the Book and Candle Bar, he had set Banks to work looking for any discrepancies in his phone and financial records. Since this left him without a partner to have a run at Greene, Kitt had tagged along. Considering she was conducting a parallel investigation it made sense, and Halloran had been able to square it with his superiors due to the complexity of the case and their particularly stretched resources.

'What are we going to do if he won't talk?' said Kitt. It was uncharacteristic of her to look on the negative side but she had rather hoped all along that the last place this investigation would lead would be here. To the doorstep of a man they couldn't touch. Couldn't pressure. Couldn't even arrest for not cooperating with the investigation. Men like Greene were protected to the hilt. And, of course, if he was behind the poisoning of both Bell and Ripley then he would have been counting on that fact to make sure he got away with it. For all Kitt knew, Nathan Greene's actions had been sanctioned by his superiors. In which case he wouldn't even consider poisoning Bell and Ripley as murder. Following orders in the military was categorised differently. Even if it did amount to murder if you looked at it in black and white terms.

Halloran's eyes lowered at Kitt's question and she noticed his jaw tighten. 'There's nothing we can do.'

'These people must be accountable to someone,' said Kitt.

'The defence secretary,' said Halloran.

'Oh,' said Kitt. 'Yes, I suppose that's right.' Even she wasn't enough of a positive thinker to imagine a politician would be any help in a matter like this. All they cared about was what the press would say. No doubt they would want to keep an incident such as this buried just as much as the Defence Medical Agency did.

'Let's hope we can get something from him off the record,' said Halloran. 'Maybe get him to let something slip by accident. The only trick I've got left up my sleeve after that is to try and get a search warrant for his property.'

'Is a judge going to go for that?' said Kitt.

'Only if I can convince them that a huge miscarriage of justice will happen if they don't grant it,' said Halloran. 'And I'll have to persuade them that I think Greene has gone rogue. That he's not working on the say-so of his superiors. Even if there's a chance that he was working on sanctioned orders for reasons we've yet to understand, I can't let the judge even suspect that. No judge in the land is going to get embroiled in a fight with a military agency.'

'As you say,' said Kitt. 'Let's hope that Greene is a bit more forthcoming out of the office. Oh . . . that looks like him.'

Kitt pointed to a figure walking away from them in the direction of town at quite the quick pace. Like most people in the city, it seemed Greene walked to work. Getting embroiled in the traffic, whether in a car or a bus, often wasn't worth it. You'd get most places quicker on foot.

Halloran started up the car, drove past the figure and pulled up about twenty feet ahead of Greene.

The pair waited a moment or two, until Greene was about ten feet behind their car. Greene didn't seem like the kind of person to run, but you could never tell. Halloran and Kitt looked at each other and, with a nod, they quickly exited the vehicle and waited on the pavement for Greene to close the last few strides between them.

'Can I help you with something?' said Greene, when he realised Kitt and Halloran were waiting for him. His voice was stern but level.

'Detective Inspector Halloran, we've spoken on the phone.'

Greene's expression didn't change, somehow Kitt would have expected it to but he kept all of his muscles in neutral even though he couldn't have been pleased that Halloran had come after him in person.

'DI Halloran, you're out of line to even be here. Unless you have found some kind of forensic evidence against me . . . have you?' said Greene, his question seeming almost like a dare. A dare for Halloran to push this conversation any further than it had already gone, when he knew all too well that Halloran didn't have anything concrete against him.

'I'm not here as an adversary, Mr Greene,' said Halloran. 'I'm trying to save a man's life.'

'If it were in my power to do that, do you not think I would have made sure of it for myself? Now, I confirmed to you that the theft had happened, which was more than I should have confirmed. I also confirmed that we are looking into that theft internally. Again, information I should never have shared with you but did so in good faith that you would leave the matter there. I know you want to look at certain documentation but I can't go around sharing information that's been classified with a civilian. And you of all people should know that.'

'I'm well aware of how the system works. But we are talking about a man's life. Can't you even talk to me here, off the record, and let me know what was in that report?' said Halloran. 'If you can confirm what's in there, even unofficially, it might lead to me being able to build a concrete case against the culprit. Isn't it worth that to save the life of a man you've worked with?'

'In my line of work, DI Halloran, someone's life is always on the line. I can't go into details, but on one or two occasions, that life hanging in the balance has been mine. I've accepted that as a risk of the kind of work I do. I can't say I blame Ripley for coming to you after what has befallen him, but it is completely against protocol and not in keeping with the spirit of self-sacrifice we favour at the agency. Self-sacrifice for a greater good, you understand?'

'How was that toxin you created in your laboratories for the greater good?' said Halloran through gritted teeth. 'I've seen what it does to a human body. Inhumane doesn't cover it. You're just going to let that happen to Kevin Ripley when you could cooperate and help me find who stole that toxin?'

'If it were possible to find the third party who stole the toxin and the antidote, we would already have found them ourselves,' said Greene. 'The fact that Kevin discovered the toxin in his system yesterday and thus likely won't be with us in three or four days' time is a source of great sadness for me but the moment you start to weigh one life as more important than any other, you put a lot of people at risk. You know better than me that information about what we do is like a disease. No matter how discreet you think you're being, it spreads like a terrible contagion. That's not a risk I can afford to take. Not even for Kevin Ripley, with whom I have worked for several years. Much as I understand his actions, I can't help thinking he was foolish to come to you and ruin his reputation at the agency. We have more resources for tracking down the missing agent than local law enforcement. Going to the police wasn't going to save him.'

'Was he really foolish? Or just desperate?' Kitt said, unable to keep her peace any longer in the face of Greene's clinical view of the situation. The thought also occurred to Kitt that Ripley had told them he didn't trust the agency, not completely. Which was why he had gone to the police. From all Kitt understood about the agency thus far, she wouldn't have trusted them if she were in Ripley's position either.

'In my experience those two words are interchangeable. And you are?' Greene said, resting his brown eyes on Kitt.

'Kitt Hartley, I—'

'Oh yes, I know who you are,' Greene said, looking Kitt up and down as he spoke. 'I've read about some of your exploits in the paper. I believe you've had quite the investigative career when it comes to small fry local matters. But this is not the place for tinpot investigators, Ms Hartley. This is a matter of national security and some hard decisions have to be made.'

Kitt opened her mouth to contest Greene's use of the phrase 'small fry' but Halloran interjected before she had a chance. Likely guessing that Kitt wasn't about to say anything to ingratiate herself with this man who had hindered the investigation from the beginning.

'Just a copy of the report, Mr Greene. That's all I'm asking for. I've already got Ripley's testimony about what's in the file so it's not telling me anything I don't already know, I just need the file as evidence,' said Halloran.

'I am deeply sorry for what happened to Leonard Bell, truly. And for what will inevitably happen to Kevin Ripley. Neither of them deserve such a fate but, sometimes in this world, we don't end up with what we deserve. In fact, we rarely do. That report doesn't have any bearing on this situation and contains a lot of sensitive information about the agency's work. Whichever third party has the toxin and the antidote should be the focus of your investigation now. That is certainly where our eyes are turned. You'll gain no traction on your case coming after me. That much I can assure you of. It is a waste of your time and only makes Kevin's death more likely. Now, unless you are going to arrest me, I am leaving for work.'

With that Nathan Greene turned on his heel and stalked off down the street.

'Small fry,' Kitt fumed. 'Tinpot! I'll show him small fry. I'll show him tinpot.'

Slowly, Halloran turned to look at her. 'I'm not sure insults to our investigative prowess are the priority right now.'

'I know,' said Kitt. 'But with him behaving like that I don't know what chance we have of saving Ripley. He says there's sensitive information in that report and if that were true I would understand him not turning it over to us. But, I don't know. Can we even trust him given that he's the one who classified the document to a level that the person who wrote it can't even access it? And then there's the fact that he's a regular at the Book and Candle, the venue in which Bell was poisoned in the first place.'

'You think the idea that there's sensitive information in the document is a smoke screen?' said Halloran. 'You think there's something in there he doesn't want us to see?'

'It just seems to me that all indicators are pointing to him. He was the one that Bell and Ripley reported their findings to. Recommending that the toxin be destroyed. Then the next day the toxin and the antidote mysteriously disappear. I showed Flick who owns the Book and Candle several photographs, Greene was the only one she picked out of the line-up as someone she recognised.'

'What about Simmons and Cryer?' said Halloran. 'From the way you described your meeting with Simmons, it sounds as though they're just as likely to be the culprits.'

Kitt nodded. 'I agree, there's something off about the pair of them. I'm just not sure if it's the fact that they're murderers. There was something about the way Simmons was talking. It was creepy but, on reflection, I actually got the feeling that Simmons might be a bit afraid of the agency. He said the people who worked there think they are gods. That they have the right to say who lives and who dies.'

'That is a pretty ominous thing to say about an organisation,' said Halloran. 'I can't dismiss it but considering the source we're going to have to proceed with some caution. We don't have any concrete evidence on Simmons to apply for a search warrant, but the type of spring trap on his property Joe described to you, gin traps, have been outlawed for decades. We could probably go to Simmons's house and arrest him on that basis.'

'What's the penalty for using traps like that?' said Kitt.

'Maximum penalty is six months in prison,' said Halloran.

'And I can't believe that someone like Simmons is unaware of that. If he's afraid of the agency coming after him since he's been dismissed, maybe that's why he's set the traps.'

'And if you get him into an interview under caution you could maybe get him to admit that and perhaps even give you more information about the agency. With the promise that he won't go to prison over the gin traps, of course,' said Kitt.

'That's the hope,' said Halloran. 'In the meantime, I also need to file for a warrant to search Greene's property and pray that Banks has found something in his financial or phone records that will help us in persuading a judge that the search is necessary. The fact that a man's life is on the line might move a judge more than it moved Nathan Greene. Given his status I doubt he'll be expecting that. He probably expects me to back down. Which is actually what I should do, but if at the end of this I can't say I tried everything to save Kevin Ripley's life I won't be able to live with myself.'

'I'm right there with you,' said Kitt. And it was then in that moment that she realised there was something she could do. 'Hmmm. Now that I really think about it, I may have another trick up my sleeve, too,' she said.

'Oh really?' said Halloran. 'What's that?'

'I can't tell you anything just yet,' she said with a knowing smirk. 'It's classified.'

CHAPTER TWENTY-SIX

Kitt was just approaching the premises of Hartley and Edwards Investigations when she heard a familiar voice call to her from across the street.

'Eeeeeee, there you are, love, I was just about to pay you a visit.'

'Oh, hello Ruby,' said Kitt, secretly wondering how she was going to extricate herself from this conversation as quickly as possible. It was nothing against Ruby, Kitt was very fond of the woman. Time was of the essence. She couldn't just sit and listen to the omens and warnings Ruby's 'familiars' had been sending her way over the last few days. When the case was over, she wanted to find some way of talking to her about the strange dreams she'd had after drinking the mulled wine, just to get her expert esoteric opinion on whether she should go and see a doctor about her hallucinations. But now really wasn't the time. 'I'm sorry I can't stop and talk today,' she said, paving the way for making a polite exit from the interaction. 'It's just I'm working a case and somebody's life is in jeopardy. Every minute counts.'

'Oh dear, that does sound serious, very, very serious indeed, you must be run off your feet with a job like that, it doesn't bear thinking about,' Ruby said without once taking a breath. 'Obviously I've been in that boat myself,' she added. 'You saved my life a few years back, and I won't 'assle you while you're trying to do the same for someone else.'

Ruby began to hobble off in the direction of town but Kitt stopped her.

'You're never hassling me, Ruby,' said Kitt. Not completely the truth but it was the right thing to say. Unwelcome as the interruption at work could be at times, she never wanted Ruby to think she was a burden. 'I expect you've got your own stuff to be getting on with anyway,' said Kitt. 'It being so close to Christmas.'

'Not really, love,' said Ruby. 'Get to my age, you spend most of your Decembers alone. Everyone else you know is gone, you see?'

'Oh,' said Kitt, chiding herself for not thinking before opening her mouth. 'What about Christmas Day? I know you don't quite celebrate it in the same way as the rest of us but are you at least having a dinner?'

'Eeee, I don't tend to bother with all that when it's just me, love,' said Ruby.

'Well, I've got a houseful on Christmas Day and it would

be lovely if you could join us,' said Kitt. She pulled a business card out of her pocket and a pen.

'Here,' she said, after writing her home address on the back of the business card. 'This is the address, no pressure but you're welcome any time after two p.m.'

'Oh,' Ruby said, looking at the business card she'd accepted as though it was the lost treasure of the Pharaohs. She pulled Kitt in for a hug. 'I wouldn't miss it, love, you're very kind, I will see you then and there.'

With that, Ruby set off down Walmgate, towards the centre of town. Kitt watched after her for just a minute as delicate snowflakes began to fall. Wondering how many years Ruby had spent Christmas alone without Kitt's knowledge, and then wondering just how wise it had been to give out her home address to a woman who had stalked her about town for over a decade. Still, she didn't have the time to feel guilty or mourn the peace and quiet she had likely just given away in sharing her address with Ruby, this case was just too urgent for that.

Tentatively, Kitt pushed the door at Hartley and Edwards Investigations, only to find it locked. This was precisely what she was hoping for. A locked door meant the building was empty. Grace and Joe weren't back yet from speaking to Donald Sanders. Considering the name had been given to them by somebody who was, to a certain extent, still under suspicion, Kitt didn't hold out much hope for big news on that score. But they had to check out every lead.

With the agency premises empty nobody would witness what Kitt was about to do.

Fast as she could, she rooted around for her keys in her satchel, unlocked the door and hurried inside. Flipping on the light switch, she went straight over to the bookcase near her desk and grabbed the copy of *Casino Royale* by Ian Fleming off the middle shelf. Flicking through the pages, she quickly located her bookmark, which was in fact an important document in disguise. Written backwards on the slip of paper was the phone number for an Agent Smith. A man Kitt, Joe and Grace had helped out a couple of years ago while investigating a murder in the Scottish Borders. Smith had been so grateful for their help in recovering something very precious to the government that he had given her the number on the understanding that she could call once, and only once, for a favour in return. Saving a man's life two days before Christmas seemed like a pretty worthy cause to spend her favour on.

Picking up the landline, she dialled the number.

Instead of a ringing sound, all Kitt heard was a click. Followed by a voice that didn't sound human. It was either a recorded message or the person at the other end of the line was using a voice changer. At a guess, Kitt would have said it was the latter.

'What is your request?' said a deep robotic voice that Kitt was sure would appear in her nightmares for the rest of time.

It took Kitt a moment to realise this was her cue to speak but once that thought struck, she cleared her throat and said: 'This is Kitt Hartley for Agent Smith. I'm working on a case involving the Defence Medical Agency. They've classified an important document with the reference TTYX8. I urgently need a copy of that document to prevent loss of life.'

There was a pause at the other end of the phone and Kitt was starting to wonder if her request had been heard when the android voice spoke again.

'No promises,' it said, right before the line went dead.

Putting down the phone, Kitt sighed, slumped in her office chair and closed her eyes.

Just for a moment.

All there was to do now was the most painful thing of all: to wait.

Kitt wasn't sure how long she had waited by the phone when she became aware of a small light twinkling in the far corner of the office. She sat up straighter in her seat and looked harder at the dim glow that on closer inspection seemed to be coming from the stationery cupboard just to the right of the Christmas tree.

Frowning, Kitt slowly crossed the room to get a better look at this unusual pearlescent phenomenon. It was the purest white light she'd ever seen and it was shining out of every nook and chink around the doorframe.

Taking a deep breath, Kitt reached a hand out to the door-knob. She looked again at the white beams almost bursting from behind the frame and wondered if opening the door was such a good idea. Before she could talk herself into turning the doorknob, however, the cupboard swung open of its own accord. And standing there, surrounded by an almost blinding luminosity, was a woman with long dark hair, parted in the centre and tied back in a bun. She wore spectacles, and a blazer with sharp lines with a matching shirt and tie. The white light around her seemed to fade as she stepped out of the cupboard and walked with a calm confidence towards Kitt.

'You're . . .'

'Yes.'

'You're . . .'

'Yes . . .' the woman said again, this time with an added smirk.

'Dorothy L. Sayers?'

'Yes, very good,' Sayers said, patting Kitt on the head as she passed her by and made her way towards her desk. 'You look a lot more surprised to see me than I would have expected. I thought you were brighter than that. But, oh well, there you have it.'

'You don't understand,' said Kitt, looking between Sayers and the phone resting next to a pile of papers. 'I can't afford to be asleep right now. I'm waiting on a very important call. A man's life depends on it. I need to be awake.'

'Who says you're asleep?' Sayers smiled at Kitt before walking over to sit in the seat that Grace normally favoured.

'Please,' Kitt said. 'Don't start with that. I know I must be tired. Exhausted even because I only got a couple of hours' sleep last night and I haven't stopped today. It probably doesn't help that I keep having these disturbing dreams instead of getting proper rest when I do drop off. But I need to wake up right now.'

'I can't help you with that, I'm afraid,' said Sayers. 'I'm here for one reason, and for one reason only.'

'And what is that?' Kitt said with a sigh as she plonked herself back in the seat behind her desk and looked longingly at the telephone. Which of course wasn't really a telephone at all but just part of the dreamscape she was imagining.

'To put you back on the right track,' said Sayers.

'What do you mean by that? There are only so many leads we can reasonably follow in this investigation due to the nature of it,' said Kitt. 'And you think . . . what? That we're . . . we're taking the investigation in the wrong direction?'

'Not necessarily the complete wrong direction,' said Sayers. 'But I fear you may be fixating on only one thing. That your focus may be too narrow. You see, when I wrote *Whose Body?*, I wanted to do something interesting to keep the reader guessing. Most of the time, in a mystery, you have more than one suspect to keep the identity of the killer a secret. In this instance I chose to have more than one motive.'

Kitt paused and thought for a second. 'So, in your story, the killer benefits from the crime in more than one way?'

'That's right. It muddies the waters far more than you might expect,' said Sayers.

'Yes . . . I can imagine that. If the investigator doesn't realise that there is more than one motive, they might pursue leads that only fixate on one motive, and accuse the wrong person . . . But, wait . . . is that what we're doing?'

Sayers did not answer Kitt's question directly, but kept on talking as if she were working from a pre-prepared script. 'Think back again to that story I wrote. You read it years ago when your heart was much lighter than it is today. Freke, the villain, has two motives, remember?'

Kitt thought back to the story Sayers was referencing. 'The desire to prove a scientific theory, if I remember correctly.'

'That's right,' Sayers said with an encouraging nod, 'and the biggest excuse of them all: love. Both played a part in his choices. If I were you, I would think long and hard on those themes. Especially since some of the players in your story come from a scientific background.'

Kitt thought for a moment. They had started to lean towards the idea that Greene was the true enemy. That Simmons was afraid of the agency rather than full of wrath for them. But what if they were wrong? Margaret couldn't have been best pleased when Simmons was dismissed under a cloud. Had Simmons coaxed her into stealing both the toxin and the antidote? Maybe. But then why poison two former colleagues? Perhaps it came back to what Ripley had suggested in the beginning. That it was a demonstration of power. Maybe Simmons planned to extort the agency and bring more bad press their way unless they paid him a large sum or gave him something else that he wanted? Perhaps when they learned Nathan Greene was a regular at the Book and Candle Bar, they had been too quick to lean into that piece of evidence. Maybe Kitt had misinterpreted Simmons's actions or he was putting on a show, pretending to be afraid when really he was behind it all. And perhaps Cryer had gone along with the scheme because of something Eleanor had suggested in her interview. That she might have held romantic feelings for Ripley. If they were unrequited, that may have led Cryer to a very dark emotional place.

Kitt went to ask Sayers if she was on the right track in considering Margaret Cryer and Tyler Simmons as suspects when a high-pitched trilling filled her ears.

Kitt jumped, and realised she had awoken with a start, still slumped in her office chair. There was no sign of Dorothy L. Sayers. But the phone on her desk was ringing. Was it Agent Smith's contingent with news about the document so soon?

Quick as she could, Kitt reached for the phone. 'Hello?'

'Hello pet, it's me,' said Halloran's voice.

'Mal,' Kitt said, rubbing her eyes. Since he wasn't a government agent calling to let her know that the document she'd asked for would be with her presently, she hoped he was at least calling with some good news.

'There's been a bit of shift forward here,' Halloran said, raising Kitt's hopes further.

'You've got access to the document?' said Kitt.

'No, but I did get a warrant to search Greene's home. Made sure to send the paperwork to a judge who I knew would find the way we've been stonewalled appalling.'

'Did you find something at Greene's address?' said Kitt, barely daring to breathe in case the heavy sound of it stifled Halloran's reply.

'Yes, we found the missing toxin,' said Halloran. 'So, we've finally been able to make an arrest.'

'Oh my God,' said Kitt, while chiding herself for putting any stock in these strange dreams she'd been having. It appeared Nathan Greene was the culprit after all. 'Wait, what about the antidote?'

'No,' Halloran said, his voice landing like a dull thud in Kitt's ears. 'We've searched the entire property. There's no sign of the antidote anywhere. I'm sorry pet, but we still don't have what we need to save Kevin Ripley's life.'

CHAPTER TWENTY-SEVEN

It was roughly an hour later when Kitt found herself taking a deep breath and rapping the knocker on Kevin Ripley's door. The knocker itself was quite ornate and took the form of a Celtic green man carved out of some kind of resin. The metal hoop that visitors might use to knock on the door was threaded through the green man's ears and Kitt couldn't help but think how appropriate this was given the news she was about to break. The fact that the antidote had yet to be found would definitely be something Ripley would wish he could block his own ears to.

A moment passed without an answer.

Strange, Kitt thought. She had rung ahead to say that she had news she thought best delivered in person so he was expecting her. He had seemed a little flustered on the phone, perhaps even agitated. But she had put that down to his circumstances and that she was insisting on a face-to-face meeting when time was so much of the essence. Still, the news she had to deliver might mean the end of his life came sooner rather than later. That wasn't the kind of thing she could tell a person over the phone.

Kitt rapped the knocker again. Trying not to let the worst thoughts she could think overtake her. What if the poor man had died as she was on the way over here? What if he were on the other side of this door right now, lying dead in the kitchen or bedroom? He would have died not knowing who had done this to him, or why. Kitt allowed that thought to pain her for a minute and then chose a more rational stance. If that were going to happen to him now, then the odds were that even if Halloran had recovered the antidote, they might not have got it to him on time. Moreover, if now was Ripley's time, perhaps it were better that it happened before she even entered his house, so that he never knew that his salvation had been so close and yet so far. That they had the right suspect in custody but as yet no cure for his condition, and possibly just missed out on saving him by one of Iago's whiskers.

A moment later, however, despite Kitt's concerns, there was a clattering sound from somewhere in the house and Kitt was certain she could hear the low thud of boots on carpet.

Sure enough, the door soon opened and Kevin stood behind it.

'Come in, come in,' he said, waving Kitt out of the cold. 'I'm sorry if I took a minute, I was upstairs and it takes me longer than I'd like to admit to get down them these days. Plus, I don't know, I keep imagining that I can't move as well. As though the toxin is already taking its effects on me, even though I haven't smelled the vaguest hint of cinnamon on myself, which is, of course, a terrible warning sign that the end is near. It's amazing, isn't it, the tricks the brain can play on the body?'

'No need to apologise,' Kitt said as Ripley directed her into his living room, 'I'm the one who's putting you out. Calling on you with such little notice.'

'I think with something as time-sensitive as my case, little notice is par for the course,' said Ripley, indicating a green velvet armchair for Kitt to sit in. A cushion bearing a cheery Santa face was nestled in the corner of it. This particular soft furnishing was probably dragged out of a cupboard a few weeks back and placed with that swelling feeling of good will and optimism that overcame most people when they were arranging their Christmas ornaments. The same was probably true of a small, withered imitation Christmas tree that stood in the corner, with strips of silver tinsel and silver baubles arranged on it in the most unattractive of formations. At the time Ripley had added his version of festive cheer to his living room, he'd had no idea of the nightmare that awaited him.

'I'm afraid the news I'm coming with is only halfway to being good news,' Kitt said, framing what she had to say to Ripley just as she'd planned. Focusing on what Halloran's team had achieved rather than what they had still yet to uncover. Ordinarily, a police officer would have gone to Ripley's door but Halloran was adamant that he needed all of his resources split between breaking Greene, interviewing Simmons who had also been taken into custody on the off-chance that he provided information that could be used against Greene, and searching for the antidote. This seemed like good sense to Kitt. Until they had the antidote in their possession, there technically wasn't anything of note to tell Ripley. And with him likely having so little time left, he probably wouldn't have thanked Halloran for sending an officer to his door when that officer could have been looking for the substance that was going to save his life.

'Right now, I'll take that,' said Ripley. 'Right now, I'll take anything. We've been hunting for the killer for two days now, you know? And it feels like a whole lifetime to me.'

'I know,' said Kitt. She'd barely slept in those two days and yet, despite the discovery of the toxin at Greene's address, she still felt as though she'd achieved next to nothing.

'I think it's a small Christmas miracle all on its own that I'm still here. Maybe I was only poisoned the day before I came to see you at that police station. Maybe I was poisoned the very night Leonard died and still have at least two more days to find the antidote.'

'That's my greatest hope,' said Kitt. 'That you got to us very quickly after your poisoning took place. The thing is,

Kevin. We have found the person who stole the toxin. A search of their property was undertaken and the toxin was recovered. But only the toxin. The antidote must be being stored somewhere separately. So, we're getting closer but we still don't have what we need.'

Ripley closed his eyes. A pained expression crossed his face as though Kitt had driven a knife through his heart and in truth she felt like she had.

'Who was it?' he asked. 'I appreciate they're just a suspect right now but if this person is in possession of the toxin then I think there's little doubt they're responsible for what happened to Leo. And for what is about to happen to me. I want to know this person's identity.'

Kitt pressed her lips together before speaking. As much as time was of the essence, she had deliberately withheld Greene's identity up until now. Not to save Greene's reputation. But to save Ripley receiving all of the worst news at once. It was bad enough that they had only recovered the toxin and not the antidote. But for Ripley to learn that the person behind this was someone he had worked closely with for some years, and likely trusted – as far as anyone can trust another person in his line of work – was likely to take some processing, to put it politely.

'According to what Halloran told me, the toxin was buried in some flower beds outside a property,' Kitt said. 'I'm afraid it belonged to Nathan Greene.'

Ripley swallowed hard and then began nodding very

quickly to himself. 'So, my suspicions were correct. He saw that report me and Leo wrote and decided he didn't want to follow our recommendations. He wanted to develop the toxin further. Make it more lethal. So, he wanted us out of the way so the agency could pursue their agenda unchecked.'

'We don't know his motives yet, I'm afraid,' said Kitt.

'I'm pretty sure of them,' said Ripley. 'They knew me and Leo wouldn't keep quiet about them working on a toxin so deadly, so cruel.'

'I understand you wanting to know why Nathan Greene did this, when we're talking about a man you've worked with for quite some time,' said Kitt. 'But with time being so short we have to spend our efforts on the things that matter most. Halloran's focusing all of his energies on getting him to reveal the location of the antidote. His thinking is, he can find out the whys and wherefores after your life has been saved.'

A small, bitter smile crossed Ripley's lips. 'Even if Halloran has a couple of days to spare, I'm afraid I don't think there is much chance of that now.'

'Of saving your life?' said Kitt. 'Whyever not?'

'When you work in our game, you learn how to cover your tracks. Keep information strictly confidential. You are also trained in . . . how to withstand torture,' said Ripley.

'I didn't realise that,' said Kitt, frowning. She had perhaps expected military personnel who might find themselves in war zones to undergo such training. But it had never dawned on her that desk workers might get a crash course in it too.

'It's part of your initial training programme at the facility. You're keeping secrets in your head that the enemy might want to access. So, if you find yourself under duress, you're supposed to follow protocol and not tell them a thing. Despite all the training I've had, I think I always knew I'd last no time at all under such circumstances. I'm a scientist. I'm not built to withstand such horrors no matter how much training I have had. I just prayed I'd never be in that situation.'

'I think you've just described most of us,' said Kitt. 'Not many people have what it takes to withstand torture, even if they have had training. There's a breaking point for everyone.'

'But Nathan Greene, he's made of sturdier stuff than me,' said Ripley.

'Well, Halloran isn't using torture,' said Kitt. 'He's using tried and tested methods of getting criminals to confess their crimes. Perhaps Nathan Greene is wise to a lot of them, but they are surprisingly powerful tactics. So, at the very least, let's give Halloran a chance.'

'Oh, don't get me wrong,' said Ripley. 'There's nothing I want more than for Halloran to ascertain the location of the antidote. And despite my scepticism, I will be hoping for that until my dying breath. But ... I know Nathan. If Halloran does manage to get any information out of him. I suspect that he will only learn it when it is far too late.'

CHAPTER TWENTY-EIGHT

Having said her goodbyes to Ripley, Kitt bustled down the steps outside his house and took a right into the alleyway she'd cut through at the side of the property on her way there. She needed to get back to the office at once. Perhaps a message was waiting from Agent Smith's contingent. Something that would shed light on where this missing antidote could be. Or perhaps Halloran had managed to get some information out of Tyler Simmons that they could use to break Greene. After what Ripley had said about how unlikely it was Nathan Greene would talk, it seemed they needed all the help they could get in uncovering that cure sooner rather than later.

As she walked along the alley, however, something caught her attention. Kitt noticed a dark object, lying flat in the melted snow.

She approached the item to get a better look. Once she was near, she saw that it was a mobile phone. Not a particularly swish one. It didn't even have a touch screen.

Kitt was just about to pocket the phone so she could take it back to the agency and have a stab at finding the owner when something quite unexpected happened. A very hard, sharp blow to the head. From behind. A hit so swift and so strong that Kitt didn't even have time to cry out in pain or protest. She simply hurtled to the ground with the force of it and everything around her went black.

When Kitt opened her eyes again, she found herself standing in a graveyard. She recognised it at once as the cemetery in Fishergate, situated on the edge of York city centre. On a clear day in the Vale of York University Library, it was possible to look across the river and see the Grade II listed chapel built of limestone and boasting strong, antiquated pillars so she was quite certain that was where she was.

What on earth was she doing in a cemetery, though? And more to the point, how had she come to be here?

She looked around the gravestones topped with heaps of snow until her eyes locked on a figure in a dark suit standing about twenty feet away. He had a mane of black shaggy hair and a moustache to match. Since he was the only person in sight, Kitt trudged through the thick snow towards him.

She stopped a few paces from the figure. Right at the moment at which she recognised him.

'Once upon a midnight dreary, while I pondered, weak and weary—' she began to recite but was cut off by the man who waved his hands at her to stop.

'Please, anything but that, I have written other things, you know?' came the man's protests, in a rich American accent.

'Edgar Allan Poe,' Kitt said. There was no surprise in her voice. What surprise was left in a person once they had already held counsel in their dreams with Charles Dickens, Wilkie Collins and Dorothy L. Sayers in the space of just a couple of days? 'Am I . . . dead?' she asked, looking around the cemetery in the fading winter light.

'Dead? Ha!' said Poe. 'What on earth makes you think that?'

'I don't know, maybe you're about to point to one of those gravestones and my name will be carved into it.'

Poe pulled a face at Kitt as though he thought she were mad. And maybe she was, imagining all of these dead authors had been sent to help her solve a case.

'Human beings are always so dramatic,' said Poe. Which, given his literary style and tone, Kitt thought was a bit rich. 'No, you're not dead. Not yet, anyway. But to be here with me, you must not be conscious.'

'I . . . I don't know what happened,' said Kitt.

'It doesn't much matter what *has* happened,' said Poe. 'It's what could and will happen that should have your attention, missy.'

Kitt's nose crinkled. She could do without a dead writer dishing out pejorative nicknames for her just now. The last thing she remembered was a great deal of pain, she knew her waking self was on the brink of exhaustion and they still didn't have what they needed to save Kevin Ripley's life.

'What exactly is that supposed to mean?' asked Kitt, doing her best to ignore Poe's tone.

'You've read my story, "The Murders in the Rue Morgue", I take it?' said Poe. 'It's a classic!'

'I'm . . . not sure if the author is the one who gets to decide if their work is a classic,' said Kitt, with a wry smile. 'But, yes, I've read that one a couple of times over the years.'

'So, you know, in that story, I underline how even the most complex of problems can be solved through analytical reasoning,' said Poe. 'That, in fact, analytical reasoning is the fundamental method through which any problem might be solved.'

'Yes, I'm familiar with the thrust of the narrative argument,' said Kitt.

'Kitt,' Poe said, taking Kitt's hands in his in a most familiar manner. Though in this strange dreamscape the gesture did not raise her hackles the way it might have done in waking life. 'The answer to the mystery you are working on relies on those same faculties of observation, deductive reasoning, analysing human behaviour and synthesising seemingly unrelated facts. When it comes to the first three, you have all of the intelligence you need to know who is truly behind the murder of Leonard Bell.'

Poe squeezed Kitt's hands before releasing them. The

pressure of his hands against hers felt so real, even though Kitt knew it couldn't be.

'Then why can't I do the last part?' said Kitt. 'Why can't I weave the facts together to get to the truth? Synthesise the facts as you would say? I'm well-read. I'm open-minded. I'm experienced in solving mysteries. I should be able to take that last step and yet the truth is somehow still out of reach.'

'There is a piece missing,' said Poe. 'And I am not sure that missing piece will be revealed to you in time. I have no control over that so it cannot be relied upon. You must work with what you already know, and re-examine all you think you know, in order to get to the truth. Possibly even without all of the pieces.'

'But how will we ever get to the truth if the vital piece of information we need is still missing?' Kitt said with a shake of her head.

'Would it help you to know you have already spoken with the true culprit?' said Poe. His blue-grey eyes fixed on Kitt's with this question and she felt her whole body turn cold at the thought that the person behind this was within her grasp and yet still evaded her.

'Who is it?' said Kitt. 'Please, a man's life depends on the answer. We may have the man who did it in custody but we can't be sure. And without the antidote, whoever is behind this is still going to claim the life of another victim. No more games or riddles.'

Poe smiled. 'If I could tell you that, I promise you, I would. But in truth, you don't need me to. This person, they have already given themselves away before your very eyes. You just have to think over your interactions and it will become clear.'

'So, you're saying the murderer is already on our radar but that it isn't Nathan Greene?' Kitt said.

But when she looked up to face Poe again, he was gone. The world around her was shaking. The gravestones, the chapel, the snowy earth, all seemed to be caught in some strange kind of quake. Kitt scrunched her eyes shut, not wanting to witness yet more unsettling absurdity. When she did so, she could hear a voice calling to her. Somewhere distant. A woman's voice. Calling her back to the world she had temporarily left behind.

CHAPTER TWENTY-NINE

'Hello, hello,' said a woman's voice. 'Are you alright?'

Kitt's eyes fluttered open. The first thing she saw was the face of a woman she did not recognise. She had deeply bronzed skin and piercing blue eyes that even in the darkness of the alleyway seemed to sparkle.

'Are you OK?' she said. 'Shall I phone for an ambulance?'

'No . . .' Kitt managed to mutter. 'I mean, I'm OK, thank you. I don't need an ambulance. I must have . . . slipped on some ice and fallen over,' she lied. There was no doubt in her mind that what had happened to her was no accident. From the agonising thud at the back of her head, she was certain that somebody had hit her, hard. Hard enough to render her unconscious. But she didn't need to drag an unsuspecting bystander into the fray. Especially not somebody who'd been kind enough to stop and see if she needed help when quite a few people might have passed her by out of fear. Better she concoct a cover story and then regroup with Joe and Grace as soon as possible.

'Are you sure?' said the woman, as she helped Kitt to her feet.

'Yes, I'm quite sure, but thank you for your concern,' said Kitt. 'I suspect most of the bruising is to my pride.'

The woman chuckled. 'Everybody has to fall over on the ice at least once a year. If you're really sure you're OK, then I'll get on. But my car is just around the corner. I could drop you at a doctor's or a hospital if you want to get checked out?'

'It's really not necessary,' Kitt said with a wave of her hand. 'But I am so grateful to you for stopping. Who knows how long I would have been out for if you hadn't woken me?'

The woman smiled, and then, picking up the hem of the purple skirt she was wearing, said her goodbyes and continued to navigate the slush further down the alley.

Once she no longer had to keep up appearances, Kitt's attentions turned to the throbbing she could feel at the back of her skull. She pressed a hand to her head. There was no blood. But there definitely was a small bump forming.

The next thing Kitt thought to do was check her pockets and her satchel. Her phone, wallet and keys, everything of importance was still there. She hadn't been mugged. She hadn't thought it was a random incident, but she had to be sure. The question was, why would somebody knock her out? Something to do with the case they were working on, undoubtedly. She had been looking at the phone she had found when it happened. And then it dawned on Kitt that this was the one item missing from the scene. Slowly, she walked up and down the small stretch of alleyway to see if she had merely forgotten the precise place it was lying in. But it was nowhere to be seen.

Of course, somebody could have come along the alleyway before the good Samaritan who had woken her. But surely, if they had, they would have quickly stepped past her if that was what they were going to do? If they meant her ill, they would likely have gone for her valuables, rather than pick up a decidedly old-school phone lying nearby.

No, that phone had been taken. But why? And by who?

Somebody didn't want her to have it in her possession, that much was for sure. And if what had happened to her was connected to the case, then surely the person who attacked her was the person behind this mess? Halloran had found the toxin at Greene's house. Perhaps he had an accomplice? Simmons was also in custody, so who did that leave? Margaret Cryer, or maybe even Jordan Ascher? They had dismissed the latter because, as Evie had pointed out, he wouldn't have been able to gain access to the facility, but what if he was somehow connected with Greene? Jordan wouldn't need a way in if he and Greene were somehow connected. Greene had all the access anyone would need to pull off what this murderer had.

Kitt shook her head at quite a loss with it all. She had yet to hear back from Grace and Joe about Donald Sanders, maybe they shouldn't have put off interviewing him for so long. But then, there had been so much else to contend with, they couldn't have got to him any quicker than they had. On a case like this, it was easy to see why Halloran so often complained about not having enough staff for the job.

Then, another thought struck Kitt.

How had the person who knocked her out known that she would be there? All the time that she'd been working this case, had the person or persons behind it been watching her? Might that indicate that the agency as a whole was behind the poisonings of Bell and Ripley? It wasn't as though Kitt was the only player in this situation, not even the most important player of them all. It was difficult to think that anyone else in the mix would have the resources to watch everyone they needed to.

The other, and more likely, explanation, however, was that the person who had poisoned Bell and Ripley was still watching their soon-to-be second victim. Kitt was, after all, just around the corner from Ripley's house. The killer was probably waiting to see when the poison would work its will on his – or her – victim. Perhaps in the course of that surveillance they had dropped a burner phone they'd been using and the last thing they could afford was for Kitt – of all people – to uncover an item like that.

Without taking another minute to think about what her

being knocked unconscious meant for the case, she dialled Grace's number.

'Kitt?'

'Grace, are you on your own?'

'No, Joe's here with me, we're just checking into Donald Sanders' alibi. It took us quite a long time to track him down but it's all been confirmed so I think we can rule him out,' said Grace. 'Why?'

'Thank goodness Joe is with you,' said Kitt, relief flooding through her that what had just happened to her wasn't going to happen to Grace. There was always strength in numbers. 'I know you're following up leads from Ripley's diary but I need you both to finish up where you are and meet me back at the office. Whatever you do, stick together until you get back to the agency. I'm going to text Evie in a minute to check in on her. She's not an official part of the investigation but the people behind this might not realise this.'

'Kitt, what's going on?' said Grace.

'It's not safe for us to work alone anymore.'

'What makes you say that?' Grace replied, this time with a mild note of alarm sounding out in her tone.

'Well, I've sort of just been attacked,' said Kitt, doing her best not to make it sound too dramatic. There was work to do and things to fathom out. The last thing she needed was a big fuss making over a bang to the head.

'Oh my God, are you OK? Because you know if you die or

get badly injured, I'm really only left with Joe to tease and it's just not as much fun,' said Grace.

'I'm fine, thank you for your concern,' said Kitt. Though she made sure her tone was dry enough to join in with Grace's little joke, she knew, in truth, that the news she had been attacked would truly concern her somewhat giddy counterpart. 'But I might have got off lucky. So until we know who attacked me, we stick together.'

'Have you alerted Halloran to the attack?' said Grace.

'He's my next call, I just wanted to make sure you were safe first,' said Kitt.

'Why were you attacked?' said Grace.

'That, I don't know ... at least, not exactly,' said Kitt. 'I'm not far from Kevin Ripley's house so I'm assuming it is related to the case. And I have a feeling that if we can figure out who attacked me, we might just be able to work out who is behind all of this.'

CHAPTER THIRTY

Kitt hadn't been back at the offices of Hartley and Edwards Investigations more than twenty minutes when Grace and Joe walked through the door.

'No Rolo?' Kitt asked when Joe walked in sans canine.

Joe shook his head. 'The hound is sleeping off the morning's excitement at the hotel.'

'I never thought I'd be jealous of a dog,' said Kitt. 'But I'd give anything for a good sleep right now. I think I've had more than enough excitement to last me a lifetime.'

'How's your head?' asked Grace as she threw her bag on a nearby chair and walked straight over to Kitt.

'I'll live,' said Kitt, instinctively rubbing the bump that was still throbbing at the back of her crown. 'I think I was knocked out because I found a mobile phone that had been dropped. Probably a burner phone. Probably belonging to someone involved in the death of Bell and the poisoning of Ripley.'

'Oh my God,' said Grace. 'If that phone really does belong to someone who's behind this, it probably has all the answers on it.'

'Don't rub it in,' said Kitt. 'If I'd been just a little bit quicker, I'd have had the phone in my pocket and likely noticed the assailant approaching me in time to make a run for it.'

'Even with something like that at stake, I can't believe someone knocked you out in broad daylight,' said Joe. 'Well, actually, after all I've seen in this business, I can believe it, but it's a big risk for whoever did it. Anyone could have witnessed that.'

'Agreed,' said Kitt. 'I rang Halloran on the way over here. He's charged Nathan Greene with the murder of Leonard Bell after finding the toxin in his house and, given what has just happened to me, he is working on the assumption that Greene has an accomplice. I had wondered if there was a possibility that Greene might have been set up but Halloran isn't willing to entertain that as a theory unless there's evidence for it. He says it's much more likely Greene has someone working with him. Since whoever knocked me out did so for a phone, however, the search team are going to be on the particular lookout for another burner phone on any future searches they carry out. They didn't find anything like that at Nathan Greene's property though.'

'How is Greene responding to the arrest?' asked Joe.

'He is doing what he's done from the outset: denying all involvement and saying no more. Apparently, he has a particularly fierce lawyer and there's been no admission of any guilt even in the face of them finding the toxin on his property. Let alone any sign of Greene giving up his accomplice or the location of the antidote,' Kitt explained.

'This can't go on much longer,' said Grace. 'Tomorrow will be day three of us working on this case. Christmas Eve. With all the luck in the world, Ripley probably won't see Boxing Day if we don't have a breakthrough soon.'

'Much as I admire Halloran, breaking a man like Nathan Greene . . . it's probably not going to happen quickly,' said Joe. 'It's really down to us to work out where that antidote might be stored.'

'Well, to think clearly, after a knock to the head like that, at the very least I'm going to need a cup of tea in hand,' said Kitt.

'I'll make it,' said Grace. 'I wanted to make myself a hot chocolate anyway. Joe?'

'Hot chocolate sounds good,' he said. 'It's still freezing out there.'

'Soft southerner,' Kitt teased.

'I live in Manchester . . .' said Joe.

'That's south to me,' Kitt said.

'And me,' said Grace, before trotting over to the kettle, which at present was standing right next to the Christmas tree.

'I was so relieved you and Grace had stuck together after checking into Sanders,' said Kitt.

'Of course,' said Joe. 'Time is of the essence here, where else would I be but on the case?'

'Oh, I don't know,' Kitt said. 'I think you could legitimately pay another visit to the Book and Candle Bar on the pretence of business if you wanted to see a certain someone again. From where I was standing, she seemed quite keen on you.'

Kitt, ordinarily, would not shamelessly dig for gossip like this. But she had a feeling when it came to Joe that maybe he was a bit stuck, personally. A perfectly understandable place to be after being widowed so young, and Kitt wouldn't think of pushing. But if he needed a little nudge in a direction that might serve to make him happier, she wasn't above that.

Joe looked at Kitt for a whole minute before responding and she was about to apologise for having overstepped. He opened his mouth first, however, and said, 'Actually, I like someone else.'

'Oh,' said Kitt. 'That's wonderful news. Anyone I know or is it a secret?'

Slowly, Joe looked over in the direction of Grace who had her back turned to them as she made the tea and appeared to be in deep conversation with Titania the Tyrannical Archangel.

'Grace?' Kitt said, far louder than she meant to. Joe's eyes widened as Grace turned from what she was doing.

'Yes?' she said, raising her eyebrows in expectation.

'Oh, er. Dig the Lady Grey out, will you? I've had enough of the Christmas stuff.'

Looking towards the top of the tree, Grace offered a firm nod and replied, 'Titania consents to your request.'

With that, she returned to the drink preparations and resumed her conversation with the angel on the top of their tree.

'Sorry,' Kitt murmured. 'I'm usually more discreet than that. You've kept your cards close to your chest on that score.'

Joe smirked. 'She's . . . not like anyone else I've ever met.'

Kitt looked over at Grace to see that the conversation with Titania had turned into a heated argument. 'That much I'll grant you,' she replied with a wry smile.

'But when it comes to keeping my cards close to my chest, I will for a while longer if it's all the same to you,' said Joe. 'I'm only just coming to terms with the fact that I've got these feelings, I'm not ready to act on them.'

'Understood,' said Kitt. 'Your secret's safe with me.'

'Right,' said Grace, walking steadily towards them with a tray of hot drinks and dishing them out as appropriate. 'Where do we think this antidote is?'

'Halloran's team has searched Greene's house from top to bottom, it's not there,' said Kitt. 'They're starting with properties owned by family members next.'

'The thing is,' said Grace. 'Because of what happened to

Kitt, we know Greene must have an accomplice out there and we're completely clueless as to their identity. It might be one of the people we've interviewed, but it could just as easily be someone not on our radar at all. If they're the ones storing the antidote, how do we go about finding them?'

'If there's more than one person behind this, as we've suspected for some time, then it also means that looking into the alibis of the people we've already questioned is only going to get us so far.'

'Just because they have an alibi for the night Bell was murdered doesn't mean that they didn't send an accomplice – likely someone unknown to us – out to do their dirty work,' said Joe.

'Precisely,' said Kitt. 'And as for Simmons and Cryer, they've given each other as their alibis but for all we know they were in it together.'

'We could check into their local chippie,' said Joe. 'At least corroborate that part of their story. But I think, from the way Simmons was talking, that either happened before the window Ripley gave us or very early into it, so even that isn't really going to get us very far in ruling them out.'

'Halloran is looking into triangulating Cryer's mobile phone signal for the last few hours,' said Kitt. 'See if he can prove she is likely the person who knocked me out in that alley.'

'That's a start,' said Joe. 'Assuming she's not smart enough to leave her phone at the office or at home if she's out and up to no good.'

'You're right, she probably is smart enough to do that,' said Kitt. 'And that's why she, or whoever the culprit is, is using burner phones that can't be linked to their identity.'

Before Kitt could share any more theories, there was a hard knock on the door.

'Is anyone expecting a visitor?' said Kitt, walking over to answer it.

Both Joe and Grace confirmed that they were not.

As such, Kitt was very tentative while opening the door. After this afternoon, who knew where the next sharp blow to the head might come from?

On opening it, however, she quickly saw that a young bike messenger stood outside with a clipboard in one hand and a manila envelope in another.

'Delivery for Ms Kitt Hartley,' said the messenger.

Kitt signed the clipboard and took the envelope inside. The envelope itself was completely blank. No writing on the front. No postmark or other stamps suggesting who the packet might be from. Out of sheer curiosity, Kitt tore off the flap and pulled out the contents.

From the Defence Medical Agency logo stamped on the top right-hand corner of the paper and the reference number TTYX8 stamped across the top, she knew exactly what this was. 'It's a copy of the report Bell and Ripley wrote,' said Kitt.

'How did you get that?' said Joe.

'Our friend, Agent Smith,' said Kitt.

'Wait, you used your favour with Smith for this?' said Joe, shaking his head. 'You were supposed to hold onto it until the aliens attacked so you could get into the secret survival bunker with the rich and the elite.'

Kitt looked hard at Joe. 'I think you've been spending a bit too much time with Grace.'

'I object to that slur,' said Grace, standing from her seat.

'Take it up with Tatiana the Tyrannical Archangel,' said Kitt.

'You can be sure I will,' said Grace.

'Well, while I'm waiting for your filed complaint, if you don't mind, I'm going to turn my attentions to this rather more important document, here,' Kitt said, and before Grace could come up with some kind of inane retort, she began at once to read.

The moment Kitt began reading, she knew she had the key to unpacking all of the questions they had pondered over on this case. All of the things that didn't quite add up. Kitt turned the pages, faster and faster. Not quite believing the words that were scrolling before her eyes. And as she read, a picture began to form that should have been quite obvious to her all along and yet had evaded her understanding until she had this final piece of the puzzle.

'I think I know who's behind this whole plot,' said Kitt.

'And if I'm right, we never had a chance of solving it on our own. I think . . . I think this might just be the most insidious crime we've been involved in yet.'

CHAPTER THIRTY-ONE

'Mal,' Kitt said, as he entered the agency with DS Banks following closely behind him. 'Did you find what you needed to in the search?'

Halloran nodded. 'The antidote and two burner phones used to communicate about the plot.'

'What about your side of things?' asked Banks. 'Are they on their way?'

'Yes, our first suspect should be arriving any minute,' said Kitt. 'We have about half an hour to break them before the second arrives.'

'It should be long enough,' said Halloran. 'I would say this whole thing has been a waste of police time the way we've been tearing around but of course, in finding out who's behind the antidote theft, we've also found Bell's killers. So my superiors will at least be happy about that.'

'And they won't be the only ones,' said Grace, who was sitting with Joe in the corner. The pair wanted a front-row seat for what was about to unfold, but it had been agreed they wouldn't talk once the suspects arrived. Halloran, Banks and Kitt would lead the questions. Faces the guilty were more familiar with. Faces they had done their best to con, right from the beginning.

'I know what you mean,' said Joe. 'I can't believe what they've done, to be honest. And I've seen a few things in the last two years. The sooner this case is closed the happier I'll be.' He was about to say something else but was interrupted by a knock at the door.

'That's her,' said Kitt. 'Right, everyone, let's keep this as streamlined as possible. We need to make sure we break her before her partner in crime arrives.'

With that, she walked to the door and opened it.

'Eleanor,' Kitt said, tacking a practised smile to her face. 'Come in, I appreciate you coming down.'

Eleanor walked in but stopped after a couple of paces. Once she noticed Halloran and Banks were also in attendance.

'Sit down, Mrs Meadows,' said Halloran, in a tone that must have left her in no doubt whatsoever that he meant business.

Kitt wondered if she knew even then. That the jig was up. Certainly, the expression on Eleanor's face changed from one of ease to one of questioning. Kitt went back to the chair behind her desk and sat there, silently looking at Eleanor.

'What's going on?' said Eleanor, looking between Halloran, Banks and Kitt. 'Have you found the antidote for Kevin?'

'Yes,' said Halloran. 'We have.'

Eleanor's eyes widened as Halloran said this but Kitt noticed her catch herself in the act and attempt to turn it into a look of happiness.

'Why that's wonderful, Kevin won't die then?' said Eleanor. 'I mean, assuming he is still with us? He's still with us . . . isn't he?'

'You know very well that he's still with us as you've just been out to meet him,' said Halloran.

'That was . . . twenty minutes ago . . .' Eleanor tried. 'With a condition like Kevin's anything could have happened in that time.'

'Could it?' Halloran said, glaring at Eleanor. 'Aren't you curious to know where we found the antidote?'

'Well, I'm sure wherever you found it is probably confidential police information,' Eleanor tried. 'And I wouldn't want to—'

'We found it at your house,' said Banks.

'At *my* house?' said Eleanor. 'That's . . . that's impossible. Even if the antidote was somehow at my house, you would need a search warrant to—'

Halloran thrust a piece of paper into Eleanor's hands.

'With Kevin's life allegedly in jeopardy, my superintendent managed to authorise an urgent search and seize warrant. We waited for you to leave before we searched the property, first,' said Halloran. 'After everything that's happened we needed to know for sure how many people were involved. Who they were. And luckily, at your house, we found all the evidence we needed.'

'I don't understand,' said Eleanor, 'I had no idea that the antidote was present at my address. Leonard must have brought the antidote home with him without my knowledge and hidden it somewhere. I can't be held responsible for—'

'I think you can,' said Halloran. 'And I'm not the only one. We found the burner phone you used to communicate with your accomplice.'

'Burner phone?' said Eleanor. 'This is ridiculous, I've never used a burner phone and you can't prove I have.'

'You mean we can't prove it because you didn't sign the messages off with your name?' said Banks.

'Yes . . . I mean, if the messages are not signed, how can you prove I sent them? I have no idea what this is all about,' said Eleanor.

'Well, we don't need your name on those messages. Because we've already tracked down your accomplice and he's confirmed he conspired with you to kill Leonard Bell.'

Eleanor's bottom lip began to tremble. 'I don't believe you. He would never . . .'

'Never what? Tell the truth about what you did?' said Halloran. 'Oh, he told us. He told us everything. Including whose idea it was to poison your husband with the toxin in the first place.'

Eleanor's mouth fell open at this. Her eyes darted from side to side as she tried to process what was happening. 'No, no, no, it wasn't *my* idea. It wasn't.'

'That's not the way he tells it,' said Halloran. 'According to his statement, you wanted Leonard out of the way so that you could be with him. You were lonely in your marriage and you persuaded him to poison your husband and frame his boss for the whole thing.'

'I didn't, I didn't!' Eleanor half-screamed. 'It was Kevin. Kevin came up with the idea. I just went along with it because I was so lonely. Do you know what it's like to be lonely in a relationship you can't get out of?'

'There's this new-fangled thing called divorce,' Kitt said, unable to control herself in light of Eleanor's skewed reasoning.

'I couldn't afford to get divorced,' said Eleanor. 'My business is in debt.'

'Yes, we know,' said Halloran. 'And that was another red flag that told us you were the culprit behind all of this. We did search your financial records initially but we looked at your personal holdings. The business is a separate entity. The second we looked at that, however, it became clear that you were in debt up to your eyes.'

'Business has been slow, and I have overheads. So I borrowed a little bit . . . It just got out of hand,' said Eleanor.

'I needed to find a way to repay the debt otherwise I'd never survive on my own. But Leo hadn't cheated on me or anything. Well, not with a woman, though he spent every minute of his time at work. He might as well have been cheating. So, if we'd divorced, I would have been left with next to nothing.'

'But if he died, you got to benefit from the generous pension scheme offered by the Defence Medical Agency, clear off your mortgage and your debts. And get rid of the man who hadn't lived up to the hopes you'd had when you married him,' said Banks.

There was a long pause as the truth about Eleanor's actions hung in the air.

'It was you who attacked me in that alley this afternoon,' said Kitt. 'You were hoping I would think it had been Margaret Cryer. That's why you told me she had feelings for Ripley when we talked to you. To plant the seeds of suspicion. Divert attention away from yourself. Ripley did the same. Handed us the prime suspects of Cryer and Simmons on a plate. You nearly got away with it. I thought it might have been Margaret at first. But no. It was you. Because I found your phone. The phone you must have lost on your way to his house this afternoon when you were no doubt canoodling and conspiring further together. You dropped it on your way in. You were probably at Kevin's house the whole time I was there. And then, a few minutes after I left, you followed me to see what I would do.'

'I-I-I . . .' Eleanor stammered.

'You're going to have to do a lot better than that,' said Halloran. 'We're talking first-degree murder, here. Not to mention the obstruction of justice that's taken place in framing Nathan Greene for the murder. Did Ripley bury the toxin in the flower bed in Greene's back garden? Or did he get you to do his dirty work?'

'I really didn't want to go along with Kevin's plan,' Eleanor said in the quietest voice Kitt had ever heard. 'But there was no other way. I was so unhappy. He said it would be quick. That Leonard wouldn't feel any pain.'

'He lied,' said Halloran. 'It might have been quick but it was not painless. Your husband died one of the most horrific deaths you could wish on a person. And for him to realise at the last minute what was going to happen to him. When the toxin gave out its signature scent. That is a form of psychological cruelty you wouldn't wish on your worst enemy, let alone the man you were married to.'

Tears started to sneak down Eleanor's cheeks but Kitt could not be sure, given the horrible conspiracy she'd been a part of, whether those tears were for all her husband had been put through before he died, or whether they were for herself now that she'd been caught.

'I didn't want to go through with it, but there was no other way,' she said with a shake of her head. 'It wasn't my idea. Kevin is lying.'

'And so am I,' said Halloran.

'Wh-what do you mean?' said Eleanor, frowning over at Halloran.

'Kevin never told us it was your idea. We have yet to confront him with all we found when we searched your property and his, but you've just named him as the chief instigator of this crime. So, your testimony will be all we need to see he goes away for a very long time, and you with him.'

'I-I won't testify against him,' said Eleanor, sniffing back more tears.

'We'll see about that,' said Halloran. 'If he really is the chief instigator of the crime and you don't testify, you'll be looking to serve the same sentence he will. We've got more than enough to convict you. You may not have signed all those text messages planning to kill your husband but your fingerprints and trace DNA is all over that burner phone. When a court sees that, failing to sign the messages with your name isn't going to matter one bit.'

The pair looked at each other for a long moment and, just as Halloran was about to speak again, there came another knock to the door.

'I imagine that will be your accomplice,' said Halloran. 'He's a little early. Probably eager to spin some more lies. Let's see what he's got to say for himself, shall we? And what he's got to say about the fact that you've named him as a co-conspirator in the murder of your husband.'

CHAPTER THIRTY-TWO

Again, Kitt walked to the door and welcomed Kevin Ripley into the room. She and Halloran had agreed that she would be the one to greet their guests of honour to reduce the likelihood of them guessing the jig was up too early and making a run for it.

Kevin's face didn't alter when he saw Halloran and Banks standing near Kitt's desk. When he locked eyes with Eleanor, however, his jaw visibly tightened.

Kitt returned to her desk and indicated Ripley should sit in a seat a few feet away from Eleanor's.

'Is everything OK?' said Ripley. 'You said on the phone that you had some important news for me.'

'I do,' said Kitt. 'I managed to get a copy of the report you and Leonard gave to Nathan Greene.'

'You . . . how did you do that, exactly?' said Ripley.

'I have contacts in high places,' said Kitt. 'It made for very interesting reading.'

'I imagine it did,' said Ripley. 'Look, I know how that report might appear but, remember, I knew my superiors would see that report. That they wouldn't take kindly to me taking an overtly moral stance.'

'I see, so you're changing your original story, are you, Mr Ripley?' said Halloran.

'Am I?' said Ripley.

'Sounds like it to me,' said Halloran. 'I've got you on record as saying that you made an ethical stand in that report against further research into the toxin that killed Leonard Bell. You said that Nathan Greene was the person in favour of continuing the research. But that wasn't true at all, was it?'

'You lied to us about what was in that report,' said Kitt. 'And it's not the only lie you've told, is it?'

Kitt watched Ripley's face carefully as he looked from her to Halloran and back again. His breathing had turned almost to panting. A sure sign that he was starting to panic. Kitt wasn't going to waste the advantage of having him turned around.

'Leonard wanted the toxin project shut down. Now that the report is in our hands, Nathan Greene has at last confirmed, as it states in the report, that he wanted the same. But the part of the report that bears your signature isn't against further research into the toxin. In fact it makes a compelling argument for keeping the research strand going. Despite the inhumanity of the toxin, you discuss at length the financial and reputational benefits of making the toxin even more deadly. So you could sell it to other parties. So you could use it to teach the enemies of our country a lesson about what should happen if they threaten our national security.'

'I was merely pointing out some of the factors the agency might want to take into consideration in order to ensure a balanced view was presented,' said Ripley. 'Just because I said those things in my report, does not mean that it was my personal view that research into the toxin should continue.'

'And yet that's exactly what Nathan Greene has confirmed,' said Halloran. 'That you came to him with a personal plea to keep the research running. You explained that you'd been promised by one of Greene's superiors that you and Leonard would be in line for a large monetary bonus should the toxin research be a success. That the superior in question had a broad definition of success, in that so long as the sub-stance was a credible threat to our enemies, one that set us apart from other countries in terms of defence, they would pay up. You offered to share that bonus with Greene if he just recommended that research into the toxin continued.'

'If that conversation took place, and I'm not saying it did, it would only have taken place between myself and Nathan Greene. Which would make it his word against mine,' said Ripley.

'Perhaps, if we hadn't read your report, we could believe that,' said Halloran. 'You knew that Greene was trying to shut the project down, jeopardising the extra payment you'd been promised from the higher ups. And you saw all the work you'd done for the last three years amounting to nothing. In your mind, you'd already spent that considerable bonus that was due to you.'

'And besides,' said Kitt. 'You were already having an affair with Bell's wife, so both Greene and Bell had become an inconvenience to you. What better way to get everything you wanted than to kill two birds with one stone? Poison Leonard Bell and frame Nathan Greene for it. Your girlfriend has already confirmed that you came up with the plot to kill her husband.'

Ripley looked at Eleanor, raising his eyebrows at her in disbelief.

'I'm sorry,' she said, more tears falling down her cheeks. 'I didn't mean to. It was an accident. They already knew.'

'They couldn't have,' he said. 'They just tricked you.'

'We did use a bit of trickery,' said Halloran. 'But Eleanor's right. We did know. You see, we found your burner phones at Eleanor's house. A search of your property is underway right now, Mr Ripley. I wonder what else we will find there, or if you were clever enough, mindful enough, not to leave a trace of evidence there in case we ever suspected you.'

Ripley's eyes were already wide but at this revelation they only got wider.

'There's about a month of messages on those burner phones, all told,' said Kitt. 'Planning murder and plotting how you'd get away with it. The many tactics you'd use to fool the police. Starting with the fake robbery.'

'Yes, funny how you failed to mention that you were present at the lab the night the security system went down and it was later discovered that both the toxin and the antidote were missing,' said Halloran.

Ripley opened his mouth to speak but no words came out. Even he must have known that any attempt to lie was pointless now that the burner phones had been found.

'According to the text messages you sent to Eleanor,' Halloran continued, 'you hacked the security system and used the confusion to hide the toxin and the antidote somewhere on the premises. Somewhere nobody else would think to look. You then reported them missing. Everyone would be searched on the way out that evening, you knew that. But when nothing was recovered, suspicions about personnel dwindled. At least in terms of them physically carrying something off the premises. The agency still thought that someone might have been involved in orchestrating the thefts. But they weren't body searching anybody.'

'As soon as the body searches stopped, you removed the toxin and the antidote,' said Kitt 'You hid the antidote with Eleanor, somewhere accessible but a place it was highly unlikely anyone would look for it. And then you used the toxin to poison Leonard when the three of you were out at the Book and Candle Bar.'

'Between poisoning Leonard, and him dying, you watched

Nathan Greene's house,' said Banks. 'You waited for the house to be empty and you buried the toxin in the flower beds. You had no use for it anymore now that Leonard would soon be out of the way. It was only useful in framing Greene.'

'But you had to make sure that the police were looking at the Defence Medical Agency in the first place,' said Halloran. 'And you had to do something to avoid suspicion, you were one of the key researchers on the project after all.'

'So you printed off some of the blood tests taken from the human trial you undertook when researching the toxin and doctored it to look like your own,' said Banks. 'Making it seem to the police, and the Defence Medical Agency, as if you too had been poisoned.'

'According to the texts we recovered from your phone,' said Kitt, 'once Nathan Greene had been arrested, your plan was to conveniently remember seeing Greene go off to an old allotment site on the edge of the city, where the police would find the antidote and you would be "cured".'

'Except you were never poisoned to begin with,' said Halloran. 'Still, neither the police nor the agency would ever know that. After the antidote had been recovered, and after all you'd been through, the agency would welcome you back to the fold with open arms.'

'You'd get to continue your research, you'd get the girl, and you'd get that big fat bonus you were hoping for,' said Kitt. 'You know, because of you, Leonard Bell never got to finish his story. Not the one he was living. Not the one he was telling at the Christmas Book Fair. But you better hope that Dickens was merely writing fiction and not channelling some greater truth in his work. Because if all our deeds in this life count for something in the next, you're going to find yourself rattling some very heavy chains indeed.'

A silence fell on the room and Kitt felt suddenly very close to tears. She'd worked some cases in her time in which people had killed for greed or jealousy, but there was something about this case that cut deeper than all the others. Perhaps it was merely the time of year and the sentimentality that tended to strike people when the days grew short. Or perhaps it was because Leonard Bell had met his end by the hand of a person he'd considered to be a friend. Someone who was supposed to lift him up. Not shoot him down for his own gain. Added to that was the fact that the victim's own wife had conspired to kill him just because she didn't have the money for a divorce. This really was one of the cruellest crimes she'd ever had the misfortune to investigate.

'I think it's best I don't say anything else until I have a lawyer present,' Ripley said at last.

'That's your call,' Halloran bit out. 'But you should know that with all the evidence we have against you, it's not going to matter one bit who your lawyer is or what you do or do not say. Still, for the sake of procedure, Kevin Ripley, I am arresting you—' But he did not get to finish the caution he was about to issue.

Without a moment's warning, Ripley stood from his chair, moved behind it and pulled three vials from the pocket of his long, grey trench coat.

'Kevin, what're you doing?' said Eleanor.

'I wouldn't come any closer if I were you, Inspector Halloran,' Ripley said when the officer made a step forward to grab at him. 'You can be sure I didn't tell you everything about this toxin. It can be ingested and injected, as I told you. But if I should throw it at you and it makes contact with any stretch of skin, it will seep through your pores and kill you that way.'

'Kevin . . .' Eleanor repeated.

'Shut up,' Ripley barked at her. 'I'm not going down for this.'

'That toxin isn't much of a threat when we have the antidote,' said Halloran.

'True,' said Ripley. 'But since we only did one human trial and that person unexpectedly died after the five-day incubation period, we didn't get a chance to test the antidote. Do you really want to risk your life with this stuff and bank on an untested antidote to save you?'

Halloran's jaw tightened but he didn't move any further. Nobody in the room moved in fact. 'That's very sensible of you all,' Ripley said. 'Ms Hartley, Ms Edwards, the keys to the premises if you please.'

'No,' said Kitt.

'The keys to the premises, or I start throwing this stuff

in the direction of the people you care about,' Ripley said, popping open one of the vials.

'Alright,' said Kitt, sighing. 'Grace, do as he says.'

'But . . .' Grace started.

'Come on, it's not worth it,' Kitt said, pulling the keys out of her pocket and throwing them down on her desk.

'Ms Edwards, pick up those keys and bring them to me along with your set,' said Ripley.

Slowly, Grace complied. Stretching her arm as far out as she could towards Ripley so she didn't have to get too close to the toxin.

'If anybody tries to follow me out of this door before I lock it behind me, I will throw this liquid right in their face,' Ripley said backing slowly away.

All Kitt and her companions could do just then was watch on as Ripley opened the door to the agency and locked it tightly behind him before disappearing into the snowy night.

CHAPTER THIRTY-THREE

'Mal, tell me you brought your spare key with you,' said Kitt, the moment the door was locked.

'I have, but you're not coming after him. Not when he's carrying a deadly toxin,' said Halloran.

'Don't be ridiculous. Goodness knows how long it will take back-up to arrive. If I catch sight of him, I won't approach, I'll just follow and let you know where he is. Here,' Kitt handed Halloran and Banks a comms radio apiece. 'I'm on channel two. Grace, Joe, I'd be grateful if you'd keep a sharp eye on Eleanor while we're gone.'

'Happy to be as far away from that toxin as possible,' said Grace.

'I'll stay and hold the fort with Grace,' said Joe. 'Just be careful.'

Clearly aware of the fact that he didn't have time to stand there arguing with Kitt, Halloran marched towards the door and, pulling his spare key from his pocket, reopened the door of Hartley and Edwards Investigations. Cautiously, he opened it a crack, then a touch wider before looking in all directions.

'He's long gone,' said Halloran.

'He probably hasn't got that far,' said Kitt. 'He thinks we're locked in here for the foreseeable and have to wait for someone to come and get us out. He might have a head start but I think we can still catch him up if we're quick.'

'I agree,' said Banks. 'I'm not sure he's got a plan other than to get away from us. He probably is trying to think where to go next. He knows the police are at his house so he might just be looking for somewhere to hide. A business or a pub of some kind.'

'Alright,' said Halloran, 'Banks, you take the route towards Barbican Road, he might be looking to hop on one of the buses that pass on the outskirts of town and just skedaddle out of the city. I'll take a look down the side streets here, Hunter's Lane, Margaret Street, et cetera. Kitt, you take the Walmgate route into town. I think it's more likely he's ducked down one of these side streets to try and get out of sight quick. But if you do spot him in the middle of town, do not approach him. Considering he's carrying the toxin, we need to get him as isolated as possible before we apprehend him and preferably take him off-guard so he doesn't have time to open the vials.'

'OK, let's not spend any more time talking,' said Kitt, reaching around the doorframe and grabbing her coat off the peg before heading off in the direction of town as Halloran had instructed.

Wrapping her navy coat around her, Kitt walked as quickly as she could through the snow, which stung at her cheeks and threatened to make her slip whenever she increased her speed. She had her low court shoes on, the same shoes she wore every day to work. They looked professional but they certainly weren't built for breaking into a run in icy conditions. She had to make sure she stayed in the game and didn't take a nasty fall.

Kitt's eyes darted everywhere as she strode along the street in the dark of the winter evening. She passed numerous restaurants and inns, any of which Ripley could have ducked into. But would he really have had the audacity to hide out somewhere so close to the agency? Surely, he would want to get a bit of distance between himself and the people who had uncovered his crimes? Then again, he was happy to hide out under their noses the whole time they had been working this investigation, so perhaps that line of logic didn't count for much when it came to a man like Kevin Ripley.

Still, she couldn't stop at every establishment en route to search for him, she just had to hope his instincts were to get as far away as possible.

Picking up the pace as much as she could while still staying upright, Kitt passed over Foss Bridge and it was then that she thought she saw something familiar. The long, grey trench coat that Ripley had been wearing. It was there, just for an instant and then in a flash disappeared into the crowds of late-night Christmas shoppers and revellers.

Kitt's body turned completely cold at the thought that Ripley could be heading into a highly populated area armed with several vials of a lethal toxin. Was it definitely him though? She had to be sure before alerting Halloran and Banks. She sped up as much as she dared in the snowy conditions, and kept her eyes fixed on the undulating sea of people ahead of her. It took a minute but eventually she did get another glimpse of that familiar trench coat and she recognised the back of Ripley's head. The short grey hair that matched his attire.

'I see him,' Kitt said over comms.

'Where?' came Halloran's scratchy reply.

'He's just about to cross The Stonebow and head onto Colliergate,' said Kitt.

'Alright, stay on him, but don't let him see you. I don't know what he might do if cornered in an area where there's hostages he could take,' said Halloran.

'I've copied his location and am heading back towards town now,' said Banks. She sounded quite breathless, as though she might be running. Kitt wasn't going to attempt that in this weather but Banks was probably wearing much more sensible shoes.

'I'll keep him in my sights and update you on his movements,' said Kitt, trotting after the subject across The

Stonebow, keeping him just in sight in case he turned around for any reason. The last thing she needed was for Ripley to see them coming. That said, given the pace at which he was walking there didn't seem much chance of that. He was stepping it out in a very assured manner. As though he already knew where he was going. Had he always had a contingency plan in case he got caught? If so, what on earth might it entail?

'We've just passed the Christmas Carousel. He's slowing down a bit,' said Kitt, also slowing herself. For all Ripley knew, they were still all locked up back at the agency, which was perhaps why he wasn't spending any time looking over his shoulder. 'He's heading down Goodramgate.'

'I'm going to try and cut him off by swinging round the back of Aldwark,' said Halloran.

'Got it,' said Kitt, glad to be on the flatter surface of Good-ramgate where there weren't any cobbles. 'He has really slowed down his pace. Maybe he's run out of adrenaline, or maybe he just thinks he's home free with us locked in at the agency.'

'Good, I've got a chance of beating him to the end of the street and surprising him then,' said Halloran.

'I'm still about five minutes away,' Banks panted out over comms.

'Oh, wait, Mal,' said Kitt. 'That's not going to work. He's turned off on Deansgate and looks to be . . . yes he's going up College Street. I think . . . I think he might be headed towards the minster.'

'Damn,' said Halloran. 'Two days before Christmas. That place is going to be heaving with people. You can't let him go in. Try and distract him. Don't get too close. Tell him we split up to look for him so he thinks you're on your own. But, Kitt, be careful.'

'Copy that,' said Kitt. Taking a deep breath and walking as quickly as she could to follow after Ripley.

'Where are you going, Kevin?' she said, when she caught up to him at the bottom of the minster steps. Ripley froze at her words and turned to face her.

'Not in there, I hope. Not with what you've got in your pocket,' said Kitt, nodding up at the minster. Golden light shone through the stained-glass windows and, beyond the stonework of the medieval buildings, a choir was singing 'In the Bleak Midwinter'.

Ripley didn't answer Kitt's question but shoved a hand in his pocket.

Kitt looked around the paved, open space of Minster Yard. There weren't many people milling around in this part of the city at night. A busker sat twenty feet or so away at the corner where the yard funnelled into Stonegate. He was playing 'O Holy Night' on the violin but couldn't really be heard over the music coming from the minster. From the volume of the voices singing along with the choir, however, Kitt could tell that there was a good number of people inside that building. And it was clearly Ripley's plan to walk among them with a deadly toxin in hand.

'You don't need to threaten me with the toxin,' Kitt said. 'I'm not going to try anything physical.'

'Why not?' said Ripley, looking Kitt up and down.

'I saw what happened to Bell when the toxin killed him, remember?' said Kitt. 'I'm not going anywhere near that stuff. Not for anyone or anything.'

'Where is Inspector Halloran?' said Ripley. 'If you're free, safe to say he is too.'

'He is, but he's on the other side of York. We split up to look for you. Personally, I was rather hoping I wouldn't be the one to find you. I have no idea how to stop you. No idea what to say to you. How to make you understand that running will do you no good. Hurting others with that substance or taking them hostage with it won't change the outcome. Except that maybe you'll end up dead rather than in prison.'

'Maybe I'd prefer that,' said Ripley, removing his hand from his pocket. He had decided against pulling out a vial of the toxin, Kitt noted. He must believe her story, that she was alone and wasn't about to try anything physical.

'Would you? Really?' said Kitt. 'Remember what I said about cutting Leonard Bell's story short? I know you're a man of science and I myself have no idea if there's any penalty in the next life for what we do in this one, but if I were in your position, I might want to put off finding out as long as possible.'

Kitt did her best not to react as she saw Halloran running down the minster steps behind Ripley. He must have
climbed them further along, out of both Kitt and Ripley's
fields of vision so he could manoeuvre himself into a position where he could take Ripley by surprise.

'If I were standing in your shoes,' Kitt said, trying to
maintain Ripley's attention and prevent him from turning
around to see Halloran charging towards him, 'I might come
to the realisation that it was over.'

Ripley was about to say something in response when Halloran tackled him to the ground from the side. Ripley was
tall but not very well-built and folded straight over, falling
flat to the paving. Kitt thought that was going to be the end
of the matter. But Ripley issued Halloran with a hard punch
to the gut, winding him.

In a flash, Ripley was on top of Halloran and reached into
his pocket to produce the toxin. Ripley moved his free hand
and clamped it around Halloran's throat as he repeatedly
tried to open the vial one-handedly and each time wasn't
quite able to manage it.

Halloran reached his arms up to Ripley, trying to fight
back, but between the punch to his stomach and the hand
wrapped around his windpipe, he probably had no air in his
lungs, and thus no fight in him.

Kitt quickly looked around the space for something, anything, she could do that wouldn't result in her accidentally
being poisoned by the toxin. She spotted that lone busker

again and ran over to him and grabbed his violin case which was standing up right next to him.

'Hey!' the busker shouted at her.

'I'll bring it straight back,' she called to him, running in the direction of Halloran and Ripley. The scene she returned to turned her blood cold. The vial had been opened alright. It lay on the paving right next to where they were struggling. Kitt could see the toxin spilled in a pool, darkening the paving. Ripley was trying to push Halloran's face down into the liquid and was about to succeed.

Without giving it another moment's thought, Kitt held the thinner end of the violin case in her hands, positioned herself just behind Ripley where he couldn't see her and swung the case as hard as she could at his head, like she used to swing a rounders bat back in school.

Since she wasn't a regular at the local gym, Kitt very much doubted she had managed to hit Ripley hard in real terms but the blunt force of it was enough of a surprise that it knocked him clear off Halloran and sent him flying to the ground.

Carefully avoiding getting his hands or any other appendage anywhere near the toxin that had spilled, Halloran pulled himself up, walked over to Ripley and wrenched his arms behind his back before cuffing him.

'As I was saying before you rudely interrupted me,' Halloran began, panting from the struggle. 'Kevin Ripley, I am arresting you for the murder of Leonard Bell. You do not have to say anything. But it may harm your defence if you do not mention when questioned something which you later rely on in court. Anything you do say may be given in evidence.'

After taking a minute to collect himself, Halloran pulled Ripley to his feet. Kitt sighed in relief to see Kevin Ripley finally in police custody. It was just another minute or so before a breathless Banks caught up with them. Halloran called for back-up and so all there was to do now was wait in the shadow of the minster for Ripley to be taken to the station. For the spilled toxin to be cleaned up to the extent that nobody would even have known it was there.

Watching a light snow fall over the spires of the minster and listening to the choir singing 'Carol of the Bells', Kitt hoped that now that the murderers had been caught, some of that well-documented peace of the season could be hers.

It was at that moment, however, that Kitt remembered that she had invited Ruby for Christmas dinner.

CHAPTER THIRTY-FOUR

'Ooooh!' Kitt said as she tore the wrapping paper off the gift Grace and Joe had clubbed together to buy her. 'It's the Montblanc Meisterstuck 146 LeGrand Platinum Trim Fountain Pen! How did you know?'

'Because you shamelessly dropped hints at every opportunity,' said Grace.

'I did not,' said Kitt.

'So, it was just an accident you left a stationery catalogue on your desk open at a particular page with this pen circled in red Sharpie?' said Grace. 'That's hardly subtle.'

'Actually,' said Kitt. 'I was sort of hoping Halloran might swing by and see it. But if he did get the hint and has bought me that as well, I certainly don't mind having two. You can never have too much stationery. Or books. Or books about books.'

'Yes, alright,' said Grace; for once she was the calm one and Kitt was the overexcitable one. 'We get the picture.'

'Funny how the same principle doesn't apply to vintage clothing and homewear when we're out shopping,' said Evie. 'You've assured me on more than one occasion that I have enough of those.'

'I'm just trying to save Banks from going out under an avalanche of the stuff,' Kitt teased. 'That would be ironic for a police officer, facing danger on a daily basis and meeting their end under a tonne of your antique store purchases.'

'Oh, please,' said Evie. 'Like Halloran would ever make it out of here alive if there were a fire.'

'Mmmm, you may have a point about that,' said Kitt with a wry smile.

'Eeee, let's 'ave a look at that pen, love,' Ruby said, and Kitt reluctantly handed over her new fountain pen. 'Oooh very swish, I can see you putting your signature on some important documents with that.'

'Thanks, Ruby,' Kitt said with a smile. On learning Ruby would be joining them, they had cleared out the York gift shops of crystals and candles. She had been quite over-whelmed when she opened them all but Kitt couldn't help but go a little bit overboard after hearing Ruby had spent quite a few Christmases on her own.

'What time will Halloran get here?' said Joe. 'Rolo loves Halloran, and it might cheer him up a bit after the reception he got off Iago.' Rolo sat at Joe's feet with his chin pressed to the floor and his ears flat against his head. When it had been agreed that Joe would join them for Christmas dinner, it seemed neither Kitt nor Joe had any idea just how far they were about to test the limits of dog–cat relations.

Rolo had entered on a lead and started growling at Iago. Iago flounced up to Rolo as if he couldn't hear a thing and gave the dog a hard swipe across the nose with his paws. Rolo yelped and stopped growling at once, and the hierarchy was immediately established.

'Whether man or beast, all visitors learn quickly that growling at Iago is not a prudent course of action,' said Kitt, looking over at Iago, who was sitting like a pot model on the window ledge. An insolent flick of his tail the only sign that he was in fact animate.

'Charley said she and Halloran finish their shift around six,' said Evie, looking at her watch, 'so they shouldn't be far away. Maybe another ten minutes. Depends on traffic.'

'Well, frankly I think it's disgusting that we've had to delay Christmas dinner to this time of day,' said Grace. 'Couldn't they have both feigned some kind of flu bug? Sprouts don't not eat themselves, you know.'

'Um, actually, Grace, technically,' Evie said, 'I think they do.'

'Halloran and Charley will be with us as soon as they can, I'm sure,' said Kitt, in an attempt to interrupt the nonsensical conversational loop Evie and Grace could so easily generate for themselves. 'With the amount of paperwork Kevin Ripley and Eleanor Meadows have generated for them, we might need to show a little patience when it comes to having our Christmas dinner.'

'Kitt,' said Evie. 'Come on, we promised there'd be no shop talk today. I know you only wrapped up the case the day before yesterday. I know it's all very much fresh in your mind. But try and leave it be. Just for today.'

'I'm sorry, I'll try,' said Kitt. 'But it's very difficult.'

'What's very difficult?' said Halloran's voice as he and Banks bundled through the door, shaking snow off their coats.

'You're here early!' said Evie, standing to walk over to Banks and putting her arms around her wife.

'I thought it'd be at least another half hour before we saw you,' Kitt said, standing to lean in and give Halloran a quick kiss.

'Our two suspects have been surprisingly cooperative today,' said Halloran. 'We achieved so much we managed to bunk off early for the first time in history. It's not like they don't owe me about a million years for all the extra ten minutes and half an hours here and there they've had for nothing over the course of my career.'

'So you got full confessions out of both Ripley and Eleanor?' said Kitt.

'Aaargh. Lalalala lalalalala,' Evie said, louder and louder with each passing moment, while placing her hands over her ears.

'This is Evie's subtle way of telling you she doesn't want to hear any shop talk today,' said Kitt.

Smiling, Banks gently tugged Evie's hands away from her ears. 'It's alright, shop talk's over, love.'

'Yes,' said Kitt. 'But Halloran, why don't you help me with a couple of things in the kitchen?'

Smiling, Halloran followed Kitt through the kitchen, hanging his sodden coat over a nearby chair as he did so.

'So, come on, tell me all about it,' said Kitt. 'Have all the loose ends been tied up?'

'Oh, I thought you invited me into the kitchen so we could canoodle in private,' Halloran said, looping his arms around Kitt's waist and pulling her in close.

Kitt smiled. 'Well, it's not like I'm against that or anything.'

'But you want to hear about what happened with Ripley and Eleanor first?' said Halloran.

'Consider it an extra Christmas present?' said Kitt, with a sparkle in her blue eyes.

'We got full confessions,' Halloran confirmed. 'I never thought it would happen but the pair of them have just crumbled today.'

'Ripley admitted that he poisoned Leonard at the bar?' said Kitt.

Halloran nodded. 'And that he never had the toxin in his system in the first place. His life was never in jeopardy. He just wanted the agency and the police to think it was, to avoid suspicion.'

'Well, that explains why Bell and Ripley were poisoned at different times. Ripley was the poisoner and thus was never poisoned himself. But my God he took a terrible risk telling us he'd put something different in that report he filed to Nathan Greene. What if Greene had just handed it over?'

Halloran shook his head. 'Ripley knew the agency protocol well enough to know that would never happen. He knew they would refuse and then classify it. He also knew that Nathan Greene wouldn't talk about the contents.'

'Which would make us suspicious that he had something to hide, when in fact it was just the routine procedure of the agency,' said Kitt.

'Exactly,' said Halloran. 'Ripley never expected you'd actually find a way to get hold of a copy of the report.'

'Well, perhaps both he and Nathan Greene won't be so quick to underestimate Kitt Hartley in future.'

Halloran smiled. 'Officially, neither Greene nor the agency are willing to comment on the events that have unfolded, which of course is driving the press mad. But unofficially he asked me to pass on his thanks to you for foiling Ripley's plan to frame him.'

'Not bad for a tinpot investigator, eh?' said Kitt with a chuckle.

'You don't need me to tell you that you did very well, pet,' said Halloran.

'Oh, I'm so glad the nightmare is over,' said Kitt, wrapping her arms tighter around him and feeling the familiar warmth shoot through her as he held her tighter in return. 'All that urgency and fire we had in us to solve the case because we thought Ripley's life hung in the balance. I've never worked such long hours, and that's saying something. In truth though, there wasn't any urgency at all, except that of a normal case in making sure you follow up leads as quickly as possible. Ripley's life was never in danger. We needn't have gone through all that stress.'

And in saying those words out loud, Kitt knew those strange literary visitors she had must really have been all in her head. Her subconscious trying to make sense of the strange series of events she was grappling with. Because each and every one of those ghostly authors had talked about how time was important to solving the case. How important it was that she solve the case quicker. But that wasn't reality. That was just her perception. Just what Kevin Ripley had told them.

'Well, I wouldn't be too sure about that,' said Halloran. 'Time was very much of the essence, just not in the way we thought it was.'

'How do you mean?' Kitt asked with a frown.

'It's come to light that if we'd taken even a couple more days to solve it we may have lost at least one of our suspects for good.'

'Really? Which one?' said Kitt.

'Eleanor had plans to leave the country between Christmas and New Year. She had a one-way flight booked to Algeria. We found the ticket when we searched her property.'

'Algeria . . .' said Kitt. 'Oh, we don't have an extradition treaty with them, do we?'

'That's right. Even if we'd found out about her involvement in the crime at a later date, unless she voluntarily returned to the UK, we wouldn't have been able to arrest her for it,' said Halloran.

'I guess it wasn't true love between her and Ripley then,' said Kitt.

'Given what she's said in interview, I think he just gave her the attention she was missing in her marriage. And I got the impression he liked her a lot more than she liked him,' said Halloran.

'Ah, then the relationship is doomed,' said Kitt. 'The only way a relationship survives is if the person you like likes you back just as much.'

'We should be OK then,' Halloran said, smiling down at Kitt, his blue eyes gleaming with the love she had seen in them for a good ten years now. Slowly she reached a hand up to his face, petted his soft beard and pressed her lips against his.

'Ahem,' said Grace, who had appeared in the doorway. 'I'm only getting hungrier, you know?'

'Oh, alright, Grace!' said Kitt, shooing her back into the dining area. 'I'm just serving it up now.'

Kitt asked Halloran to get the glasses out of the drinks cabinet and make sure everyone had a beverage prepared while she served up the meal that had been warming and browning in the oven. A huge turkey, not dissimilar to the one Scrooge himself took to Bob Cratchit's house in

A *Christmas Carol*. Golden roast potatoes. Lush green beans. Piping hot carrots. And Kitt's pièce de résistance, perfectly risen homemade Yorkshire puddings with a large gravy boat waiting to be filled.

As she was transferring the vegetables to a serving tray, Ruby appeared in the doorframe.

'I don't want to bother you while you're cooking, love,' said Ruby.

'I can multitask, Ruby,' said Kitt, spooning out the green beans. 'It's not a bother at all.'

'I just wanted to say, thank you for 'avin' me,' said Ruby.

Kitt stopped what she was doing and looked Ruby in the eye. 'It's my pleasure to have you. But, Ruby?'

'Yes, love?'

'What the hell was in that mulled wine I drank?'

'Well, er, it's a bit of a secret that recipe, love. Why do you ask?'

'Because after drinking it, I . . . saw things.'

'Things?'

'People,' Kitt clarified. 'Dead people. As in, Haley Joel Osment has nothing on me.'

'What?' said Ruby.

'Never mind,' said Kitt. 'My point is, all the ingredients in that wine . . . they were legal, weren't they?'

Ruby took a longer pause than Kitt would have liked before answering. 'Of course it's all above board,' she said at last. Though Kitt wasn't very convinced by her tone. 'I might 'ave to rethink the formula for next year, like. If it's opening the third eye that wide, well, nobody wants their third eye opening too wide, do they?'

'No, Ruby,' said Kitt with a little shake of her head. She should have known better than to try and get some sense about her strange festive episode out of Ruby. But, based on the woman's reaction to her question about the ingredients, she had a strong inkling that the mulled wine was definitely to blame. 'Why don't you go and make sure Halloran serves you a glass of something you like at the table? I'll be serving the food up any second.'

'Aye love, aye of course,' Ruby said, trundling off back towards the group.

Kitt listened to all the merriment happening on the other side of the wall as her guests filtered into the dining room and filled their glasses. Halloran, Banks, Evie, Grace and Joe, none of them had had the easiest festive season for one reason or another, and Kitt couldn't imagine Ruby had either, spending so much of it alone. And yet, somehow, they were still all finding it in themselves to laugh and raise their glasses to the spirit of Christmas, and the hopeful prospect of a new year.

A warm sensation spread through Kitt's chest as she realised how truly lucky she was to have this particular group of people around her. She knew in her heart, it couldn't be forever. One didn't need to regularly investigate murders to understand that nothing in this world truly was. Even the luckiest of all those living only had a certain number of Christmases where all of their loved ones found their way to their table. So, no, it couldn't be forever. But she had them now, and she was grateful for that. For if there was one thing she had learned keeping company with death for just over a decade, it was that life was made up of nows. They were all anybody ever really had. Kitt intended to make the most of hers and the dear ... if somewhat eccentric friends that she shared them with. While they were all here, healthy, happy and together.

ACKNOWLEDGEMENTS

These books would not make it into the hands of readers without my agent, Joanna Swainson and my publisher Quercus Books. Specifically, I'd like to thank Stef Bierwerth and Kat Burdon who continue to champion and nurture me as an author. Heartfelt thanks belongs to all three of these kind and inspiring individuals.

I am also supported by two wonderful writing partners, Dean Cummings and Ann Leander who offer much solace and warmth on those days when the writing journey can feel tough.

Thanks are due to Hazel Nicholson who scours every Kitt Hartley adventure so that she can offer feedback about police procedure. My books are much stronger for this invaluable assistance!

And, lastly, I owe much gratitude to my loved ones. Those who listen to the latest update on the writing of these books with much patience and impressively straight faces. I could not live a creative life without you.